Some Like It Wicked

TERESA MEDEIROS

Some Like It Wicked

AVON

An Imprint of HarperCollins*Publishers*

This is a work of fiction. Names, characters, places, and incidents are products of the author's imagination or are used fictitiously and are not to be construed as real. Any resemblance to actual events, locales, organizations, or persons, living or dead, is entirely coincidental.

AVON BOOKS
An Imprint of HarperCollins *Publishers*
10 East 53rd Street
New York, New York 10022-5299

Copyright © 2008 by Teresa Medeiros
ISBN 978-0-7394-9936-8

First Avon Books paperback printing: August 2008

Avon Trademark Reg. U.S. Pat. Off. and in Other Countries, Marca Registrada, Hecho en U.S.A.
HarperCollins® is a registered trademark of HarperCollins Publishers.

Printed in the U.S.A.

To the memory of our nephew Daniel Lee Medeiros. We were blessed by God to have you in our lives for twenty years.

For my prayer buddy Teresa Farmer, whose laughter brings delight to my life and always makes me feel much funnier than I am.

And for my Michael—I would have waited for you forever, darling, but I'm so grateful that I didn't have to.

Acknowledgments

Every happy ending requires a fairy godmother and this book had three. My heartfelt thanks to Carrie Feron, Tessa Woodward and Andrea Cirillo for wielding their magic wands on my behalf.

Chapter 1

England
1805

A throaty feminine moan disturbed the cozy peace of the stable loft. As Catriona Kincaid jerked up her head, the drowsy bit of fluff draped over the back of her neck let out a shrill mew.

Fortunately, the kitten's protest was drowned out by another moan from below, this one underscored by a husky, knowing chuckle that sent a warm shiver tingling down Catriona's spine.

Still gripping the book she'd been reading, she used her elbows to wiggle forward on her stomach through the slanting beams of shadow and sunshine. The kitten began to gnaw at her hair with the ferocity of a lion cub. As an insipid giggle drifted to her ears, along with the intriguing rhythms of labored breathing, she leaned down and pressed her eye to a generous crack between two boards.

Even in the faded light, her cousin's hair gleamed like a tousled blond halo around her flushed face. Alice was pinned against a stall door opposite the loft, caught in the fervent embrace of an officer of His Majesty's Royal Navy. As he pressed his open mouth to the pale column of her throat, she tilted her head back, revealing shuttered eyes and moist lips parted with some indefinable hunger.

Catriona's own mouth fell open. She'd never seen her vain cousin so unconcerned about smearing her powder or rumpling the elegant train of her garden gown. This dashing new beau of hers must weave a powerful spell indeed.

Catriona's curious gaze shifted to his back. The young officer's dark blue dress coat had been tossed over a nearby stall door. His dazzling white shirt was stretched taut over his broad shoulders while his waistcoat hugged his lean waist. White breeches clung to his narrow hips, tapering down over muscular calves and thighs to disappear into a pair of shiny black Hessians.

It wasn't the sculpted beauty of those hips that drew Catriona's eyes back to them, but the subtle movement that accompanied each of his forays against her cousin's throat. The provocative motion struck such a delicate balance between coaxing and demand that it was as if his lean, clever body had been created for just such wicked pursuits by God Himself. Or by Lucifer.

When he shifted his avid attentions from Alice's throat to her parted lips, Catriona gaped, mesmerized. Not even in her most wicked dreams had she imagined such kissing! It bore no relation to the grudging buss on the cheek her aunt allowed her uncle each night before they retired to their separate chambers. She touched her fingertips to her own tingling lips, wondering how it might feel to have them devoured with such tender ardor. Her parents had been generous with both their hugs and their kisses but since coming to live with her uncle's family, she hadn't received so much as a dry peck on the brow.

The shameless scapegrace took advantage of her cousin's distraction by dipping his long, tapered fingers into the lacy décolletage of her gown. Alice murmured a halfhearted protest. Catriona rolled her eyes. Alice had pitched a more convincing fit at breakfast that morning when

Catriona had wolfed down the last kipper. Between one breath and the next, Alice's objection melted to a mewling gasp of pleasure. She arched her back to better fill the officer's skilled fingers with her ample breasts.

Catriona wanted to turn away in disgust, but couldn't. She hadn't been quite so captivated since Monsieur Garnerin had crashed his hot-air balloon into a flock of bleating belles at Vauxhall Gardens.

With a grace more deserving of a minuet, the man pivoted, gently backing Alice toward the bed of hay directly beneath Catriona's perch. The sun-dappled shadows flirted with his face, making it impossible to get a clear look at him. Catriona suppressed a groan of frustration as they disappeared from view. If the man could handle a warship with half that finesse, she thought, Britain's victory over Napoleon's navy should be assured.

The intriguing rustle of both hay and clothing being rearranged whetted her curiosity beyond bearing. Scrambling to her hands and knees, Catriona crawled forward until she could hang her head over the edge of the loft.

She had forgotten about the kitten perched on her shoulder until he dug ten tiny claws into her tender nape. Sucking back a yelp of pain, she let go of her nose and made a grab for the kitten. A cloud of dust and pollen flew up her nose. A mighty sneeze gathered in her lungs. Even if the good Lord had blessed her with three hands, she wouldn't have had time to decide which one to use to grab the kitten, muffle the sneeze, and maintain her teetering balance.

As it was, she could only bat wildly at the air as she tumbled headfirst out of the hayloft and crashed into the imposing back of the man preparing to settle himself between her cousin's pale, shapely thighs.

Simon Wescott could feel the hot breath of hell blowing down his neck.

It wasn't the first time he'd experienced that particular whiff of brimstone, nor was it likely to be the last. Hazardous experience had taught him that enraged papas, the self-appointed guardians of their daughters' virtue (either real or illusory), were even more dangerous than irate husbands. Fearful that it was just such a papa who had landed on his back, he waited for a muscled forearm to tighten around his throat.

But the thing on his back just lay there, wheezing down his neck like a consumptive walrus.

His confusion mounted as something began to nibble at his freshly trimmed hair. He frowned.

Good Lord, had one of the earl's ponies fallen on them? Gingerly, he reached around and extracted the tiny culprit from his head, holding it by the scruff of the neck to avoid its windmilling claws. The bit of orange fluff hissed and spit at him like a suckling demon.

The weight on his back shifted. "He takes poorly to being handled that way. I'd let him go if I were you." The merry voice bore the faintest trace of a lilt. The breath stirring his hair was warm and smelled faintly of cinnamon biscuits.

When he failed to heed the warning quickly enough, the kitten twisted, sinking its teeth deep into the tender pad of his thumb.

He shook off the animal, gritting his teeth against a bellow of pain. The weight on his back scrambled away. The woman beneath him shrieked in outrage and shoved at his chest. He rolled off of her, forced to shuffle and refasten clothing with a haste that challenged even his adept hands.

"You horrid beast!"

For a dazed moment, Simon thought Alice's hissed denouncement was directed toward him.

Jerking up her bodice, she sprang to her feet, her fashionably pallid cheeks blotchy with rage. "You nasty, wretched little troll! How *dare* you spy on me?"

Brushing hay from his breeches, Simon climbed to his feet to discover the object of Alice's fury crouched behind him, cooing to the rabid kitten without a single trace of remorse. Strawberry blond curls that looked as if they had been trimmed with a wheat scythe fell over a face of indiscernible age. The curious being's slender body was wrapped in a faded blanket.

"I wasn't spying." Alice's tormentor pointed at the book dangling by its broken spine from the loft above them. Simon tilted his head. Even in the dim light, he recognized Sir Walter Scott's *Minstrelsy of the Scottish Border.* "I was reading."

As Simon's gaze traveled higher to the loft, his lips quirked in a knowing grin. He might have indulged in just such a bit of boyish mischief himself had his own curiosity not been satisfied at the age of thirteen by an eager young housemaid with indiscriminate morals and insatiable appetites.

Alice had considerably less appreciation for the foibles of youth. Whistling through her clenched teeth like a teapot about to overboil, she advanced on Catriona, her elegant hands curved into claws.

Catriona warily climbed to her feet, nudging the kitten out of harm's way with her foot. She'd grown accustomed to having her ears boxed by her quick-tempered cousin, but somehow the prospect of having them boxed in front of this dashing stranger made her chin come up and her spine stiffen.

As Alice drew back her arm, the officer stepped into her path and caught her heaving shoulders, gifting her with an angelic smile. "Come, now, Ally. 'Twas a mere mischance. There's no harm done."

Catriona stood transfixed by his bold maneuver. No one had ever dared to defend her against Alice's bullying. Her aunt might *tsk* beneath her breath when Alice's taunts grew particularly shrill and her uncle might occasionally murmur, "Stop pinching your cousin, dear," before disappearing behind his morning paper, but they all pretended not to see the vivid bruises that so frequently marred the tender skin of her upper arms.

For the first time in his twenty-four years, Simon's considerable charm failed him. Alice turned on him, baring her fangs with a venom that made the kitten seem tame in comparison. Her transformation from purring dove to shrieking shrew made Simon silently, but fervently, renew his vow never to marry.

"A mischance?" she spat. "The only mischance around here was that creature's invasion of our household!" Tearing herself from his grip, she flung an accusing finger at the inept spy. "You've been nothing but an embarrassment to this family since the day my father took you in."

As Catriona saw the officer flinch in pity, she almost wished he'd step aside and let Alice slap her insensible instead.

"You skulk around like a wild animal, wrapped in that filthy rag, making a mockery of everything Papa has worked his entire life to achieve. I'm warning you—from this day forward you'd best keep your homely nose buried in one of your ridiculous books where it belongs and out of my business!"

Alice tried to turn back into her young man's arms, but something of his distaste must have shown in his expression. She shot Catriona a look of pure loathing and burst into tears. "You miserable little monster! You spoil everything!"

Throwing the train of her skirt over her face, she fled the shadowy stable, leaving the sunshine streaming through the open doors in her wake. Catriona blinked rapidly to dispel the sudden glare, finally getting a clear look at the officer's face.

For the second time that day, she had the breath knocked out of her. It wasn't difficult to figure out why Alice had succumbed so eagerly to his charms when they were displayed in such dazzling abundance. He looked like a young Icarus who had flown too close to the sun but had been rewarded for his arrogance instead of punished. His tawny hair was neatly trimmed, barely brushing the collar of his shirt. The sun had kissed his high cheekbones with a bronzed glow and the striking brackets around his mouth provided the perfect frame for his rueful smile. His lips were full with just a tantalizing hint of a pout, yet firm and sculpted enough to be utterly masculine.

Fearful she was about to start wheezing again, Catriona jerked her gaze from his mouth to his eyes. Their moss-green depths sparkled with dormant mischief. It was those devil's eyes set squarely in that angelic face that proved her undoing. Catriona bowed her head, blinded anew by his radiance.

Mistaking his companion's stance for one of dejection, Simon reached down to ruffle the inclined head. "Don't take it so hard, lad. I was once an inquisitive young fellow myself."

The boy jerked up his head, brushing his curly bangs out of his eyes. Eyes as soft and gray as a misty loch on a summer morn. Eyes framed by silky, curling lashes as undeniably feminine as their owner.

Simon would have judged his jaded self incapable of blushing, yet a traitorous heat crawled up his throat. Truth be told, he was more mortified at miscalculating this child's sex than at being caught seducing her cousin.

Eloquent words of apology had always flowed smoothly from his lips. God knows he'd had ample use for them. But for once his glib tongue failed him. He stole a longing glance at the door. Weren't hasty exits his forte? Climbing out windows in the dead of night? Shimmying down trellises? Sneaking barefoot through dew-drenched gardens, boots in hand?

"You might as well go after her. Perhaps you can still coax her into letting you make love to her."

Simon jerked his head back around to find the girl still surveying him. He answered her glare with one of his own. "And what would an impudent little bit of a girl like you know about making love?"

She snorted. "I'm glad to see that I've risen from 'lad' to 'little girl' in your estimation. But I'll have you know that I'll be sixteen only next month. And you needn't pretend there's anything mysterious about making love. The male simply bites the back of the female's neck to hold her still while he mounts her from behind."

It took Simon several dazed blinks to absorb that extraordinary assertion. He had to clear his throat twice before he could choke out a word. "Although the idea has merit, I had hoped to demonstrate considerably more finesse. May I assume your previous intelligence efforts consisted solely of spying on your uncle's stallions?"

"And tomcats," she confessed. "Robert the Bruce's papa fancied himself quite the rake."

Simon's confusion was relieved when she reached down and scooped up the kitten butting its head against her dusty ankles. He studied her, piecing together her reference to an obscure Scottish hero, the faded plaid he'd mistaken for a blanket and the intriguing lilt in her voice.

"Are you Scots?"

"Aye, that I am." She tossed back her head and Simon's breath caught as pride transformed her shabby figure. Buried beneath the layers of dust, tartan and the painful awkwardness of youth was an enticing promise of beauty. "All the Kincaids are Scots, although many, like my uncle Ross, have spent the last fifty years denying it. After our parents were murdered for daring to defend the Kincaid lands against the English when I was but a wee lass, my brother Connor packed me off to live here. 'Tis the curse, you know."

"And what curse might that be?" he inquired gently, suspecting that the girl was cursed only with an overactive imagination.

"Why, the curse of the Kincaids, of course!" Straightening her shoulders, she recited by rote, "The Kincaids are doomed to wander the earth until they're united once again beneath the banner of their one true chieftain. 'Twas pronounced by old Ewan Kincaid himself as he lay dying with an English sword through his breast."

"Why would anyone levy such a frightful fate on their own kin?"

"Because my grandfather—Ewan's son—sold out the clan at Culloden for an earldom and thirty pieces of English silver."

Simon shrugged. "People do what they must to survive."

Her eyes blazed. "I'd rather be dead than survive without honor!"

Her words sent a chill of shame down Simon's spine. He'd never defended any principle with such conviction unless it involved the pursuit of his own pleasures. Or an opportunity to infuriate his father.

He shook off the unfamiliar sensation. Regardless of her claims, she was only a child. A starry-eyed child who'd seized on a romantic obsession to ease her longing for a home and family she most likely would never see again. Her uncle was a very wealthy and influential earl. In time she would grow out of her silly fancies and find herself concerned with nothing more pressing than choosing the sprigged muslin for her latest ball gown or comparing the size of her suitors' inheritances. Simon felt an odd pang of loss at the thought.

"I gather your uncle doesn't share your sympathies for the Scottish cause?"

She ducked her head. "Uncle Ross says I'm as much a fool as my father—always dreaming about castles in the clouds when I should be keeping my feet planted firmly on the ground. Something that's very hard to do in those ridiculous slippers my aunt expects me to wear."

Simon couldn't bear to see her in defeat. He wanted to see her standing tall and proud again, her eyes glittering with courage and defiance.

He reached down to brush the bangs from those extraordinary eyes. "Had he lived, I'm sure your father would be very proud of you."

Catriona had to summon her last shred of pride to keep from turning her cheek into his hand. No man had ever looked at her in such a manner. As if she were the only girl who existed in his world. But hadn't he favored Alice with just such a look only minutes before? She hid her miserable flush of jealousy by ducking beneath his arm and out of his reach.

"If you intend to court my cousin," she said brusquely, "you'll have need of a steady income. Since he has no sons, my uncle is set on making solid matches for both Alice and Georgina. Alice's dowry should support the two of you until you make commander. Provided, of course, that—"

"Whoa!" Simon caught her arm, keeping his fingers well out of reach of Robert the Bruce's teeth. "Before you start planning my nuptials, you might want to know that I'm shipping out on the *Belleisle* tomorrow."

"The *Belleisle*? Why, that's one of the ships under Admiral Nelson's command!"

Her awed response made Simon chafe a bit beneath his starched collar. He'd always worn the blue and white of His Majesty's Navy with the same casual disregard as the rest of his wardrobe.

"Nelson's a true hero and a bonny fine fellow, he is! For an Englishman, of course," she hastily added.

She cast him another shy glance and Simon recognized instinctively that the hero worship simmering in her eyes wasn't for Nelson, however bonny she might think him. But Simon had done nothing to earn her regard. His half-brother Richard had always been the hero in the family. The legitimate heir and the apple of their father's eye. He was nothing but the unfortunate result of a few drunken nights his father had spent in the arms of a pretty young opera dancer.

He was seized by a strange desperation to wipe that moon-eyed look off her face, to make her see him for the man he was, not the man she believed he could be. "Nelson is indeed a 'bonny fine fellow,' but the army is the province of heroes. The navy is for common-born blokes like Nelson and expendable second sons like me." He leaned against the stall door, folding his arms over his chest. "I'll be at sea for several months. As long as your cousin expects nothing from me, she won't be disappointed."

The girl buried her nose in the kitten's fur. "Alice will wait for you if you ask, although I can't promise that she'll be faithful. She's always been a bit fickle."

Simon grinned. Ah, now, here was a game he understood! He had played the delicate rivalries between women to his advantage more than once.

He cupped the girl's cheek in his hand. Startled by its downy softness, he tilted her face up for his tender perusal. "What about you, Miss

Kincaid? How long would you wait for the man you loved?"

"Forever," she whispered.

Her vow seemed to tremble in the air between them, binding and irrevocable. A shudder of unexpected yearning passed through him. He had asked the question in jest only to find himself the butt of his own joke. As she gazed up at him, her moist lips parted in a disarming blend of innocence and invitation.

He lowered his hand, suddenly frantic to escape this dangerous flirtation with a child. Avoiding her eyes, he shrugged on his coat, then rescued his bicorne hat from where Alice had raked it off his head in a moment of passion, and slapped it against his thigh. "Any woman who waits for me is wasting her time. I learned long ago the folly of making promises when you have no intention of keeping them."

The girl cradled the kitten beneath the challenging tilt of her chin. "I suppose that would make you an honorable man."

Donning his hat, Simon gave her his cockiest grin—the one he saved for displaying his winning hand over the whist tables at Boodle's. "On the contrary, Miss Kincaid. That would make me Lieutenant Simon Wescott, a bastard in both birth and deed."

He left her haloed by a crown of shimmering dust motes—a bedraggled Celtic princess without a kingdom, a kitten her sole subject. It was only as he flung himself onto his saddle and kicked his horse into a furious canter that he realized he had never learned her Christian name.

Catriona ran to the stable door, gazing after the brash young lieutenant until nothing remained of him but the clouds of dust stirred up by his mount's hooves. When even those had drifted away on the wind, she sank against the splintery doorframe, still clutching the kitten.

"What say you, Robert?" she whispered, burying her wistful smile in the kitten's downy fur. "Perhaps our Lieutenant Wescott is more honorable than he realizes. If he's brave enough to throw himself in front of Alice on my behalf, facing down Napoleon's cannons should be no more taxing than a stroll through Hyde Park."

Robert the Bruce butted his small head against her chin, purring in assent.

Chapter 2

1810

Catriona Kincaid ducked as a silver hairbrush went sailing past her head.

It was hardly the first object her cousin had
hurled at her head during the ten years of their
acquaintance and she doubted it would be the
last. Fortunately, Alice's normally keen aim had
been weakened by the wrenching sobs buffeting
her slender frame. Her weeping was so piteous
it had stirred even Catriona's sympathy, but it
was Catriona's cautious offer of comfort that
had resulted in the flying hairbrush.

She backed toward the doorway of Alice's

bedchamber, prepared to beat a hasty retreat should any more items come winging her way.

Alice was sprawled full-length across the elegant four-poster. She submitted to her older sister's ministrations with slightly more grace, allowing Georgina to pat her heaving shoulder and murmur, "There, there, pet," in soothing tones.

Alice's tear-streaked face briefly emerged from the nest of pillows to glare daggers at Georgina. "You can't possibly know how much I'm suffering. You *have* a husband." Her voice rose to a wail. "Oh, how could a fat cow like you snare a husband when I can't?" She rolled over and dove back beneath the pillows, punctuating each sob by driving a fist into the feather tick.

Georgina may have been a little on the placid and plump side compared to the temperamental and sylphlike Alice, but she was hardly bovine. Patting with just a fraction more force, she cast Catriona a helpless look over her shoulder. They both knew Alice and Georgina's mother would be of little assistance. Aunt Margaret was huddled in the wing chair by the hearth, weeping copiously, if silently, into her lace handkerchief. She hadn't budged since drawing all of the damask drapes in the bedchamber as if her daughter were suffering from a fatal illness rather than a broken engagement.

"What did you do, Alice?" Catriona asked softly. From the abrupt silence that fell over the room, she knew no one else had dared to ask. "A man like the Marquess of Eddingham isn't going to stir up the scandal broth of a broken betrothal for naught."

Alice rolled back over, her disheveled blond head reemerging from the pillows. She sniffled sullenly. "I only allowed him one kiss."

Catriona drifted closer to the bed, frowning in puzzlement. "Virtue is a quality highly prized by most gentlemen. Surely the marquess wouldn't be so cruel as to end your engagement just because you refused to allow him a second kiss."

Alice sat up, plucking fretfully at the satin counterpane. Her eyes were swollen, her fair skin mottled and grubby with tear tracks. "It wasn't the marquess I kissed." Despite a visible effort to sustain her pout, a dreamy smile curved her lips. "It was the other fellow in the garden. Lord Melbourne's cousin."

Georgina's pale blue eyes widened with shock. The soggy handkerchief Aunt Margaret pressed to her lips failed to muffle her dismayed cry.

Catriona folded her arms over her chest, her worst suspicions confirmed. Her cousin had always had a weakness for pretty boys. Despite her best efforts, Catriona had never forgotten the prettiest of them all—a young naval officer with an angel's smile and the devil's eyes whose touch had made her shiver with a yearning she had been too young to understand. She had hoped it would fade with time, not sharpen.

"And I suppose the marquess caught you kissing this fellow in the garden?" she asked her cousin.

Alice nodded. Her lower lip began to quiver anew. "He humiliated me in front of my friends and refused to speak to me all the way home in the carriage. I had no idea he had such a cruel and jealous streak. Perhaps it's just as well I discovered it before we were wed."

"Just as well for him, you mean," Catriona muttered.

Alice's eyes narrowed. "Catriona's being hateful to me, Mama. Make her go away."

Drawing breath for a fresh wail, she snatched up a Meissen shepherdess from the table beside the bed. Catriona didn't wait for her aunt's dismissal. She slammed the bedchamber door an instant before the delicate porcelain shattered against the other side of it. Her cousin's strident sobs followed her down the corridor.

Catriona hastened down the long curving staircase of the stately Palladian mansion she had called home since she was ten years old. Despite its tasteful combination of elegance and grandeur, there were times when Wideacre Park felt more like a prison than a palace. The graceful arched windows and her uncle's expectations caged her far more effectively than any iron bars. Although she had striven to reward him for his charity by becoming the proper young English lady he had always longed for her to be, there was still a wild and rebellious part of her that yearned to throw on her old plaid and scamper barefoot over the freshly cut grass.

But on this afternoon she had no choice but to heed the demands of duty. Uncle Ross had best learn the truth about what had transpired between Alice and her fiancé before he called the marquess out for publicly humiliating his eldest daughter. From the gossip she'd heard, Eddingham—a devout hunter—possessed both a steady hand and deadly aim.

When she reached the half-ajar door of her uncle's study, she was surprised to hear the deep rumble of male voices.

She crept closer, wondering who would be thoughtless enough to intrude at such a delicate time. But before she could identify the unfamiliar baritone, her uncle's voice rang out. "Is that you, Catriona? Do join us. The gentleman and I have concluded our private business."

Catriona slipped into the study, startled to

discover that the *gentleman* lounging in the brass-studded leather chair across from her uncle's desk was none other than the Marquess of Eddingham himself. He looked far more composed than her cousin. His dark eyes were clear, his cool smile untainted. He revealed no overt signs of a broken heart, deepening Catriona's suspicion that he had always possessed more affection for Alice's ample dowry than for Alice herself.

With both his heavy jowls and the bags beneath his eyes drooping, her uncle looked more heartbroken than either Alice or the marquess. Catriona couldn't really blame him. Finding the scandal-prone Alice a husband had been no easy task.

Her uncle beckoned her into the room. "I believe you made my niece's acquaintance at Lady Stippler's soiree last month," he said.

Eddingham rose, an artful arrangement of raven curls falling over his brow as he sketched her a flawless bow. "Always a pleasure, Miss Kincaid. Even under these trying circumstances."

He was a handsome man, she supposed, if you fancied the dark, brooding sort. "I'm afraid my cousin can be rather rash and impetuous," she said. "I assure you that it's a reflection on her character, not yours."

"Perhaps it was for the best." He sighed, striking just the right note of tragic resignation. "I've suspected for some time that our temperaments might not be suited." As Catriona chose a brocaded stool to spread her skirts upon, he settled back into his chair. "Your uncle Ross and I were just discussing the many other interests we have in common. A fondness for fine horseflesh. A love of the land." His hawkish gaze lingered on her face. "The pleasure of a good challenge. Tell me, Miss Kincaid, are you and your uncle any relation to the Scottish Kincaids?"

"Why, yes!" Catriona blurted out, startled by the unexpected question.

"I should say not," her uncle rumbled at the precise same moment, drowning out her reply. "Our branch of the family has been sturdy English stock for decades."

Barely one decade in her case, Catriona thought, helping herself to a crumpet from the tea tray in the hopes that its buttery sweetness would take the edge off of the bitter taste in her mouth.

Eddingham took a genteel sip of his tea. "I was curious because I've just purchased a large tract of land in the Highlands near Balquhidder. My financial advisers tell me there's a fortune to be made there in Cheviot sheep."

Her uncle ran a thumb along the edge of his

leather desk blotter, suddenly having great difficulty meeting Eddingham's eyes. "So I've heard."

"I was able to purchase the land from the Crown for little more than a song because for years it's been plagued by a pesky band of outlaws led by a man calling himself the Kincaid."

Catriona tried to swallow, but the crumpet had crumbled to sawdust in her throat.

The marquess favored her with an indulgent smile. "I can't tell you how relieved I am to learn that this rogue and his kin are no relation to such a lovely young lady."

"Has anyone ever seen this notorious outlaw?" she asked lightly, pouring herself a cup of tea to hide the sudden trembling of her hands.

The marquess didn't look nearly so handsome with his thin upper lip curled into a sneer. "I'm afraid not. He prefers to skulk in the shadows like the bullying coward he is. In the past year he's vanished completely, as men of his ilk so often do. If he's not already dead, we'll flush him and his men out when the spring thaw begins. I've English troops at my disposal only too eager for the task."

Thundering feet. Red-coated figures looming out of the darkness. A blaze of light, then choking blindness. Staccato gunfire. A man's bellow of anguish as he threw himself across his wife's limp body. Then noth-

ing but the ghostly creaking of a rope as it swung in
stark relief against the moonlit sky. Burying her
tear-streaked face in her brother's shirt, trying to blot
out a sight forever etched in both their memories.

Catriona's own voice seemed to come from
very far away. From that misty Highland night
when her parents had died at the ruthless hands
of the English soldiers. "Would you care for some
more tea, my lord?"

Eddingham held out his cup to her. "Why, I'd
be delighted."

Her lips frozen in a numb smile, Catriona
tipped the spout of the silver teapot an inch past
his cup, pouring a stream of lukewarm tea into
his lap.

Biting off an oath, Eddingham shot to his feet.

"Catriona!" her uncle barked, pounding on
the desk. "What in the devil has got into you,
girl? I would have expected that from Georgina,
but it's not like you to be so ham-handed!"

Catriona's gracious smile didn't waver as she
gently rested the teapot back on the tray and
handed the marquess a linen serviette. "Forgive
me, my lord," she said smoothly. "I promise to
take greater care in the future."

"That would be well advised, Miss Kincaid,"
Eddingham said through clenched teeth, dabbing at the unsightly stain spreading across the

front placket of his buff trousers. Tossing the towel back on the tray, he forced his grimace into a smile and sketched her uncle a curt bow. "If you'll be so kind as to excuse me, my lord, I'd best retire to my town house to make the necessary repairs."

While her uncle escorted Eddingham to the door, Catriona remained on the ottoman, her hands folded serenely on her lap—the very portrait of a dutiful niece. But the minute the door closed behind their guest she surged to her feet to face her uncle, the study becoming a smoldering trench in a battle of long standing.

She rested her hands on her hips, glaring at him. "I can't believe you're still denying your own kin! Didn't you hear the man? He plans to hunt down what's left of them like wild game as soon as the mountain snows thaw. What if this 'Kincaid' he speaks of is my brother and your very own nephew?"

"All the more reason to deny him! Didn't you hear Eddingham?" Her uncle sought refuge behind his desk, putting it between them like a shield. "This fellow is an outlaw, a thief, a highwayman who robs innocent folk for his own gain. He's naught but a common criminal whose only possible destiny is to end up dangling from a hangman's noose."

Catriona stiffened. "Just like your brother?"

Her uncle shuffled through a thick sheaf of papers, his face still hard but his eyes softened by an old grief. "Your father chose his own fate."

"As did yours," she said, reminding him of the devil's bargain her grandfather had struck with the English. A bargain that had saved his life but cost him his clan's land and soul. "But because I'm a woman I'm not free to choose mine."

He tossed the papers back down on the desk. "And just what fate would you choose, Catriona?"

She stepped closer to the desk, leaning over to brace both palms upon its gleaming mahogany top. "I want to return to Scotland to search for my brother."

Her uncle simply gazed at her for a long moment before saying softly, "If Connor was this outlaw . . . if he was still alive, don't you think he would have tried to contact you by now? He was fifteen years old when he sent you to me and he's had ten long years to practice his penmanship."

Catriona had expected her uncle to counter her demand with fury and bluster or perhaps even mocking laughter. Logic was the one weapon she was not prepared to parry. "Perhaps he thought I'd be better off if I forgot our life in Scotland. Forgot him."

"Then he was right. But the one thing you should never forget is that he sent you to me so you could have a better life."

"He sent me to you because he believed it was the only way to *save* my life after the redcoats shot our mother and hanged our father."

"And you expect me to send you back so they can murder you as well? I think not." He snorted. "Your father's head was full of clouds and dreams too. He stood right where you're standing today, his eyes blazing with righteous indignation, and demanded that my father allow him to travel to Scotland and try to reunite the Kincaid clan. When he was refused, he defied my father's wishes and snuck away in the dead of night. He abandoned the wealthy fiancée my father had chosen for him and ended up wedding some penniless Highland chit. We never saw him again." Her uncle shook his head. "Davey threw away everything to chase some ridiculous dream. I won't allow you to make the same mistake."

Catriona straightened. "I'll be twenty-one in three months and can go wherever I choose." She allowed the faintest hint of a lilt to creep into her speech, knowing it would gall her uncle more than any words she could utter. "Aye, Uncle Roscommon," she said, calling him by the name no one else in the family dared to use. "I'll be free to pursue my own destiny then and I'll walk all the way to the Highlands to find Connor and my clan if need be!"

Catriona realized too late that her open rebellion had been a mistake. Her uncle's broad face went ruddy, betraying his Scots heritage more effectively than any burr. He wagged a sturdy finger at her. "That you won't, *lass*. Because I'm doubling your dowry and I'm going to wed you to the next man who walks through that door and asks for your hand. He'll bed you, get you with child and then you'll be too busy practicing your scales on the pianoforte and pasting pretty seashells on colored paper to pursue this idiotic notion of yours!"

To her horror, Catriona felt tears sting her eyes. "I've always been grateful for your charity, Uncle, and I can understand why you might wish to be rid of such a cumbersome burden. But I never dreamed that you could despise me so much." Although she wanted nothing more than to burst into tears and storm out of the room just as Alice would have done, she forced herself to turn and walk calmly out the door, her head held high.

As the door closed behind his niece, Ross Kincaid sank heavily into his chair. After his younger brother had defied their father's wishes and run off to Scotland, their father had ordered that every likeness of him be taken down and burned. But Ross needed no sketches or portraits to remember his brother. Catriona—with her unruly strawberry blond curls, obstinate chin, and misty gray eyes—was Davey's living, breathing image.

He would never forget the day the mail coach from Edinburgh had dumped her on his doorstep—a thin, bedraggled creature with enormous gray eyes and a thick thatch of curls falling in her face. Her only possessions had been the clothes she wore on her back and the ragged plaid wrapped around her shoulders. Despite the hungry gleam in her eyes and the dirt smudging her fair cheeks, she had alighted from the back of the mail coach as if she were arriving at Buckingham Palace to take tea with the King.

His lips curved in a reluctant smile at the memory. In truth, he didn't despise his niece. He loved her. Loved her enough to marry her to a man she did not love if it would keep her safe in England. Keep her from making the same fatal mistakes her father had made.

Ross drew a small gold key from his waistcoat pocket and unlocked the bottom drawer of the desk. He reached inside, his normally steady hand trembling faintly as he drew out a yellowing bundle of letters tied with a ragged bit of string, all addressed in an awkward masculine scrawl to a Miss Catriona Kincaid. He turned them over in his hands, studying the unbroken wax seals through troubled eyes.

He hadn't lied to his niece, Ross told himself, ignoring the acid burn of guilt in his gut. The letters from her brother had stopped arriving over three years before. The boy must surely be dead.

He tucked the bundle of letters back into the drawer, slid the drawer shut and turned the key, locking his secrets away along with all of his regrets.

When Catriona emerged from her uncle's study, her eyes still burning with unshed tears, the last sight she expected to see was the Marquess of Eddingham leaning lazily against the opposite wall.

He held up his ornately carved cane in a white-gloved hand. "I forgot my walking stick." The glitter of amusement in his eyes warned her that he had overheard the entire conversation, including her uncle's threat to double her dowry and marry her off to the first man who asked for her hand.

She dashed a stray tear from her cheek, sensing that it wouldn't be wise to betray any trace of weakness in front of this man. "Have you forgotten your way to the front door as well? Shall I ring for one of the footmen to show you out?" she asked pointedly.

He straightened, looming over her in the shadowy corridor. "That won't be necessary. However, you might want to inform your uncle that I'll be away on business for the next few days but that I have every intention of calling on you as soon as I return on Monday afternoon. You might also wish to tell him that I'd like a word with him then. In private."

Catriona remained frozen in place as Eddingham reached to drag his gloved thumb over the curve of her cheek, the motion no more a caress than the warning flicker of a cobra's tongue.

He leaned closer, the warmth of his breath an unwelcome intimacy against her ear. "Perhaps it's not too late for you to save those savages you so boldly claim as your kin, Miss Kincaid. With a willing and eager bride to warm my bed, I'd have far less time to devote to their extinction."

Then he was gone, the sprightly tap of his walking stick on the parquet floor mocking her dread. Catriona collapsed against the door. She didn't realize she had been holding her breath until it escaped her in a ragged rush. She nearly jumped out of her skin when something warm and fluffy brushed against her leg.

She glanced down just as Robert the Bruce butted her in the ankle with his enormous head, nearly knocking her off her feet.

"Why, there you are, you cheeky little rogue!" she exclaimed, bending down and hefting the cat into her arms. His rumbling purr reminded her that there was no longer anything *little* about him. "Just where were you a few minutes ago when I could have used a stout-hearted gentleman to defend me?"

Catriona caught a glimpse of their reflection in the gilt-framed oval mirror hanging on the opposite wall. She rested her chin on Robert the Bruce's broad head, savoring his solid warmth and remembering how she had once held him in exactly the same manner while standing in a stable door and watching a handsome young man ride off to do battle with the world. Her gray eyes were no longer misted with tears, but flashing with the steel of crossed swords.

"Uncle Ross is wrong, isn't he, Robert? We don't need a husband. What we need is a hero." She watched her lips curve into a determined smile. "And I know *exactly* where to find one."

Chapter 3

Somewhere within the dank walls of Newgate Prison was housed every manner of rogue and miscreant who had ever plagued the broad thoroughfares and narrow alleys of London. Murderers, rapists, thieves, kidnappers, debtors and scoundrels of every stripe crowded the prison's long, narrow cells, all contributing to the miasma of misery and squalor that seemed to hang over the place.

The gallows stood in the courtyard directly outside the prison windows, their forbidding shadow a stark reminder that many imprisoned behind those walls would only make their escape at the end of an executioner's rope.

Catriona gingerly followed the gaoler down a

dank brick tunnel, struggling to keep the scalloped hem of her redingote from brushing the filthy straw that littered the floor without losing her grip on the handkerchief pressed to her nose. She could only be thankful that she had sprinkled the lace-trimmed scrap of linen with lavender water earlier that morning. The floral scent helped to block out the stench of unwashed flesh and other, even more unthinkable insults to her delicate nostrils.

The gaoler lurched to a halt and swung around. The lantern gripped in his bony hand cast a sallow arc of light over his broken nose and rotting teeth. Sparse strands of ginger hair clung to his misshapen skull. "Are you sure you want to do this, miss? Newgate is no place for a lady. If you was my sister, I'd want you safe at home darning my stockings in front o' the fire, not traipsing 'round 'ere with a bunch o' sodomites and cutthroats."

Catriona lowered the handkerchief and cast a nervous glance over her shoulder, fearing a sodomite was about to spring out of the shadows to cut her throat. "I appreciate your concern, sir, but I feel it my Christian duty to seek out my wayward brother and offer him what comfort I can give."

The gaoler snorted. "Suit yourself, miss. But

the only comfort most of these rotters is lookin' for can be found in the bottom of a gin bottle or under a doxy's skirts."

Still shaking his head, he proceeded down the tunnel, whistling a tuneless melody through the gap in his remaining teeth. Catriona might have joined him had she believed it would bolster her faltering courage. The tunnel soon opened up into a broader corridor, flanked on one side by the bars of a long common room almost too large to be called a cell. It would have appeared even larger if every inch of available space hadn't been occupied by the most motley-looking horde of men Catriona had ever encountered.

Some were slumped on wooden benches, while others milled restlessly about or sprawled in the straw like barnyard animals. A handkerchief soaked in lavender water for an entire night couldn't have masked their stench.

A chorus of hoots and catcalls greeted her appearance. Catriona kept her gaze fixed straight ahead, steadfastly feigning deafness.

"Why, look there, Charlie!" one of the men shouted. "It's a lady come to call! Or is it your wife lookin' for a *real* man to warm 'er bed?"

Another prisoner shoved his grime-encrusted hand through the bars, crooking his finger at her. "Maybe she's one o' them there missionaries.

Come over 'ere, luv, and I'll give you a reason to get on your knees."

Both Catriona and the prisoner flinched as the gaoler slammed his wooden truncheon into the bars, missing the prisoner's fingers by a hair's breadth. "Mind your tongue in front o' the lady, Jack, or I'll be forced to come in there and teach you some proper manners."

Although the men's bawdy taunts quickly subsided to sullen mutters, Catriona could still feel their hungry gazes burning their way through the sturdy scarlet wool of her redingote. By the time she followed the gaoler through the far door, it was all she could do not to collapse in relief. But her relief was short-lived. The tunnel sloping down into the shadows was even danker and narrower than the one that had come before it.

She cleared her throat to mask the faint quaver in her voice. "Is this where you lock away the most incorrigible prisoners?"

The gaoler cast her a sly glance over his shoulder. "There's some that might say that."

By the time they reached the thick oak door at the foot of the tunnel, Catriona was beginning to question anew the wisdom of her quest. An iron grate was set high in the door, too high for her to peep through even if she stood on her tiptoes.

She reached into her reticule with shaking

hands and handed the gaoler her crumpled permit. "I was promised an hour alone with my brother."

Holding the permit upside down, the gaoler squinted at it, his lips moving as he pretended to read. Catriona slipped a guinea from her reticule and waved it in front of his eyes, confident that its universal language would be understood.

He beamed at her, pocketed the coin, then unhooked a clanking loop of iron keys from his belt and slid the largest, most forbidding-looking one into the keyhole. As the door creaked outward on its massive hinges, Catriona drew in a deep breath, steeling herself for the worst.

That breath escaped her in a disbelieving puff as her gaze swept the interior of the cell. If it could indeed be called a cell. The room might not possess all the comforts of home, but it certainly possessed all the comforts of a lavishly decorated bawdy house. Or at least the comforts Catriona imagined a bawdy house might possess, having never visited such an establishment.

The dank walls had been draped with scarlet and gold embroidered scarves that were both gauzy and gaudy. An Oriental carpet in glowing emerald and ruby tones warmed the stone floor. A pair of half-naked plaster nymphs cast Catriona coy glances from their mismatched pedestals set in the far corners of the cell. The statues might be chipped and the carpet a tad threadbare, but a trio of oil lamps hanging from wooden pegs set into the wall cast their cozy glow over the entire scene, giving it the enticing allure of a sultan's tent.

There was no bed in the chamber, but the overstuffed settee would doubtlessly serve just as well. As was proved by its current occupant. All Catriona could see from the doorway was a pair of shiny black Hessians crossed at the ankle and a graceful curlicue of smoke drifting up to join the faint cloud hovering near the ceiling.

"That you, Barney?" the settee's occupant drawled without even bothering to uncross his boots, much less rise to greet his guests. "Did Mrs. Terwilliger send over that girl I requested? You can't begin to imagine how bloody lonely it gets in here with nothing but your imagination to keep you company."

The gaoler scratched his head, giving Catriona an abashed look. "I'm afraid not, sir. But I 'ave brought you some company to ease your loneliness. It's your dear sister, come to bring you a dose o' Christian comfort."

The boots didn't budge. A thoughtful puff of smoke drifted toward the ceiling. Just as Catriona was seriously considering bolting and taking her chances with the men in the common cell, the prisoner sat up and swung his long, muscled legs over the edge of the settee.

As he came into full view, Catriona barely managed to swallow her gasp.

Simon Wescott was no longer a pretty boy.

His hair was in desperate want of a cut, spilling to a spot just past his shoulders. It was a shade darker than the honeyed hue she remembered, as if those silken strands had seen more of midnight than sunlight in the past five years. A day's growth of beard shadowed his jaw, accentuating its strong cut and the Slavic hollows beneath his high cheekbones. Dissipation had taken its toll around his eyes, carving a fine web of lines that gave his face more character than he probably possessed. A jagged white scar bisected his left eyebrow, as if he'd finally been punished for daring to fly too close to the sun by a lightning bolt hurled from the fist of a jealous god.

He stubbed out his thin cigar with deliberate care, then peered at her through the lingering haze of smoke, wariness darkening his eyes to the color of a forest glade in the breathless lull just before a storm breaks.

Catriona was about to open her mouth to stammer something—anything at all—when he spread his arms wide, his lips curving in the

dazzling smile that had no doubt charmed countless young women out of their undergarments
and into his arms. "Why, hello, sweeting! Why
don't you come over here and let me bounce you
on my knee as I used to when you were but a
wee poppet?"

Given no choice but to play along with her
own charade, Catriona edged toward him,
clutching her reticule in white-knuckled hands.
"Hello, brother, dear," she said stiffly. "I do hope
they've been treating you well."

"Not as well as you always did, pumpkin," he
replied, reaching around to give her rump a
playful swat. Her outraged glare only deepened
the sparkle of mischief in his eyes.

"Given your grim circumstances," she said,
"I'm glad to find you in such high spirits." Her
lips pressed into a rigid pucker, Catriona leaned
down to brush a chaste kiss over his cheek. But
he turned his head at the last second so that her
lips grazed the corner of his mouth instead.

Blushing furiously, she straightened and stepped
out of his reach.

Moved by their tender reunion, the grizzled
gaoler drew a filthy handkerchief from his pocket
and began to dab at his eyes. "Your sister wishes
to have some time alone with you, sir, so I'll let the
two o' you get reacquainted while I take my tea."

"No!" Realizing that she had made a terrible mistake, Catriona made a frantic lunge for the door. But it was too late. The gaoler had already slipped from the cell and was turning the key from the outside, leaving her locked in the tiger's cage.

And unless she wanted to become his dinner, she knew she had best try to repair her crumbling composure.

As she slowly turned to face him, Simon rose from the settee. He was taller than she remembered. Broader in the shoulders, leaner in the hips. He wore no coat or waistcoat, just a pair of doeskin trousers and a white lawn shirt with full sleeves laid open at the throat to reveal a wedge of muscular chest lightly sprinkled with golden hair. In her boldest imaginings, she had never dreamed that his charms would grow even more lethal with time, honed by that mysterious masculine alchemy of age and experience.

"I'm a wretched liar," she confessed.

"I know. That must be why Mummy always loved me best." At her reproachful look, he cocked his head to the side. "If you're not another one of my father's bastards, then why are you here? Did you come to assassinate me or"—his skeptical gaze dipped to the slender waist revealed by the flattering *princesse*-cut of her redingote—"to accuse me of siring your future progeny?"

"Why, I—I—" she sputtered before curiosity got the best of her. "Does that happen frequently?"

He shrugged. "At least once a week. Sometimes twice on Tuesdays." The wry twist of his lips made it impossible to tell if he was mocking her or his own reputation. "If you've come to assassinate me, then I'm afraid I'm at your mercy. I'd offer you my cravat so you could strangle me, but they took it away so I wouldn't hang myself. Wouldn't want to deprive the executioner of the pleasure."

"The last time I checked, getting oneself nearly seven thousand pounds in debt and seducing a magistrate's daughter wasn't a hanging offense."

"You haven't met the magistrate." He sank back down on the edge of the settee and reached beneath it.

Half expecting him to whip out a weapon of some sort, Catriona took a nervous step backward. But when his hand reemerged, it was brandishing a half-empty bottle of port.

He whisked two glasses out from under the settee with equal aplomb. "I've been remiss in my manners. Would you care to join me?"

"No, thank you." Watching him pour a generous splash of the ruby liquor into one of the glasses, she said, "I forgot that you were expecting company of a different sort altogether. You must be very disappointed."

He slanted her an unreadable look from beneath his gilt-tipped lashes. "I wouldn't say that. Surprised, perhaps, but not disappointed."

"We've met before, although I can hardly expect you to remember me."

Just as she could never expect herself to forget him.

"Then you do me a grave disservice"—Simon's gently chiding look could have melted an ice floe—"Miss Kincaid."

Catriona's mouth fell open in shock.

He lifted the glass in a mocking toast. "I never forget a lovely face."

Her mouth snapped shut. "You thought I was a boy."

His lips twitched with amusement as he glanced ever so briefly, yet boldly, at the generous swell of her bosom. "A mistake I can assure you I won't make again." He took a sip of the port, a teasing lilt infusing his voice. "Surely you didn't think I'd forget a bonny Scottish lass who smelled of fresh-cut hay and cinnamon biscuits and whose only champion was a savage orange kitten named Bonnie Prince Charlie."

"Robert the Bruce. I suppose you remember my cousin as well?" she could not resist asking.

He blinked at her, all doe-eyed innocence. "You had a cousin?"

"You really should remember Alice. You were about to complete your seduction of her when I tumbled out of the hayloft onto your back."

"Ah, yes, how could I forget dear sweet . . ." He frowned. "What was her name again?"

"Alice."

"Ah, yes, dear sweet Amelia." He clapped a hand to his heart. "I've thought of her fondly nearly every day since the cruel hand of fate tore us apart."

Biting back a reluctant smile, Catriona reached out to flick the end of one of the scarves that draped the stone walls. "What sort of prison affords you the luxuries of wine, tobacco and women of easy virtue?"

"I hate to corrupt your delicate sensibilities, my dear, but incarcerated men of means have always honored the age-old tradition of bribing the gaoler." He hefted the glass in another toast, giving him a valid excuse to drain it dry. "God bless his money-grubbing little soul."

She frowned. "I don't understand. If you have means, then why are you locked up as a debtor?"

He winced. "Perhaps I should have said the

illusion of means. Everyone here knows that the Duke of Bolingbroke is my father. And they believe that surely not even the most icy-hearted of noblemen would be so cruel as to allow his bastard son to rot away in Newgate. They expect him to charge up to the gates in his coach-and-four at any minute, tossing coins from his overflowing purse to the slavering peasants."

"Is that what you expect as well?" she asked lightly, trying to hide how critical his answer might be to her plans.

The ghost of a bitter smile tugged at his lips. "I expect him to provide the rope for my hanging. I'm afraid I've always been a dreadful disappointment to him. My most recent transgression was to survive my encounter with Napoleon while my brother Richard died an ignoble death from dysentery on a mud-soaked battlefield in Malta, leaving him with no proper heir."

"I'm sorry," Catriona said softly.

"That my brother died? Or that I survived?" He leaned back on the settee and patted the cushion next to him. "Enough about the rot in my family tree. Why don't you trot over here, rest your pretty head on my shoulder and tell me just how word of my sordid crimes reached ears as refined and lovely as yours?"

Ignoring his audacious invitation, Catriona gingerly settled herself on a rickety three-legged stool a few feet away. The thing tottered wildly, nearly upending her before she recovered her balance. She sought to reclaim her dignity by briskly removing her bonnet and resting it on the floor next to the stool.

"As I'm sure you're well aware, your most recent incarceration is the talk of every drawing room in London." She drew off her gloves and placed them on top of the bonnet. "But you really shouldn't be so modest about your accomplishments, Mr. Wescott. Or should I call you *Sir Simon?* You didn't just survive Napoleon. You were knighted for valor after Trafalgar because you saved the life of your captain on the *Belleisle* by throwing yourself in front of a musket ball intended for him. Upon your return from Spain, you were hailed as a hero before all of London."

He snorted. "This city has always been quick to embrace any fool with a handful of shiny medals and a bit of braid on his shoulders."

"Oh, but it wasn't your rise to glory that truly captured the city's imagination. It was your rather spectacular fall from grace. Or should I call it a plunge? Instead of accepting the promotion to commander that the navy offered you, you resigned your commission and proceeded to wench, drink, and gamble away every ounce of respectability your valor had earned you."

He stretched out on the settee and folded his hands behind his head, looking thoroughly bored. "You left off brawling and dueling. I haven't killed a man yet, but I've winged several."

She continued as if he hadn't spoken. "Not a fortnight has gone by since then without some torrid mention of you in the scandal sheets."

"Which you no doubt pore over every night in your virginal white nightdress before you slide between the cold sheets of your lonely bed."

His taunt struck uncomfortably close to home. He would never know how many times his memory had warmed both those sheets and her dreams.

She lifted her chin. "How do you know I sleep alone?"

"Because you look like you're in desperate need of a good—" He met her unwavering gaze for a long moment, then finished softly, "Husband."

Catriona rose to pace the cell, avoiding his eyes. "I've heard other rumors about you since your return as well. Rumors not printed in the scandal sheets but whispered in drawing rooms and back alleys. They say that you're willing to use the skills you acquired in the navy to provide certain services for those in need of them— protection, transportation, retrieval of lost items." She paused before one of the plaster statues, running one finger lightly along the nymph's dimpled cheek. "All for a price, of course."

"Devoting oneself to a life of debauchery doesn't come cheap, you know."

Behind her, she heard the settee creak as Simon sat up. "Is that why you came here today, Miss Kincaid? Because you wish to hire me?"

"No, Mr. Wescott," she replied coolly, turning to face him. "I came here today because I wish to marry you."

Chapter 4

$\mathscr{S}$imon had received some unconventional proposals in his life—many of them too lurid to whisper in mixed company—but none of them had involved anything as shocking as the prospect of matrimony.

His nimble tongue failed him as he gaped at his visitor, wondering if she was as balmy as she was lovely. The promise of beauty he'd glimpsed in that barn five years ago had been fulfilled beyond his wildest expectations.

Hers was the sort of beauty that required no cosmetics or artifice to enhance it. She didn't need a beauty patch to draw attention to the kissable plumpness of her bottom lip or rouge to heighten the natural roses in her cheeks. There were those who might have judged her nose a fraction too sharp or her jaw a shade too strong, but Simon would have condemned them as fools. He found her flaws to be as endearing as her charms, especially the unfashionable hint of strawberry in her hair and the delicate scattering of freckles that dappled the cream of her skin. As far as he was concerned, trying to bleach them away with buttermilk or Gowland's Lotion should be considered a hanging offense.

His jests had held a damning ring of truth. He could barely remember her cousin Alice. Hell, he could barely remember the face of the randy young countess who had taken him to her bed the night the magistrate's henchmen had dragged him out of it and into this cell. But he had never forgotten this girl or the look in her eyes when he had so recklessly cupped her cheek in his hand and seduced her into meeting his gaze.

He'd admired his own reflection in the eyes of countless women through the years, but the man gazing back at him from those misty gray mirrors had been a stranger. A man who might actually be worthy of such admiration. A man who still had a chance to make both his country and his father proud.

This time Simon didn't bother with the glass. He simply lifted the bottle of port to his lips and took a deep swig of the liquor, welcoming its familiar and numbing burn. "Your driver must have taken a wrong turn on the way here, Miss Kincaid. This is Newgate, not Bedlam."

"I'm well aware of how mad such a notion must sound to you." She reached up to swipe away a stray curl that had escaped her neat chignon, reminding him of the awkward girl she had been. Her years in England had finally succeeded in polishing the lilt from her voice. Simon was surprised by how much he missed it. "But what I'm offering you is very much a business proposition. Isn't that what most marriages are anyway?"

"Why, Miss Kincaid," he drawled, "I had no idea the heart of a true romantic beat beneath that lovely bosom of yours."

That lovely bosom heaved in a sigh of frustration. "You can mock me if you like, but you know I'm telling the truth. An impoverished duchess weds a wealthy merchant to save the fortunes of her family. Two young people who grew up on adjoining estates pledge their troths simply to please their families and unite their lands. Hearts are bartered all the time and for far less noble pursuits."

"Why don't you tell me what pursuit could possibly be so noble as to drive a woman like you to storm the walls of a prison to search for a prospective husband?"

She drew nearer to him, her expression disarmingly earnest. "I want you to escort me to my brother in the Highlands."

Simon took a minute to absorb that information. "A simple enough task. Why should it require me to trade one set of shackles for another?"

"Because I don't have the means to hire you outright. But I do have a *very* generous dowry." She lowered her eyes, her thick lashes casting a shadow on her cheeks. "A dowry that's just been doubled by my uncle in his desperation to be rid of me."

"Was this before or after he found out you were going to Newgate to look for a husband?"

She gave him a reproachful look. "He doesn't know I'm here. No one does."

Simon held her gaze without blinking, watching color creep higher in her cheeks as she realized what a dangerous admission she had just made. She had risked not only her reputation but her virtue itself by allowing the gaoler to lock her in the cell with him. For all she knew, he was the sort of heartless blackguard who could have her beneath him on the settee with one hand up her skirts and the other clapped over her mouth before she could so much as draw breath to scream. Not that anyone in this godforsaken hole would care if she screamed. The men in the common room were more likely to cheer him on while demanding their turn when he was done with her.

Dragging her gaze away from his with visible difficulty, she began to pace the length of the cell once again, the graceful sway of her hips beneath the scarlet wool of her redingote drawing his jaded eye.

"I'm willing to split half the dowry with you," she informed him, speaking as if he'd already been fool enough to accept her offer. "After you've escorted me to my brother, you can return to England. The money should be more than enough to settle your debts and still leave you with a tidy little profit."

He cocked one eyebrow. "For gambling and wenching?"

"If that's how you choose to squander it," she replied with acid sweetness.

"How is it going to look when I abandon my beloved bride in the wilds of the Highlands and return to London to resume my debauched ways?"

Her snort was less than ladylike. "You weren't concerned with appearances last summer when you stripped off all your clothes and went swimming in Lady Abercrombie's goldfish pond during the middle of her afternoon soiree, were you? But have no fear. I've prepared for all eventualities. Once you return to London, I will petition for an annulment. I doubt another scandal will tarnish *your* reputation. I'll be the only one running the risk of ruin."

"You're already running the risk of ruin," he gently reminded her. "And I hate to point this out, but the only way to obtain an annulment would be to prove that we *are* actually brother and sister, which is impossible, or that I was incapable of performing my marital duties to your satisfaction."

"Which I'm sure you believe is equally impossible," she finished dryly.

He let his shrug speak for him.

"That's precisely my point, Mr. Wescott. If I make such a claim to obtain an annulment, *I'll* be the laughingstock of London, not you. You, on the other hand, will be free to go back to devoting your days—and nights—to proving me a liar."

She had finally drawn near enough for him to snag her hand. He tugged her closer, forcing her to look at him and see that the teasing light had completely gone out of his eyes. "Once you're my wife in the eyes of the law, why should I settle for half your dowry? What's to stop me from absconding with every penny of it and leaving you abandoned and destitute?"

She blinked down at him. "Why, your word, of course."

Simon couldn't remember the last time anyone had put faith in his word. It might have been nothing more than a trick of the flickering lamplight, but for an elusive instant he would have sworn he caught a glimpse of that old adulation in her lovely face.

Catriona was taken aback when a hearty bark of laughter escaped Simon, then another. Freeing her hand, he collapsed against the cushions of the settee, laughing so hard he was forced to swipe tears from his cheeks. "I hate to disillusion you, my dear, but my word isn't worth the breath I'd waste in giving it. If you're looking for a knight-errant to aid you in your noble quest, then I'm afraid you've come to the wrong place." He offered her a fond leer. "This knight is far more likely to ravish a damsel than rescue one."

With that deliciously wicked threat making her blood sizzle through her veins, it was all Catriona could do to force her own lips into a cool smile. "You needn't work so hard to shock me. I can promise you that I have no illusions left about your character—or lack thereof. Why do you think I chose you?"

"Because you've been wearing your nightcap too tight? It must be that, because I would hate to think that you've been nursing a sentimental *tendre* for me all these years."

His gentle mockery effortlessly skewered her heart. Desperate to keep the blade from twisting and spilling her blood where he might see it, she tossed her head with a scornful ripple of laughter. "Don't flatter yourself, Mr. Wescott. I chose you because I know you can't resist turning a tidy profit for a minimal amount of effort."

Simon eyed Catriona balefully. Her offer was beginning to sound just a little too tempting. "And just how do you plan to spring me from Newgate?" He nodded toward her reticule. "Have you a pistol tucked away in your little silk purse?"

"I'm hoping that won't be necessary. I plan to pay each of your debtors a visit to announce our secret engagement and to beg both their discretion and their patience. I believe I can make them see reason. After all, they'll have no hope of recouping their losses as long as you're rotting away in prison. If they believe your debts are to be settled as soon as we return from a romantic Highland honeymoon, they're much more likely to be magnanimous, are they not?"

"You might be able to charm my debtors, but there is the little matter of that angry magistrate. The last time I saw him, he was howling for my blood."

Her smile deepened, revealing a beguiling dimple in her left cheek. "Who do you think authorized this visit? Lord Poultney knows he has no hope of seeing you hanged. I was able to convince him that being leg-shackled to one female for life would be a far more fitting punishment for a rogue like you."

Simon grew very still. He'd been a navy man just long enough to recognize when he'd been outflanked and outgunned. And he didn't much care for the feeling that he was about to be boarded against his will.

He unfolded his muscled length from the settee, towering comfortably over his guest, and was gratified to watch her inch backward.

No one had ever accused him of gallantry. But it seemed he had no choice but to try and save this misguided child before she proposed to some convict less scrupulous than himself. If such a fellow even existed.

"Very well, Miss Kincaid," he said, resting his hands on his hips. "I'll accept this devil's bargain of yours."

"You will?" Catriona replied, unable to completely hide her start of surprise at his unexpectedly rapid surrender.

"With a small stipulation of my own."

"And just what would that be?" she asked warily.

He took a step toward her. She retreated another foot, stopping just short of tumbling backward over the stool. "Although the prospect of squandering half your dowry is undeniably enticing, I'm afraid it's not enough of an incentive to satisfy my . . . *appetites*. I see no reason why I should suffer the indignities of marriage without being allowed to enjoy any of the benefits."

"S-s-such as?" she stammered.

His smile was as tender and benevolent as a priest's. "You."

She swallowed audibly. "Me? You want to enjoy *me*?"

"Surely you must have mirrors at your uncle's house. It can't have escaped your notice that you've bloomed into quite the beauty." He lifted a hand to her cheek much as he had in the barn on that long-ago summer day. "If I'm going to play the role of devoted husband to you, then I deserve a more substantial reward than just your dowry." He drew the pad of his thumb across the plush velvet of her bottom lip. At her delicate shiver, a husky note crept into his voice. "I want you. In my bed. Performing whatever wifely duties I require of you."

Simon had thought to cast his seductive spell over Catriona, but he was the one mesmerized by the misty glow in her eyes, the tantalizing way her lips parted ever so slightly beneath the coaxing pressure of his thumb. Her skin still felt like down beneath his fingertips. It was a damn shame he would never find out if she was as soft all over.

It was almost as if they were back in that barn with the smell of fresh-cut hay tickling their noses and dust motes dancing a sparkling minuet around them. Almost as if he were a much younger man full of promise and secret dreams for the future that only she could see. Before he realized it, he found himself leaning forward, lowering his head toward hers, savoring the fragrant warmth of her sigh against his lips . . .

Swearing softly beneath his breath, he abruptly straightened. His trousers had grown uncomfortably snug and his traitorous body was urging him to draw her down on the settee and consummate a mock marriage to which he had no intention of agreeing.

Folding his arms over his chest, he gazed sternly down at her. "Those are my terms, Miss Kincaid. Take them or leave them."

Catriona knew she would have to be mad to agree to his shocking terms. She had proposed a brief, sterile marriage of convenience. He had countered by demanding to defile her tender young body in whatever way was guaranteed to bring him the most pleasure and satisfy his debauched *appetites*. For her brother's sake, she might be able to recover from being married to Simon. But sharing his bed—even for a season—could very well haunt both her body and her heart to the end of her days.

She tilted her head to study him. He wore the mask of leering villain with disturbing ease, but she couldn't afford to forget that he was also a skilled gamester.

If he was bluffing, she supposed there was only one way to find out.

As the mist faded from Catriona's eyes, leaving them as sharp as flints, Simon set his jaw, bracing it for the well-deserved clout he knew was coming.

"Very well, Mr. Wescott," she said firmly. "I shall take your terms. And you."

Simon's jaw dropped in astonishment.

All he could do was stand there as she bustled back over to the stool and began to draw on her gloves as if she hadn't just bartered away her precious innocence to a complete stranger. "It may take me a day or two to arrange for your release. I'll send you a full set of instructions as soon as I'm able. I believe you're familiar with the way to my uncle's estate just outside of the city. I'm hoping we can be on our way to Gretna Green for our wedding as early as Monday morning."

As Simon watched her knot the ribbons of her bonnet into a jaunty little bow, it took him several ragged breaths to identify the unfamiliar emotion coursing through him as anger. Simon Wescott didn't get angry. He got drunk. He got bitingly sarcastic. And occasionally, he got even. But he never got angry. And in truth, he wasn't angry now.

He was bloody well furious.

He hadn't been so thoroughly duped since he'd caught Philo Wilcox at the faro table with an entire deck of aces tucked up his sleeve. He had satisfied that slight by calling the man out and shooting him in the arse when he turned to flee instead of fire. He supposed society would frown if he inflicted a similar punishment on the cunning Miss Kincaid.

But that didn't mean he was without recourse.

He stalked toward her, kicking the stool out of his path. Something in his narrowed eyes made hers widen with alarm. She scrambled backward, betraying her first trace of genuine fear since finding herself locked in the cell with him.

"Why, Mr. Wescott," she said breathlessly, "was there something else you wished to discuss?"

"Oh, I think we've done all the discussing we need to do." He backed her up against the wall until there was nowhere left for her to flee. "But I can't let you leave here believing me remiss in my duties. If I'm not mistaken, it's traditional to seal such a bargain with a kiss."

Her hand fluttered to her throat. "Oh, no . . . I really don't think . . . it would hardly be proper if—"

He bore her against the wall with his body, cupped the back of her head in his hand, heedlessly crushing her bonnet, and brought his mouth down on hers, cutting off her protest in midsqueak. If this was a devil's bargain, he was determined she would leave this cell knowing exactly which one of them was the devil.

But he hadn't anticipated that the softness of the mouth crushed beneath his would give him a taste of both heaven and hell. The scorching sweetness of her kiss tasted of nectar and ambrosia. The flames only licked higher as she twined one hand around his nape and clung for dear life, as if she were sliding down into some deep, dark abyss and was determined to take him with her.

Catriona had spent a thousand lonely nights dreaming of the kiss Simon might have given her in that sunlit barn if she hadn't been so young and he hadn't been so jaded. She would close her eyes with a wistful sigh and imagine the tender communion of their minds, hearts and souls as his lips gently brushed over hers in a chaste caress.

This was not that kiss.

She had been right about one thing. There was nothing proper about this kiss. It wasn't the kiss of a suitor tenderly wooing his bride. It was the kiss of a pirate claiming his prize. The kiss of a conquering barbarian intent upon ravishing the first village virgin he saw. Simon ruthlessly plundered the softness of her lips, taking advantage of her shocked gasp to plunge his tongue between them.

She welcomed him into her with shocking ease. The heated thrust of his tongue threatened to melt everything inside of her to thick, sweet honey.

Simon had thought to punish Catriona, but he was the one in pain—aching with a raw hunger that made him want to devour so much more than just her pretty mouth.

When her knees failed her, his knee was there, sliding between her thighs to bear her up. Even through the thickness of her skirts, he could feel the heat emanating from her tender core. He could not resist crudely grinding his knee against her, and his body surged with a wicked thrill of satisfaction when she moaned her helpless pleasure into his mouth.

Neither one of them heard the creak of the cell door swinging open on its rusty hinges.

"Aw . . . ain't that sweet!"

They sprang apart. Acting purely on instinct, Simon wrapped one arm protectively around her waist and thrust her behind the shelter of his body.

The gaoler was standing in the doorway of the cell, the blackened stumps of his teeth bared in a fond grin. "Seeing the two o' you together like that positively warms me old cockles." He shifted his gaze to Simon, sighing wistfully. "You're a lucky devil, lad. I always did wish I 'ad me a sister o' my very own."

Chapter 5

*H*e wasn't coming.

Catriona climbed to her knees in the padded window seat, unlatched her bedchamber window and leaned halfway out into the night. Except for the distant jingle of a harness and the whicker of a restless horse drifting out from the stables, there was little to disturb the bucolic peace of the evening. No matter how desperately she searched the rolling hills and neat hedgerows surrounding her uncle's estate, there was no sign of a gallant knight charging over the hill to either rescue or ravish her.

A wicked shiver danced unbidden over her skin. If the kiss he had planted on her lips at the jail was any indication, he was more inclined toward the latter.

She cast a nervous glance over her shoulder at the bed. Even Robert the Bruce seemed to have deserted her. The furry rogue was probably out courting the harem of female cats who prowled the stables, vying for his fickle attentions.

Settling back on her heels, she studied the delicate ormolu clock on the mantel. According to her calculations, Simon should have been released from Newgate over five hours ago. In the four days since they had made their pact, he'd had ample time to plot his escape from her. He had probably already fled the city, perhaps even the country. He was most likely languishing in the arms of some pretty little trollop right now, swilling brandy and making jokes at Catriona's expense.

Given the reckless promise she had made him, she supposed she ought to be grateful that he was stranding her at the proverbial altar. Agreeing to his bold demand had been madness itself. Of course, it had almost been worth it just to watch that beautifully sculpted jaw of his drop in shock.

Heat crept into her cheeks as she tried to stop her wayward imagination from conjuring up shocking images of the *duties* a man like Simon

Wescott would expect his wife to *perform*. She ran a finger over the tender swell of her bottom lip. Judging by the devastating skill of his kiss, those duties would probably afford her just as much pleasure as they did him, if not more.

The clock ticked away another minute. Apparently not even the prospect of bedding her was enough to entice him into honoring their bargain. Catriona shifted restlessly on the window seat, feeling unaccountably irritable.

The faint echo of a husky male murmur made her heart skip a beat. She craned her neck toward the copper-roofed dovecote, only to discover two of her uncle's footmen out for an evening smoke before securing the house for the night.

Despite the tender buds adorning the nearby branches of a linden tree, a crisp bite of winter still laced the March air. Curling into a corner of the window seat, Catriona tucked her bare feet beneath the hem of her nightdress and hugged her ragged plaid more tightly around her.

The green and black tartan was so threadbare it was nearly transparent in spots. Her uncle had banished it from polite company over three years ago. She'd had to rescue it from the trash heap twice after he'd ordered the maids to burn it. The cashmere shawl he'd given her for her twentieth birthday was tossed carelessly over the lacquered dressing screen in the corner while she clung to this rag.

She knew she was being childish, but she couldn't bear the thought of letting it go. It was all she had left to remind her of the life she'd once shared with her parents and her brother. Time was fading both the tartan and her memories.

As if to underscore that forlorn thought, the long-case clock on the second-floor landing began to sound, not stopping until it had chimed eleven times. As the last hollow bong rolled through the house, Catriona's spirits sank.

If Simon had betrayed her, she was done for. Eddingham was due back tomorrow afternoon and she knew his first order of business would be to petition her uncle for her hand.

Throwing off the plaid, Catriona climbed down from the window seat and stalked over to the tall cherry wardrobe in the corner. She yanked out a brocaded portmanteau and began to cram handfuls of stockings and undergarments into it.

Her uncle Ross had been right. Her head *was* stuffed full of clouds and dreams. If she hadn't been clinging to a childish romantic fancy, she never would have entrusted her hopes—and her brother's life—into the hands of a shame-less scapegrace like Simon Wescott. She'd be better off selling the few pieces of jewelry her uncle had given her over the years and booking passage on a mail carriage to Edinburgh. She might arrive in the Highlands with little more than she'd left with, but at least she wouldn't have to abandon all hope of finding Connor or her clan.

She was digging deeper into the wardrobe when her hands brushed a smooth length of rosewood. Her haste forgotten, she drew the rectangular box from its hiding place and gently lifted the lid. A thick sheaf of clippings was nestled in the box's silk-lined interior.

Which you no doubt pore over every night in your virginal white nightdress before you slide between the cold sheets of your lonely bed.

The echo of Simon's mocking words was so clear he might have been standing just behind her, near enough to touch. It hardly helped that her white nightdress with its fussy ruffled cuffs and high collar was as virginal as a novice's robes.

Catriona snapped the lid shut and shoved the box deep into the portmanteau beneath the most unmentionable of her unmentionables.

She was reaching into the wardrobe for the

sturdiest, homeliest wool gown she owned when a tremendous clatter came from the direction of the window. She tensed, her heart lurching into an uneven rhythm. The clatter was followed by a blistering oath in a man's deep familiar baritone.

She ran to the window and leaned out to find Simon Wescott lying on the ground below in a disgruntled tangle of long arms and legs, splintered trellis fragments, and rosebush branches. It was hardly the dashing sight she had envisioned in countless daydreams—Simon strolling beneath her window while strumming a lute or gazing tenderly up at her, one hand clasped to his heart while he recited, *What light through yonder window breaks? It is the east, and Catriona is the sun!*

She bit back a grin, telling herself that the giddiness coursing through her was only relief that he hadn't broken his fool neck. "Why, good evening, Mr. Wescott," she called down in an exaggerated whisper. "Why didn't you just knock on the front door and have the butler announce you? It would have been a great deal more discreet."

Swiping a trailing branch from his hair, he glared up at her. "And a great deal less painful."

"I warned you in my note that the trellis might not bear your weight."

Kicking away an offending piece of the structure, he sat up. "But you failed to warn me about the rosebush growing beneath it."

"I didn't see the need. It won't bloom for several weeks yet."

"It may not have blooms, but I can assure you it still has plenty of thorns. Or it did until I landed on it. Now I believe most of them are buried in my . . . person." Wincing, he unwound a length of vine from his throat and clambered to his feet.

Before Catriona could suggest that she sneak down to the servants' entrance to let him in, he was scaling the wall itself, using the roughened stones jutting out from the corner of the house for balance.

When his broad shoulders came within reach, she caught him by the back of his coat and helped to haul him through the window, the action giving her ample time to admire the intriguing play of muscles beneath the clinging superfine. She wondered if he had once scaled the rigging of the *Belleisle* with equal grace.

He cleared the window seat and rolled neatly to his feet. She backed away from him, rather intimidated now that she actually had a notorious libertine standing in her bedchamber. In her fantasies, he had always stayed safely outside the window, content to admire her from afar.

"I'm a bit disappointed in your lack of finesse, Mr. Wescott. I assumed you would have had ample experience at this."

Rubbing his backside, he eyed her darkly. "At what? Plucking thorns out of my—"

"Sneaking through women's windows in the dead of night," she inserted smoothly. "After all, isn't that the most expedient way to avoid their husbands?"

He shook his tawny fall of hair over his shoulders and smoothed the claret silk of his waistcoat. "I'll have you know that I stopped trifling with married women years ago. They had an annoying habit of falling in love with me and insisting on divorcing their husbands."

"How very tiresome that must have been for you. And the husbands," she added dryly.

"I can assure you that my suffering was far greater than theirs, Miss Kin—" He scowled at her. "What in the bloody hell is your Christian name anyway?"

"Catriona," she informed him, deciding this might not be the most opportune moment to chide him for swearing.

"Catriona," he repeated, the name rolling from his tongue like music. "Naturally it would be

Catriona," he muttered beneath his breath. "Not Gladys or Gertrude or Brunhilde." His expression brightened. "May I call you Kitty?"

She smiled pleasantly. "Not unless you want to land right back in that rosebush."

He edged away from the window and swept her a genteel bow. "Good evening, my fair Catriona. Per the instructions you sent to my jail cell, I've come to compromise you." Judging from his lazy, come-hither grin and the provocative way the buff doeskin of his trousers clung to his lean hips like a second skin, he looked more than equal to the task.

Catriona swallowed, her mouth suddenly going dry. "No, you've come to *pretend* to compromise me. We're not wed yet, Mr. Wescott."

"But we are practically betrothed. So don't you think you should call me Simon?" Closing the distance between them, he captured her hand and brought her palm to his lips. "Or perhaps 'darling.' Or 'sweetcakes.' Or some other endearment that indicates your passionate and undying affection for me."

Unnerved by the devilish twinkle in his eye, Catriona curled her hand into a fist. "My aunt has been married to my uncle for over thirty years and I've never heard her address him as anything other than 'my lord.'"

Simon shrugged, the twinkle in his eye only deepening. "I'm only a humble knight, but I have no objection whatsoever to you addressing me as 'my lord.'" Gently tilting her clenched hand, he brushed his parted lips over the sensitive skin on the inside of her wrist. His voice deepened to a husky purr. "You can even add 'and master' in our more intimate moments if it pleases you."

Fighting to ignore the melting sensation that seemed to radiate from the caress of his lips, Catriona jerked her hand out of his grip. "Have you always been so utterly shameless?"

He struggled to look contrite, but failed miserably. "So they tell me. My mother was an opera dancer, you know. I spent the first nine years of my life being raised backstage at the theater. The other dancers were always cooing over me, rumpling my hair, passing me from one lap to another." A nostalgic smile curved his lips. "They doted on me and I adored everything about them. The way they chattered amongst themselves. The way their hair smelled. The way their petticoats rustled when they walked. I disappeared one night during a performance of *Don Giovanni* when I was six years old and my mother claimed she found me on bended knee before one of the prettiest girls in the company, stammering out a marriage proposal."

Catriona couldn't help but smile at the image of a green-eyed, golden-haired little boy in short pants trying to woo a sophisticated dancer during an opera devoted to the dissolute life of Don Juan. "What happened to her?" she asked softly.

"She refused me, of course. Said I was too short and told me to come back and ask again in ten years when I'd grown into my ears. It was a devastating blow to both my heart and my confidence, but after a brief and bitter period of mourning, I managed to gather up the shattered pieces of my heart and carry on."

"No . . . I meant your mother."

All of that effortless charm vanished from his face, leaving its chiseled planes even more compelling than before. "She died when I was nine. And I went to live with my father."

He turned away and began to restlessly prowl the bedchamber, making it clear that no more confessions would be forthcoming. Pausing at her dressing table, he tugged the stopper from a bottle of lavender water and brought it to his nose. It gave Catriona an odd shivery feeling to watch his strong, masculine hands handling her things. It was almost as if they were gliding across her own skin.

"Are you certain this scheme of yours is going to work?" he asked, returning the scent bottle to its place before pivoting to face her. "Wouldn't it have been simpler for me to compromise you in one of the more traditional ways? I could have sent you a naughty letter proclaiming my devotion or been caught stealing a kiss behind a potted palm at Almack's."

"My uncle can be very canny. We have to convince him that I'm utterly ruined. He may suspect that I'm up to no good, but if the servants witness my disgrace, he'll have no choice but to let us wed."

"What if he decides to shoot me instead?"

She smiled sweetly at him. "Then I'll have to find another groom, won't I?"

"Heartless wench." Narrowing his eyes at her, he strode across the chamber and flung himself to his back on her bed. He looked disarmingly masculine reclining there among all of the lace-trimmed pillows and padded bolsters.

Folding his arms behind his head and crossing his boots at the ankle, he gazed morosely up at the wooden tester that canopied the top half of the bed. "I can't believe I'm about to be condemned for a crime I haven't even had the pleasure of committing." He slanted her a provocative look from beneath his lashes. "Yet."

To hide her consternation, Catriona seized his ankles and swept his lower legs over the edge of the bed, rescuing her cream-colored satin counterpane from the insult of his boot heels. "Just think of it as punishment for all of the crimes you've got away with over the years. The stolen hearts. The pilfered virtues."

Not the least bit fazed, he sat up and began to tug off his boots, pitching them one by one over the opposite side of the bed. "When they find us together in your bed in the morning, don't you think they'll wonder why I didn't steal away before we could be discovered?"

"Perhaps they'll believe we fell asleep before you could go."

He nodded. "That would make perfect sense. Naturally, you'd be exhausted after a night of my strenuous and wildly inventive lovemaking."

Catriona folded her arms over her chest. "Or perhaps I simply dozed off out of boredom."

He lifted one eyebrow and gave her a bemused look, letting her know just how unlikely a scenario that was.

As he peeled off his coat and began to unknot his cravat, she realized he had no intention of stopping at his boots.

"What are you doing?" she demanded as his deft fingers began to unfasten the cloth-covered buttons of his waistcoat.

"I'm disrobing, of course." He spoke very gently,

as if explaining a complicated mathematical equation to a slow-witted child. "We can hardly be caught *in flagrante delicto* with all of our clothes on, can we?"

He shrugged the waistcoat off of his broad shoulders and began to remove the silver studs from the front placket of his shirt, one at a time. Catriona was nearly as mesmerized by the deliberate grace of his fingers as she was by the impressive expanse of chest that was gradually being revealed as each stud slid from its neatly stitched mooring.

The well-defined muscles of his abdomen slowly came into view. A golden sprinkling of chest hair narrowed into a neat V just below his navel, like a cherub's arrow pointing the way to either heaven or hell. Swallowing hard, Catriona jerked her gaze back up to his face.

He wasn't watching his hands. He was watching her. The wicked sparkle in his heavy-lidded eyes let her know just how much he was enjoying her discomfiture.

She whirled around, feeling her freckles melt in a scalding rush of heat. Struggling to keep her voice as cold as her cheeks were hot, she asked, "If it's not too much bother, would you please let me know when you're done stripping off all your clothes?"

She could hear the smile in his voice. "Eager for a little look-see, are we?"

She closed her eyes briefly, counting to ten. "And when you're tucked safely beneath the covers."

She tapped her bare foot against the maple floor as several minutes passed.

There were a few mysterious bumps and thumps, followed by an intriguing rustling, before he finally said, "You can turn around now. There's no danger of offending your maidenly modesty."

In her bolder daydreams Catriona had dared to imagine Simon in her arms, but never in her bed. She reluctantly turned, half afraid he would still be standing there on the rug beside her bed as naked as on the day he was born. But true to his word, he was tucked neatly beneath the blankets. Well, at least half of him was.

He reclined against the headboard with the counterpane drawn up to his waist. The fingers of lamplight played lovingly over his bare chest, giving him a golden glow perfectly suited to the archangel Gabriel. But if the devilish gleam in his eyes hadn't already convinced her that he was no angel, his next words would.

"Now it's your turn."

Chapter 6 🌿

$\mathscr{A}$ s Simon nodded toward her nightdress, Catriona clutched it closed at the throat with a white-knuckled fist. "Pardon?"

"If we're going to make this convincing," he said, "I can't be the only one not wearing any clothes."

"I d-d-don't see why not," she stammered. "Couldn't you just . . ."—she waved her other hand vaguely in the air, searching her trove of limited knowledge for inspiration— "pretend that you lifted the skirt of my nightdress, then . . . um . . . covered me back up when you were . . . um . . . finished?"

He lowered his head to give her a disbelieving look. "Please don't tell me that's how your uncle makes love to your aunt."

The very thought made Catriona shudder. "They don't even share a bedchamber."

"Well, they did at least once or they wouldn't have spawned the charming Agatha, now, would they?"

"Alice," Catriona murmured weakly. "And it had to be twice, because there's Georgina as well."

Careful to keep the sheet draped artfully across his lap, Simon folded back the blankets and patted the expanse of feather mattress next to him, his crooked smile achingly tender. "Don't be shy, darling. I promise I'll be the perfect gentleman."

She wondered just how many other women he had lured into his bed with those words and that smile. His words might promise one thing, but his eyes and his smile promised pleasures no woman could resist or regret. At least not while she was experiencing them.

Her bed had always seemed decadently spacious to her—especially compared to the narrow heather-stuffed tick she had slept on in Scotland as a child—but Simon's big, masculine frame seemed to dwarf the elegant half-tester. She'd never dreamed that one man could take up so much room. Or so much air. As her gaze traveled from his smile to his broad shoulders to that enticing little arrow of hair that adorned the taut planes of his abdomen, her chest tightened and her breath grew painfully short.

Afraid she might compound her mortification by swooning, she dashed across the room, sprang into the bed and jerked the covers up over her head. Only then did she dare to wiggle out of her nightdress and toss it on the floor. With her head still buried beneath the blankets, she huddled stiffly on the very edge of the mattress, terrified that if she stirred, some wayward part of her might accidentally graze some even more wayward part of him.

"Catriona?"

"Hmmm?" she replied, halfway surprised that he had remembered her name.

"Do you plan to stay under there all night?"

Clinging to the last stitch of her dignity, if not her clothing, she sniffed. "Perhaps."

He tugged on the counterpane until her nose and eyes were exposed. She blinked up at him.

"Would you like me to douse the lamp?" he asked.

"No!" she exclaimed, her panic deepening at the prospect of sharing the darkness as well as her bed with him. She sat up, clutching the sheet to her breasts and shaking her hair out of her eyes. "I have a much better idea."

Within seconds, she had put her hands on every pillow and bolster she could reach. She plumped them up and began to build an impenetrable wall between them. When it was done, she could barely see over the top of it. She doubted Napoleon himself could have constructed such an impressive blockade.

"I feel as if I'm back in Newgate," Simon said, his voice muffled.

"If my plan doesn't work, you may very well be," she reminded him, rolling over and presenting her back firmly to his side of the bed.

With a long-suffering sigh, he settled back on his side of the makeshift barricade. Catriona closed her eyes. Despite her best efforts to relax and ignore him, she was still keenly aware of his presence. He no longer seemed to bear any kinship to the boy she had adored for so long. He was a stranger—as large and exotic and dangerous as an African tiger drowsing in the sun. An indefinably masculine scent wafted from his warm skin. It reminded her of melted toffee mingled with the bracing sea breezes at Brighton.

She rolled restlessly to her back and glared up at the tester. She'd never done anything as scandalous as sleeping without her nightdress. There was something deliciously decadent about the way her naked limbs glided over the sheets, the way the crisp linen tickled her nipples and made them pucker. Something that made her want to stretch and purr like a contented cat.

She flopped over to her other side and glared at the mountain of pillows, knowing that neither one of them would get so much as a wink of sleep on this night.

A muffled snore reached her ears.

Clutching the sheet to her bosom, she sat up and peered over the pillows. Simon's eyes were closed, his mouth slightly open, his breathing deep and even. With his gilt-tipped lashes resting on his cheeks and a wayward strand of hair falling over his brow, he looked as innocent as a newborn babe. Or in his case a hellborn babe.

The sheet had slid all the way down to his hipbones. Catriona chewed on her lower lip, fascinated against her will by the mysteries that lay beneath. Thanks to Aunt Margaret's reticence, her knowledge of male anatomy had never progressed beyond what she had gleaned from the mating rituals of the tomcats and stallions in her uncle's stables. What would Simon do if he awoke to find her lifting the sheet to steal a peek?

All too afraid that she knew *exactly* what he would do, she settled back into the lonely nest she'd built for herself. He'd probably slept next to so many naked women in his lifetime that she was no more a distraction to him than if Robert the Bruce had been curled up against his leg.

She sighed, abandoning all hope of rest. But before she knew it, the cozy rhythm of Simon's snoring had lulled her into a sweet and dreamless sleep.

Simon awoke with a warm female body snuggled against his bare back and a raging erection. Although he was still more than half asleep, he knew exactly what to do with both. But before he could roll over and cover that warm female body with his own, seeking an oblivion even sweeter than sleep, he remembered exactly *whose* warm female body it was.

His eyes flew open.

Wondering if he was still dreaming, he lifted his head just enough to peer over his shoulder. No, there she was—Miss Catriona Kincaid herself, with her strawberry blond curls streaming over his pillow, her cheeks rosy with sleep, her breath a beguiling whisper on the back of his neck. As he stirred, she slipped one arm around his waist and drew him even deeper into the lush cup of her body, so deep he could feel the softness of her naked breasts pressed against his back. Although he wouldn't have thought it physically possible, he grew even harder.

Groaning beneath his breath, he sank back into the pillow. Even though all of the other bolsters and pillows had been flung off of *her* side of the bed, she would never believe that he wasn't to blame for this. He glanced downward. She had curled her hand innocently against his rigid abdomen, just a finger's breadth away from both their ruins.

Shuddering with lust, Simon abruptly sat up and nudged her arm away from him. Instead of waking as he'd hoped, she simply scowled, let out a disgruntled little snort, then nestled deeper into the mattress.

The sheet still draped all of her more pertinent parts, but in that moment Simon found the graceful curve of her throat and the delicate wings of her collarbone nearly as enticing as the dusky shadows of her nipples beneath the sheet. She smelled warm and feminine and musky with sleep. No French perfumier could have concocted a fragrance more erotic or irresistible to a man's nostrils.

It might astound the casual observer, but he'd always prided himself on his self-control— especially where women were concerned. Every seductive word that flowed from his lips, every lingering kiss, every deft stroke of his fingertips was carefully calculated to bring about his lover's loss of control, not his. But here he was on the brink of losing that winning advantage with little more than an artless touch from an innocent girl.

The lamp had gone out during the night. He squinted through the shadows but couldn't quite make out the face of the clock on the mantel. The pearly light drifting through the window could be either moonlight or dawn. It could be minutes before they were disturbed or hours.

He studied Catriona. Her parted lips were as lush and tempting as rose petals kissed with the first drops of morning dew.

I promise I'll be the perfect gentleman.

His own words came back to haunt him. Hadn't he told her in that barn all those years ago that he wasn't in the habit of making promises he couldn't keep?

To so much as steal a kiss while she was vulnerable and defenseless just to satisfy his own carnal appetites would be unthinkable, unscrupulous . . .

He leaned over, gently brushing her lips with his own.

Unforgivable . . .

Catriona was being kissed by a man who'd been born to the art. His lips were firm yet soft, grazing hers over and over, using just the right amount of pressure to coax them apart. She kept her eyes pressed tightly shut; if this was a dream, she never wanted to wake.

But she could not help stirring when he entered her mouth with his tongue. Her hips arched off the bed of their own volition, seeking the answer to some question she did not even have the words to ask. His tongue toyed with hers—teasing, tantalizing, stroking. Making wordless promises she could no longer distinguish from lies.

Desire stirred thickly in her veins, pulsing in secret places she had dared to touch only in the dark, lonely watches of the night. His kiss promised that was but a shadow of the pleasure he could give her. He made love to her mouth with the same exquisite attention to detail she knew he would give the rest of her body if she was bold—or foolhardy—enough to surrender it into his hands.

Hands that were even now tracing the vulnerable curve of her throat, the delicate flare of her collarbone, the aching swell of her breasts. He gently cupped one of them through the sheet, testing its weight in his palm and flicking her distended nipple with the pad of his thumb. As he did so, he sucked softly on the very tip of her tongue, showing her exactly what wonders he could work if she would just let him. She moaned, the provocative motion sending a shiver of yearning deep into her womb.

She might have been able to convince herself she was still dreaming if she hadn't felt truly awake for the very first time in her life. Her every sense was alive and tingling, a willing slave to the tender mastery of his mouth and hands. It would be all too easy to feign sleep until his seduction of her was complete. To let him bear the blame and the shame of it while she played the innocent victim, despoiled by his uncontrollable lust.

But her conscience would not allow her the luxury of such a ruse. She might not have the courage to look him in the eye and risk letting him see just how recklessly and faithfully she had loved him or how very long she had waited for this moment, but she could breathe his name into the honeyed chalice of his mouth. She could tangle her hands in the wheaten silk of his hair and kiss him back with an artless fervor that betrayed a lifetime of longing.

His response was something between a groan and a growl. The primal sound sent a heady thrill through her. For the first time she realized she had her own array of wiles—a power over him that did not require either experience or expertise.

Accepting her unspoken invitation, his tongue swept through her mouth in a kiss that was both tender and erotic, while his hand slipped beneath the sheet and glided up the bare silk of her thigh. Catriona gasped. She was about to be compromised in earnest, yet all of her moral fortitude seemed to have fled. Instead of protesting in outrage, all she could seem to do was welcome her ruin with open arms.

She had never dreamed that a man could be so gentle and so ruthlessly persuasive all at the same time. Simon coaxed her thighs apart as easily as he had coaxed her lips apart, his fingers breaching the softness of her nether curls with exquisite care.

Whatever he discovered there seemed to please him mightily. His powerful body tensed and shuddered as he dipped one finger between those tender petals.

Catriona buried her face against his shoulder and moaned deep in her throat as a sensation like no other threatened to rip the last of her inhibitions asunder. Pleasure was too common a word to describe it. It was bliss and agony and a desperate yearning all rolled into one. She didn't think she could bear it for another second, yet she wanted it to go on forever.

"Please," she whispered hoarsely. "Oh, please . . ."

She didn't even know what she was begging for. She only knew that if she didn't get it, she might very well perish from longing.

He knew *exactly* what she wanted. His devilishly clever fingers spread and stroked and teased and petted until she was writhing beneath his hand. She did not know this wanton stranger she had become. She only knew that she craved his touch and the maddening pleasure it was giving her the way an addict must crave opium. She had been right about him all along. He was both angel and demon, relentlessly urging her toward the promise of paradise even as he sought to make her soul his own.

He gently flicked his thumb over the rigid little bud nestled at the crux of her curls and for a timeless moment she hung suspended between heaven and hell. Then a shattering wave of rapture broke over her and she went tumbling head over heels into the abyss with only his arms to break her fall, only his lips to muffle her soft, broken cry of ecstasy.

She was still clinging to him, lost in a haze of delight, when her bedchamber door came thumping open and a shrill voice raked across her tender nerves. "Have you seen my pearl hair combs, Catriona? I should have known better than to lend them to you. You have no appreciation for the finer things in life. You'd have probably been just as happy with some filthy plaid ribbon or a . . ." The voice trailed off.

While Catriona lay frozen, her eyes as big as saucers, Simon gently tucked the sheet around her, then rolled over to face the intruder.

Grinning like a housecat that had just been caught with canary feathers in his teeth, he flexed his muscles in a feline stretch and said, "Good morning, Agnes. Have you come to bring your cousin and me some breakfast?"

Chapter 7 🌿

atriona's scheme was a smashing success. Alice's outraged shrieks roused the entire household, including one poor underfootman who rushed upstairs, kitchen ax in hand, convinced that murder was being done. By the time Catriona's aunt and uncle came stumbling through the door of her bedchamber, wearing nothing but their rumpled nightclothes and dazed expressions, over a dozen servants were standing elbow to elbow, gaping at the bed in dumb astonishment.

Catriona supposed she and Simon must have made a very convincing pair. Especially with her hair all atumble and her cheeks rosy with both mortification and the afterglow of the pulsing, wondrous pleasure he had just given her. She probably would have remained frozen in place until she perished of old age if he hadn't slipped his arms around her shoulders, propped her up against the pillow like a dressmaker's dummy, and brushed his lips against her hair.

"You!" Alice breathed. Her elegant cream chiffon dressing gown rippled around her as she stabbed an accusing finger at Simon. "I know you!"

He smiled pleasantly at her. "Not as well as you might have if we hadn't been interrupted all those years ago."

Uncle Ross's face went scarlet. His eyes bulged as if he were about to drop dead of an apoplexy right there on Catriona's bedchamber floor. He would have looked even more forbidding if the tassel of his nightcap hadn't kept flopping over one eye as he trembled with rage.

"What is the meaning of this, young lady?" he thundered. "Who in the devil is this man and why is he in your bed?"

Catriona hadn't anticipated how much it would sting to have her uncle believe the very worst of her. It was worse than having Alice denounce her as a savage Scot without an ounce of manners or good breeding. Worse than Aunt Margaret's exasperated sighs as the maid struggled to work a brush through her unruly hair. Worse than the footmen's snickers whenever she had shoveled her peas onto the blade of her knife instead of using the delicate two-pronged fork beside her plate. Her first instinct was to draw the blankets over her head and quail in shame.

But then she remembered just what was at stake should their ruse fail.

Disengaging herself from Simon's arms with as much grace and dignity as she could muster, she slid out of the bed and to her feet, draping the sheet around her as if it were the toga of a Greek goddess. Since Aunt Margaret didn't faint dead away, she could only assume she had left behind enough blankets to cover Simon.

Lifting her chin, she looked her uncle dead in the eye and boldly proclaimed, "His name is Simon Wescott and he's my lover."

The servants gasped as one.

"Oh, my!" her aunt exclaimed, swaying on her feet. A fresh-faced little parlor maid rushed forward to steady her.

Catriona didn't realize Simon had risen to stand behind her until his husky murmur caressed her ear. "If they'd have held off for a few more seconds, angel, that would have been true."

As his hands settled on her shoulders, she could only hope that their audience would mistake the color creeping higher in her cheeks for a flush of triumph.

"Leave us," her uncle barked.

For a dazed second, Catriona thought she and Simon were to be banished in disgrace like Adam and Eve being cast naked out of the garden, but then she realized he was addressing the servants.

They all stood paralyzed with shock until he bellowed, "*Go!* Get back to your duties immediately and don't breathe a word of what you saw here this morning or you'll be dismissed without pay or references."

Ducking their heads to avoid their master's eyes, the servants silently filed out of the chamber. Despite her uncle's threat, Catriona trusted that news of her disgrace would still reach London by nightfall. The backstairs grapevine, tended and watered lovingly both in country kitchens and on back stoops all over the city, was notoriously hardy and nearly impossible to eradicate.

Breathing through his flared nostrils like a bull about to charge, her uncle looked Simon up and down. For a man wearing nothing but a lazy smile and a blanket tucked around his waist like a loincloth, Simon looked remarkably composed. But he'd probably had ample experience staring down furious fathers and jealous husbands, Catriona thought, plagued by an unbecoming flash of resentment.

Her uncle shifted his glare to her. "How could you do such a thing? After I welcomed you into my home and treated you like my very own daughter, how could you shame me and your aunt by sneaking this . . . this . . ."—he waved a hand at Simon, at a loss for a word vile enough to describe him—"this *stranger* into my house and your bed?"

Simon spoke before she could, his hands gently rubbing her shoulders. "We can hardly expect the two of you to understand such irresistible passion when you don't even share a bed."

Her uncle's face went from scarlet to purple while her aunt clapped a hand to her breast and exclaimed, "Well, I never!"

Simon's expression softened as he winked at her. "Forgive me for contradicting you, my lady, but you did at least twice or you wouldn't have Georgina and Alberta here."

"*Alice*," Catriona's cousin hissed. "My name is *Alice*. And I don't know why you'd be surprised by any of this, Papa. You always said Catriona's mother was nothing but a common Scots trollop who seduced my uncle Davey into marrying her and then got him killed." She sniffed derisively. "With a mother like that, it's no wonder the little baggage has the morals of an alleycat."

As her mother's loving smile and sparkling eyes rose up in her memory, Catriona took an involuntary step toward Alice, her hands closing into fists. "Oh really? Then what's *your* excuse?"

Simon caught her by the upper arms and hauled her back to his side. Although his smile never wavered, his voice whipped like a cat-o'-nine-tails through the room, sharp enough to flay flesh from bone. "If I were you, *Abigail*, I'd think twice about how you address my bride."

Catriona shot him a startled glance, realizing for the first time that he might make a dangerous enemy. Perhaps even more dangerous than Eddingham.

"Your bride?" Alice echoed, going as pale as her dressing gown.

"*Your bride?*" her uncle roared.

"Oh dear," Aunt Margaret said, sinking into the nearest wing chair and pressing her ever-present handkerchief to her trembling lips.

Simon offered her uncle a conciliatory bow. "I pray you'll forgive my boldness, my lord, but from the first moment I laid eyes on her across a crowded ballroom, I knew your niece was the only girl in the world for me. All other women seemed to pale in her shadow."

While her uncle continued to glower, unmoved by the tender declaration, Simon tugged Catriona around to face him. He gently clasped her hands, his gaze caressing her face as his thumbs played tenderly over her knuckles. "I fell in love with her courage, her spirit, her beauty, and could think of nothing and no one else. If I were a better man, I would have resisted the temptation to sample her charms. But my hunger for her was so great that no power in heaven or hell could have stopped me from making her my own."

Simon's green eyes were no longer sparkling with mischief but smoldering with passion. Alice had gone slack-jawed with shock and Aunt Margaret was using her handkerchief to fan herself.

Catriona was equally flummoxed when Simon dropped to one knee before her and pressed his lips briefly but fervently to the back of her hand. He gazed up at her, his expression both earnest and beseeching. "I can only pray that she'll forgive me for taking such ruthless advantage of her innocence and will allow me to make amends by doing me the honor of agreeing to share my life, my future . . . and my name."

Catriona's own mouth fell open. She had

dreamed of this precise moment for so long that she almost wanted to beg Alice to pinch her just to prove she was awake.

Despite the warning bells sounding an alarm in her heart, she was tempted to believe his every syllable.

But that way lay madness . . . and heartbreak.

What he deserved was a round of wild applause, followed by an enthusiastic *Bravo!* Apparently he had learned more than just how to set off flash pots and look up the opera dancers' petticoats during his years backstage at the theater. Why, he'd been born to trod the boards at Drury Lane right alongside the likes of John Kemble and Sarah Siddons!

When she continued to eye him warily instead of falling, weeping with joy and gratitude, into his waiting arms, his eyes narrowed ever so slightly. "What say you, my darling Kitty? Will you do me the honor of becoming my wife?"

"Kitty?" Alice snorted and rolled her eyes. "The last time I called her that, she put a barn mouse in my bed."

Fighting the urge to hiss at the both of them, Catriona primly said, "Well, since you put it so prettily, sir, I suppose I have no choice but to accept your proposal."

Simon surged to his feet, wrapping her in a

passionate embrace that threatened to dislodge both sheet and blanket.

Alice stamped her delicate foot. "That's not fair, Papa! He compromised me first! He should have to marry me!"

"I'd rather be hanged on the gallows at Newgate," Simon murmured in Catriona's ear.

"Good God, man!" Uncle Ross bellowed, glaring at him disbelievingly. "Just how many of my female relations have you seduced?"

"Well, I've yet to meet the fair Georgina." Reclaiming Catriona's hands, Simon offered Aunt Margaret his most wolfish smile. "Nor have I had the pleasure of spending any time alone with your charming wife."

While Aunt Margaret tittered into her handkerchief, Uncle Ross snapped, "Nor will you, if I have anything to say about it!"

Shooting his wife a reproving look, Uncle Ross marched over and wrested Catriona's hands away from Simon's. His palms were hot and sweaty, a marked contrast to Simon's cool, dry grip. He had never before touched her with anything resembling affection.

"Is this truly what you want, child?" He searched her face, his gaze far more penetrating than she had anticipated. "If it's not, I'll send you abroad until the scandal dies down."

He swallowed with some difficulty. "If there are . . . complications, we can find a good home in the country for the babe. You'll never have to see it again or be reminded of this terrible night. You can remain here under my roof for as long as you like. I won't force you to marry this scoundrel—or any other man—if it's not your wish."

Catriona had managed to endure her uncle's condemnation and her own shame, but his unexpected compassion was almost her undoing. She blinked up at him, genuine tears blurring her vision. "This is what I want, Uncle Ross." She stole a glance at Simon. He was watching her with an oddly detached, yet intent, expression. Praying he would attribute the conviction in her words to a talent for playacting equal to his own, she said, *"He* is what I want more than anything else in this life."

Still squeezing her hands, her uncle turned a murderous glare on Simon. "Then, as God is my witness, *you shall have him."*

Uncle Ross was as good as his word. By early afternoon of that very day, Simon and Catriona were preparing to depart for Gretna Green in one of the earl's more modest carriages. Now that an unexpected wedding was afoot, the servants were buzzing with fresh excitement. Two footmen had been dispatched to retrieve Simon's clothing from his Piccadilly lodgings, which meant that news of the scandal had probably already reached London. But now it would be embellished with touching anecdotes about how very attentive the prospective groom was to his bride and how adoringly she gazed up at his handsome visage.

"So where is my money, darling? Were you able to convince your uncle to hand it over?" Simon murmured, bringing her gloved hand to his lips as they stood side by side in the crushed-shell drive, watching the groomsmen finish hitching a handsome team of matched grays to the carriage.

"*Our* money, you mean," Catriona replied sweetly, batting her eyelashes at him.

"Very well. Where is *my* half of *our* money?"

"All in good time, my love." Tugging her hand from his, she beamed up at him and gave his waistcoat a wifely pat that made the watching maids simper with delight. "All in good time."

As he narrowed his eyes at her, she turned to watch the footmen load a single large trunk into the spacious boot at the back of the carriage. She couldn't very well order the maids to pack all of her worldly belongings. They believed she would return to retrieve them after an idyllic honeymoon spent in her groom's arms and bed. They had no way of knowing they might never see her again.

She glanced over her shoulder at the mullioned windows and weathered gray stones of the house she had called home for the past ten years, surprised by the pang of regret that seized her heart. Had her father felt the same pang on the night he'd run away, leaving this place for the last time? He hadn't even been allowed the luxury of saying goodbye to his family.

"If you ask me, Mama, we're well shed of the little tart." Alice came strolling around the corner of the house with Aunt Margaret, her expression so sour one might have supposed she'd been lapping curdled cream straight from the saucer. She'd traded her elegant dressing gown for a bright yellow walking dress and matching parasol that only made her pinched face look more sallow. "Perhaps without her muddying our good name with her common ways, it will finally be possible for me to make a decent match."

"I've heard the Marquis de Sade is shopping for a new bride to keep him company in the lunatic asylum," Simon whispered in Catriona's ear, referring to the notorious author of *Justine* and *Juliette*.

Catriona bit back a smile before murmuring, "I should think he'd be a trifle too staid for Alice's tastes."

They turned as one at the sound of hoofbeats. Catriona expected to see the footmen returning from London with Simon's bags or perhaps Georgina and her husband in their fine carriage, rushing to bid her farewell. But it was a single rider who came thundering down the long, oak-lined drive toward them as if the hounds of hell were snapping at the hooves of his mount.

With the parasol shading her eyes from the glare of the afternoon sun, Alice was the first to recognize him. "Look, Mama! It's Eddingham. I knew he'd come to his senses and beg me to take him back!"

Without realizing it, Catriona edged even closer to Simon as the rider sawed viciously on the reins, bringing the massive chestnut to a shuddering halt. The poor horse's sides were heaving and lathered with foam.

As Eddingham threw himself off of the horse, Alice trotted forward, giving her parasol a jaunty little twirl. "I knew you'd come back for me, darling! You're probably wondering if I could ever find it in my heart to forgive you, but if you're truly sorry for the deplorable way you treated me, I believe that in time I'll be able to . . ." Her face fell as he stormed right past her.

He strode toward Catriona and Simon, slapping his riding crop against his palm in perfect rhythm to the muscle twitching in his jaw.

He halted in front of them and stabbed a finger at Simon, his handsome face mottled with rage. *"You!"*

"Have you ever noticed how many people tend to greet you that way?" Catriona murmured out of the corner of her mouth.

Simon shrugged. "What can I say? It must be a consequence of my dazzling charm." Grinning at the marquess, he said, "Hullo, Ed. Have you rushed all the way out here to offer me and my bride your felicitations?"

"Your *bride*?" the marquess spat, looking as if he might very well choke on the word. "So the rumors are true, then?" He turned to Catriona. "When I left here last week, I thought we had an understanding."

She returned his burning gaze with a cool one of her own. "Oh, I understood you perfectly, my lord. You made your intentions quite clear."

Simon clapped a hand to his heart. "Why, darling, you never told me I had a rival for your affections!"

"I wasn't aware you were the jealous sort,

dear," she replied. "But there's no need to trouble your pretty head about it. Lord Eddingham was only a rival for my dowry, not my affections."

Simon slid an arm around her shoulders and beamed at Eddingham. "I'm sure it was simply maidenly shyness that prevented Catriona from telling you that she was already spoken for. By me." Before she could react, he tilted up her chin with one finger and pressed a tender kiss to her lips. He couldn't have marked his territory any more clearly had he piddled on her kid boots like one of her aunt Margaret's ill-mannered spaniels. For a breathless moment, Catriona felt as if she truly belonged to him.

Eddingham's face looked so stricken that if she believed he had even an ounce of genuine feeling for her, she might have actually pitied him. "It can't be true, can it?" he demanded of her. "Surely you know of Wescott's reputation. Why, he's waltzed his way through half the women in London! Tell me you don't really intend to marry the . . . the . . ."—he spared a sneer for Simon—"*bastard.*"

Most men would have reacted to the insult as if Eddingham had whipped his riding crop across their cheek. But Simon's smile simply deepened a dangerous degree. "I can assure you that Catriona is well aware of my character flaws . . . and the fact that I was born on the wrong side of the blanket. We have no intention of allowing the same fate to befall our first child, which is why we're making for Gretna Green in such haste."

At Simon's blatant implication that he had already shared her bed—and her body— Eddingham took a step backward, his face paling. The look he cast her was beyond contempt. "The two of you deserve each other. I hope you both burn in hell." He started to turn away, then paused, a nasty smile twisting his lips. "Oh, and Miss Kincaid? If you happen to see any of your Scottish kin during your honeymoon, make sure and give them my regards."

He turned on the heel of his polished boot and went striding past Aunt Margaret and the crest-fallen Alice as if they weren't even there. Flinging himself on the back of his horse, he drove his spurs into the beast's sides with a force that made Catriona wince in sympathy.

"Charming fellow," Simon murmured. "Even more amiable than I remembered."

As they watched him gallop across her uncle's immaculately groomed lawn, his gelding's hooves churning up raw clots of turf, Catriona sighed. "So who did you seduce? Was it his sister? His

maiden aunt? His second cousin thrice removed?"

Simon's profile was uncharacteristically grim.
"He thinks I seduced his fiancée. But believe it or
not, I was innocent and so was she. Our dalli-
ance was nothing more than a harmless flirtation after she accidentally dropped a glove in my
path at Almack's nearly three years ago. She was
in love with Eddingham and had every intention of going through with her marriage to him.
But only a few days after he witnessed our exchange, she took a nasty tumble from her horse
during an afternoon ride in Hyde Park and broke
her neck."

Catriona shivered, a sudden chill dulling the
warmth of the spring sun. "The poor girl. You
don't think he had anything to do with her death,
do you?"

"I've always had my suspicions, but nothing
I've ever been able to prove." His voice betrayed
its first trace of bitterness. "After all, who would
believe the wild accusations of a bastard over
the word of such an upstanding *gentleman*?"
Catching her troubled frown from the corner of
his eye, Simon gave her shoulders a comforting
squeeze. "Don't worry, love," he assured her,
the casual endearment that flowed so easily to

his lips stinging more deeply than any of Eddingham's insults. "He can't hurt either one of us now."

Catriona watched the marquess ride away, her heart heavy with dread. If she told Simon just how very wrong he was, she might have to watch him disappear over the horizon as well.

Chapter 8

Catriona's traveling companions sat in opposite corners of the carriage, balefully eyeing each other across the gap between the seats.

"You never told me about Eddingham or *him*," Simon said, folding his arms over his chest and shifting his accusing glare to Catriona. She was sitting directly opposite him, having thrown herself clearly and without compunction into the camp of his rival.

Without lowering the leather-bound book she'd dug out of her portmanteau to pass the long hours on the Great North Road, she shrugged. "Since the two of you had met before, I hardly felt a formal introduction was necessary."

"I wouldn't have recognized him. What have you been feeding him? Ponies?"

Catriona gave Simon a disapproving look over the top of her book. "It's hardly sporting of you to mock his girth. He's quite sensitive about it, you know."

"What is he going to do if I offend him? Eat me?"

She slammed the book shut and tossed it on the carriage seat. "Why, Mr. Wescott, you ought to be ashamed of yourself! I realize that my Robert is a bonny fine fellow who is certainly worthy of your jealousy, but all the same, it hardly becomes you."

Still glaring at him, she reached over and hauled the enormous orange cat curled up on the seat beside her into her lap. As she began to gently stroke his coarse fur, a deafening purr rumbled up from his throat. He rested his monstrous head on his paws and blinked at Simon with his somnolent golden eyes, gloating like a paunchy sultan who had just laid claim to the last virgin in the harem.

Simon rolled his eyes. "You forget that the last time we met, he tried to bite off my finger. I've still got the scar."

She sniffed. "He was simply defending my honor, which is what a hero is *supposed* to do."

Their eyes met for a charged moment, both of them remembering that dangerous yet intoxicating moment in her rumpled bed when Simon had nearly stolen her virtue instead of defending it.

Then Simon muttered an unintelligible retort beneath his breath and sank deeper into his seat. As he scowled out the carriage window at the passing countryside, Catriona retrieved her book and lifted it to hide her smile. In truth, she rather fancied the idea of Simon being jealous, even if it was only of a cat.

She was thankful for the distraction of both book and cat. This was the first time they'd been completely alone since she'd awakened that morning with his mouth on hers and his hands . . . well, perhaps it would be wiser not to think about where his hands—or his fingers—had ended up.

Earning a disgruntled chirrup from Robert the Bruce, she leaned forward and shoved open the nearest carriage window. "It's getting a bit stuffy in here, don't you think?" she asked, bathing her flushed cheeks in the fresh air.

Simon simply lifted one eyebrow. The air had grown steadily brisker as they traveled north toward Scotland.

He nodded toward the portmanteau sitting on the floor at her feet. "Have you any other books in there?"

Remembering the rosewood box still tucked beneath the undergarments she had so hastily packed the previous night, Catriona felt a flare of panic. "No!" she exclaimed, making a frantic grab for the brocaded bag at the exact moment he caught the ivory handle on the opposite side of it.

Plainly intrigued by her violent reaction, he gave the bag a tug. "I'd be perfectly happy with a newspaper or a scandal sheet to while away the hours until we reach our lodgings for the night."

"Well, I haven't either one." She tugged back, desperation giving her the strength she needed to wrench the bag out of his grip and whisk it safely onto the seat beside her.

Simon leaned back and stretched out his long legs, looking even more smug than if he had won the humiliating little contest. "Why so secretive, darling? Is that where you're hiding my money?"

"Here. You can have this book." She tossed her book at him; he caught it without so much as a flinch.

He frowned down at the gilt lettering on the spine. *"Pilgrim's Progress?* I was rather hoping for something more . . . stimulating."

"Like *The Randy Adventures of Naughty Nell,* perhaps?"

"Oh, I've already read that one twice." A wicked smile flirted with his lips. "Rumor has it that the author based the character of Nell's most dashing and accomplished lover on me."

Trying not to remember just how *accomplished* he had proved himself in her bed, she nodded toward the book. "There's a character based on you in that book as well. They call him Satan."

Now that she had nothing to read, it was Catriona's turn to scowl out the carriage window. After several minutes of stony silence, she stole a look at Simon. He had drawn a pair of steel-framed spectacles from the pocket of his waistcoat and appeared to be thoroughly engrossed in the story. She felt her expression soften. With the spectacles perched low on his nose and a stray lock of hair falling over his brow, he looked less like a libertine and more like a professor from some hallowed university. She could only too easily imagine the subjects he would excel at teaching—dueling, gambling, flirting, wenching.

Breaking hearts.

Her smile faded. By tomorrow night, she would be his wife. She couldn't help but think how different this journey might have been if their impending marriage was more than just a business arrangement. She would probably be cuddled up in his lap right now with no need of a book to while away the tedious hours of traveling.

She sighed. She could no longer afford to indulge in such dangerous fantasies. She had promised him a marriage of convenience and she had an obligation to deliver on that promise, no matter how inconvenient to her yearning heart. She would simply have to do everything in her power to hide that heart from him.

Simon glanced up to catch her studying him. She quickly dropped her gaze to her lap, devoting all of her attention to stroking Robert the Bruce's velvety ears.

"Shall I read aloud?" he offered.

"If it pleases you," she replied, trying to sound as disinterested as possible although there was nothing she would have liked better.

He flipped back to the very first page of the book and began to read. He had a fine and expressive baritone, honed by his years of observing the actors at the opera house. As the rich music of his voice cast an irresistible spell over her, Catriona soon found herself immersed in Bunyan's grand old story as if she were experiencing it for the very first time.

* * *

Night was fast approaching, stealing the last bit of light from the page and making the words run together in an inky blur. Simon glanced up from the scene where Christian and Hopeful prepare to cross the River of Death to find Catriona slumped in the seat across from him, sound asleep. He had been reading steadily since they'd stopped at an inn to change horses and eat supper two hours ago. A reluctant smile touched his lips as he gently closed the book, laid it aside, and drew off his spectacles.

With her bonnet listing to the left and a feather drooping over one eye, Catriona looked like a little girl who had borrowed her mother's finery to parade around in. A glowing curl had escaped her neat chignon to trail around the ivory curve of her throat.

Given the shameless way he had behaved in her bed that morning, he was surprised she still trusted him enough to relax her guard. She had every right to fear that the minute she closed her eyes he would fall upon her like some sort of rutting stag with no control over his baser impulses.

He would swear before the bewigged members of Parliament itself that he had only intended to steal an innocent kiss from her parted lips. But her lips had been so soft . . . so warm . . . so inviting . . .

When she had breathed his name into his mouth with a hint of an enchanting Scottish lilt, he had been well and truly lost.

If Alice hadn't barged into the bedchamber looking for her infernal hair ribbons, he would be atoning for an even greater sin than just stealing a kiss. He still couldn't decide if it had been relief or regret that had overwhelmed him in that moment.

He would do well to remember that he was nothing but Catriona's hired gun. It would be impossible for her to petition the church for an annulment based on his failure to perform his marital duties if she returned to London with his child already growing in her belly. He'd learned how to prevent such *mishaps* when he was little more than a lad, but this morning when he had heard her moan his name and felt her shudder with ecstasy beneath his fingertips, all thoughts of *coitus interruptus* and French letters had flown right out of his head, along with caution and common sense. All he had wanted in that moment was to push his way deep inside of her and make her his own.

Desperate to distract himself from the provocative images that thought invoked, he glanced at the portmanteau resting on the seat beside her. This might be his best opportunity to find out exactly what she was so eager to hide from his prying eyes. But some ghost of conscience stayed his hand. Or perhaps it was just the fear of being caught. If she awoke to find him rummaging through her personal belongings like some Covent Garden footpad, she might never nap again.

The carriage jounced through a deep rut, bumping her head against the back of the seat. She frowned, her delicate eyelids fluttering. Simon turned to gaze out the carriage window at the rising moon, testing his resolve. He was nothing but her hired man. Her comfort was none of his concern.

The next bump jarred his own teeth and wrung an unhappy little moan from Catriona's throat. Blowing out a sigh, Simon reluctantly shifted himself to her seat. He scooped Robert the Bruce from her lap, hoping he wasn't about to lose a finger or perhaps even a thumb. The cat simply hung there in his grasp, boneless yet ridiculously heavy. He gingerly settled it on the seat he'd just vacated. The beast gave him a cross look before curling into a sullen ball and closing its golden eyes.

Simon tugged off Catriona's bonnet, then drew her into the circle of his arms so his chest could cushion her against the blows of the road. But it seemed the greedy little minx was not to be content with using his chest for her pillow. Before Simon could fully absorb what was happening, she had wiggled her rump across the seat and slid her head into his lap.

As she nestled her cheek against him, trying to find the most comfortable spot, he swore softly beneath his breath. If she kept rubbing him in that maddening manner, it wouldn't be any different than resting her head on a rock.

She curled one hand around his upper thigh and went still, her rosebud lips curving into a contented smile. She had no way of knowing that her bliss was his agony. The caress of her warm breath through the thin doeskin of his trousers was a taste of both heaven and hell. He rolled his eyes toward the carriage's roof. If this was his punishment for the morning's transgression, then God had a far more wicked sense of humor than he had ever guessed.

As the carriage bounced through another rut, he was the one forced to clench his teeth against a moan. Despite his reputation, he'd never had any problem controlling his lust when it suited him. Perhaps he was simply suffering from the novelty of denying himself a woman he wanted.

He brushed a curl from the downy softness of

her cheek. The silky tendril twined around his finger as if to ensnare him.

He realized in that moment exactly what he had to do if he was to escape this woman with his heart unscathed. She'd promised to split the dowry with him after they were wed. Once she did, it would be easy enough for him to steal away. She might despise him for the charlatan he was, but at least he would have escorted her as far as the Scottish border. She could use the rest of the dowry to get her to the Highlands and into her brother's waiting arms.

As for him, he would forget all about his London debts and use the money to flee to the Continent, where some hot-blooded Italian countess or swarthy Greek beauty would welcome him into her arms and bed and make him forget all about Catriona Kincaid with her misty gray eyes and ridiculous freckles.

Catriona drifted into wakefulness with a hand playing gently in her hair. She kept her eyes pressed firmly shut, luxuriating in the novel sensation. Her uncle's family had prided themselves on their newly won English reserve. They rarely touched one another and—unless one could count Alice's stinging pinches—they never touched her.

The hand tenderly sifting through her loosened curls stirred long-buried childhood memories. Memories of her father hefting her over his head as if she weighed no more than a feather. Memories of her brother rumpling her freshly braided hair just to make her squeal in protest. Memories of sitting before the fire in their cottage with her mother stroking a brush through her unruly curls until Catriona nodded off and her papa arrived to carry her off to bed.

She sighed and nestled deeper into her pillow, feeling cherished and secure for the first time since the English soldiers had come and wrenched away both her family and her future, leaving her with nothing but a hollow ache where they had been.

A man's husky whisper brushed like velvet across her ear. "Wake up, sleeping beauty. It's time to find you a proper bed."

Catriona's eyes flew open in horror as she realized the hand deftly tucking a wayward curl behind her ear belonged to Simon and the pillow beneath her cheek wasn't a pillow at all but his muscular thigh.

No matter how tempting the prospect had seemed earlier, she couldn't believe she had been so foolish as to crawl into his lap. What if she had murmured something both idiotic and incriminating in her sleep—something like, *Kiss me, darling,* or *I think I might love you?*

She sat up so fast she bumped her head on his chin hard enough to make her see stars.

"Ow!" Rubbing his jaw, he eyed her warily. "I haven't taken a shot to the jaw like that since the last time I boxed at Gentleman Jackson's."

"I'm terribly sorry." Desperate to escape him, she lurched away and fumbled around on the shadow-draped seats in search of her bonnet. When her hands seized upon something soft, an offended "Mrrwwww" warned her that she had found the cat instead.

"Looking for this?"

She straightened to find Simon dangling the bonnet from one long, elegant finger. "Thank you very much," she said stiffly, seizing the hat and clapping it on her head.

"Shall I make arrangements for our lodgings?" he offered, reaching over and turning the bonnet around so that its saucy little velvet-trimmed brim would be facing forward instead of backward.

She brushed his hands away. "That won't be necessary. I'll take care of everything while you arrange for our bags to be brought in."

He shrugged, retreating behind a shield of indifference. "Suit yourself. After all, you are the boss."

Without waiting for the coachman or one of the inn's grooms to assist her, she wrenched open the carriage door and scrambled out of the vehicle so fast she got her feet tangled up in her skirts and nearly fell. Regaining her footing, if not her dignity, she started across the courtyard. She was halfway to the door of the inn when she executed an abrupt about-face and marched back to the carriage.

She reached through the door and jerked out her portmanteau. After a moment's thought, she reached back in and hauled Robert the Bruce into her arms as well. As she marched back across the courtyard, she could almost feel Simon's arch gaze boring into her back. She lifted her chin, reminding herself sternly that any refuge she found in his arms was nothing but a dangerous illusion.

A short while later, Simon found himself following his betrothed up a narrow, winding staircase. The feathers in her bonnet might be drooping, but the saucy swish of her rump was as fresh as ever.

She turned right at the top of the corridor,

counting beneath her breath as she led them past a handful of narrow oak doors. She stopped at the last door and slipped the beribboned key in her hand into the keyhole. The door swung open to reveal a bedstead of whitewashed iron.

Simon nearly groaned with longing. After so many grueling hours spent bouncing around the interior of the carriage, the thin mattress with its understuffed pillows and faded patchwork quilt looked as inviting as a celestial cloud.

He started forward, but Catriona turned in the doorway, blocking his path. She blinked up at him, her dewy gray eyes as innocent as a babe's. "I'm sorry. Did I neglect to tell you that I'd arranged for separate accommodations? Since we won't be officially wed until the morrow, it would hardly be proper for us to share a room." She pointed down the corridor before offering him a second key. "You'll find your bed right down the hall—the last door on the left."

Simon slowly took the key, then nodded toward the cat cradled in her arms. "I suppose you have no qualms about letting that rascal share your bed."

"Of course not. Unlike you, I can count on him to be the perfect gentleman." With those words, she gently closed the door in his face, leaving him standing all alone in the corridor.

*   *   *

The wedding day Catriona had dreamed about for five years dawned with an ominous rumble of thunder and the steady patter of rain on the inn's roof. By the time she and Simon had dressed and broken their fast with chunks of stale bread and lukewarm bowls of porridge, they were forced to wade through chill puddles to reach their waiting carriage. The coachman huddled atop his bench, rain streaming steadily from the brim of his top hat and the voluminous shoulder capes of his greatcoat. He looked even more miserable than Catriona felt as she dragged the sodden hem of her cloak and a yowling Robert the Bruce into the carriage.

As they resumed their journey on the Great North Road, the promise of spring slowly disappeared, leaving the hedgerows and tree branches bare of buds and the landscape bleak and wintry. At least Catriona didn't have to worry about crawling back into Simon's lap. With her nerves strung as taut as pianoforte wires, she was far too tense to sleep.

The man sitting across from her wasn't some fairy-tale prince who would be content with a chaste kiss from her trembling lips. He was flesh and blood, with a man's needs and a man's hungers. Hungers she had foolishly promised to satisfy.

They crossed the Scottish border and rolled into the sleepy little village of Gretna Green just as the bleak day was fading into an even bleaker dusk. Catriona wondered how many brides had traveled this road before her—some giddy with joy, some still stinging from the scandals they had left behind, others being pursued by frantic parents and jilted lovers desperate to halt their elopements before they could be consummated in one of the seedy inns that had sprung up for just that purpose. As she took the hand Simon offered her and descended from the carriage, she realized that there was no one to rescue her from her folly.

She was about to marry the man of her dreams, yet she felt as if she were slogging through a nightmare of her own making. Instead of standing before the altar in a candlelit church and giving her his heart, Simon would take her money and her innocence. He would share her bed, but not her life.

They were directed to a smoky barn lit by the hellish glow of a forge. In lieu of a clergyman, a hulking blacksmith in a soot-stained apron strode forward to perform the ceremony. For all he knew, she could be an abducted heiress only minutes away from being ravished by her greedy groom. As long as his grimy paw was crossed with silver, he would gladly deliver her into the hands of the devil himself.

She stole a look at Simon's profile. He bore little resemblance to the charming young officer who had fueled her innocent fantasies since the day she'd caught him making love to her cousin. This man with the sinister scar on his brow and the cynical quirk to his lips suddenly seemed like a stranger to her—forbidding and dangerous. She flinched as the sweaty blacksmith slammed his hammer down on an anvil and pronounced her and Simon man and wife.

A stranger who was now her husband.

As the blacksmith boomed out, "What God joins together, let no man put asunder!" she stole a glance skyward, half expecting a bolt of lightning to sizzle her into ashes where she stood.

They had exchanged no heartfelt vows, no golden rings, no tender kiss. It was a wedding without pledges or promises, tailor-made for a man like Simon Wescott.

"Is that all there is?" she asked, desperate to forestall the inevitable.

The blacksmith's broad, leathery face split in a grin. "Aye, lass, that's all there is. Once you and yer young man sign the register over there, 'tis every bit as bindin' as a proper church weddin' in the eyes o' the law. And the Lord," he added, shooting a glance toward the dusty rafters of the barn as if to cue a choir of angels eager to lend approval to their unholy union.

Simon quickly scrawled his name in the leather-bound register, then handed her the feather quill, his warm hand brushing hers. Catriona was trying to still her trembling long enough to dot her *i*'s when another couple burst through the door of the barn, laughing and shaking rain from their hair. Although they looked like a pair of drowned rats, their faces were glowing brighter than the forge.

"Are you the bloke who can make all my dreams come true?" the copper-haired young man demanded of the blacksmith, wrapping an arm around his apple-cheeked companion.

She patted his drooping shirtfront and gazed adoringly up at his freckled face. "You made all my dreams come true on the day you defied my father and begged me to elope with you."

Her eager young groom cupped her radiant face in his hands and lowered his mouth to hers, kissing her with a tender yet passionate ardor that made a barbed blade of envy twist in Catriona's heart.

The blacksmith cleared his throat. "Unless you want yer first bairn on the way before I can pronounce you man and wife, I suggest the two o' you step over here to the anvil."

The couple broke apart, giggling and blushing. The girl glanced toward the table where the register lay, noticing Simon and Catriona for the first time.

She smiled shyly, revealing a winsome gap between her two front teeth. "Did the two of you just marry?"

Catriona nodded. "Right before you came in."

The girl rushed over and threw her arms around Catriona in an impulsive hug. "Oh, I hope you'll be as happy as me and my Jem!"

Catriona gave the girl's back an awkward pat before stepping away. Avoiding Simon's eyes, she said, "Thank you. I'm certain we will."

The young man strode over to give Simon's hand an enthusiastic pump. "May your marriage bed be blessed with sons, sir. Lots of strapping sons." He gave Catriona's hips an appreciative glance before winking at Simon. "Your new missus there looks like she'll make as fine a breeder as my Bess."

As Catriona let out a shocked gasp and his Bess smothered a giggle behind her hand, Simon winked back at the boy, his stage whisper loud enough to be heard by them all. "You've a good eye, son. That's precisely why I married the lass."

Keenly aware of Simon's presence behind her, Catriona trudged up the inn stairs to their room. There would be no leaving him standing in the hallway tonight. He had laid claim to her heart five years ago and as far as society and the law were concerned, her body now belonged to him as well.

She couldn't even count on Robert the Bruce to defend her honor tonight. Despite Catriona's protests, the innkeeper had insisted that the cat remain in the stables with the coachman.

As they reached the top of the stairs, the shadows that draped the narrow corridor threatened to consume her. No one in Gretna Green was worried about the elegance of their accommodations. The only requirement for a room was that it contain a bed. And judging from the grappling couple they had glimpsed in the courtyard, some of the more eager newlyweds were even willing to forgo that luxury. She felt her cheeks heat all over again as she remembered the man's groan of appreciation as the woman's naked breast had spilled from her bodice into his eager hand.

"Ah, here we are," she said with false cheer as they reached the room they had been assigned.

After she'd made three futile stabs at unlocking the door, Simon gently removed the key from her trembling hand and slid it smoothly into the keyhole. Their bodies brushed as he held the door open and ushered her inside, making her aware all over again of how much stronger and larger than her he was.

The innkeeper had delivered their baggage, but the stone hearth was cold, with no fire to welcome them or burn the damp chill from the air. A rough-hewn table squatted in front of it. There was no wedding supper waiting for them either. No steaming pigeon pie or even a moldy hunk of cheese and stale bread.

Perhaps that was just as well, Catriona thought. With all of the butterflies waltzing in her belly, she doubted there would be any room for food.

The single lamp cast a grudging glow over the narrow iron bedstead in the corner. It looked as if it had barely enough room for one occupant, much less two. It was a far cry from the luxurious half-tester she and Simon had shared at her uncle's house.

She was fretting needlessly, she told herself. Simon had probably already forgotten the foolish pledge she'd made in the jail. He had only been bluffing to frighten her away. She removed her bonnet and placed it on the table before turning to face him.

Eyeing her with an intensity that could only be called predatory, he leaned his back against the door as if to block any hope of escape, tugged the knot from his cravat and said, "Enough dawdling, darling. Let's have done with it, then, shall we?"

Chapter 9

atriona froze. Given Simon's reputation, she had expected at least a token attempt at seduction—a coaxing smile, a tender touch, some honeyed words flattering the silkiness of her hair or the intoxicating aroma of the lavender water she had dabbed behind her ears. She knew firsthand just how persuasive his tongue could be. Especially when employed in the service of a kiss. But at the moment he was eyeing her as if he had every intention of bending her over the table, throwing her skirts up over her head and ravishing her like some sort of marauding Viking.

She awkwardly cleared her throat. "We just arrived. There's really no need to rush, is there?"

He straightened to his full height, the impressive breadth of his shoulders making him look even more forbidding than he had in the forge. "And why not? I've done the deed and now it's your turn. I want what I was promised."

Catriona gazed at his implacable face for a long moment before slowly nodding. "Very well. Now that we're wed, I suppose I have no right to deny you."

With shaking hands she stripped off her damp cloak and draped it neatly over one of the rickety chairs. She moved toward the bed, measuring her every step as if it were carrying her toward the gallows. She settled herself gingerly on the thin heather-stuffed tick, then lay back and squeezed her eyes shut. Perhaps if he was ruthless and impersonal—taking his own pleasure without offering any in return—she would be better able to hide her feelings for him. There would be no danger of her melting beneath his tender caresses or crying out his name in a moment of blissful madness.

"What in the bloody hell are you doing?"

Catriona opened her eyes to find Simon leaning over the bed, frowning down at her as if she'd lost the last of her wits.

She blinked up at him. "Preparing to perform my wifely duties."

"You look more like you're preparing to be roasted on a spit." He grabbed her by the upper arm and hauled her to a sitting position. "If I were you, I'd sit up before someone stuffs an apple in your mouth."

Flushing to the roots of her hair, she jerked her arm out of his grip, mortified that he found her so clumsy. "As you probably guessed from our earlier encounter, I'm not particularly well versed in the art of lovemaking."

Taking his pained cough to be one of agreement, she scowled. "I've never been a professional libertine, while you, undoubtedly, have had the opportunity to practice any number of creative perversions."

"Oh, dozens. Each more creative than the last," he agreed cheerfully.

"What I'm trying to say," she continued through gritted teeth, "is that I might require your instruction. I have no idea what will please a man like you."

Simon dropped to his knees in front of her and gently folded her hands in his own. As Catriona met his eyes, she felt a reckless hope stir in her heart. Perhaps she had misjudged him. Perhaps he too had secret hopes that their marriage could be more than just convenient.

He stroked his thumbs over her knuckles, his

touch even more seductive than she'd dreamed it could be, his voice even more tender. "I can tell you *exactly* what would please a man like me."

"Can you?" She was mesmerized by his husky murmur, and her gaze wandered from the sparkling green depths of his eyes to the beguiling curve of his lips.

He leaned closer to her, his warm breath caressing the wispy curls at her temple. "Nothing would please me more than . . ."

She closed her eyes and held her breath, promising herself she would maintain her composure no matter how scandalous his suggestion.

". . . being paid the money that I am owed."

Catriona's eyes flew open. Snatching her hands out of his, she rose to her feet so quickly she nearly sent him tumbling to his backside. He recovered his balance and slowly straightened, but she was already pacing fitfully in front of the hearth.

For a few foolish seconds, she had allowed herself to forget just what sort of man she was dealing with. A rogue. A mercenary. A man who would barter away his own soul if it meant he had a fistful of farthings to squander in the brothels or at the gaming tables. Of course, she had bartered her innocence away with even less care, so she supposed she had no right to condemn him for his greed.

She swung around to face him. "I'm afraid that won't be possible."

He eyed her warily. "And why not?"

"Because you haven't yet completed the task for which I hired you."

"You hired me to marry you."

It sounded even more humiliating when stated so baldly, as if it had been the only way for her to obtain a husband. "I also hired you to escort me to my brother in the Highlands. Once you've completed that task to my satisfaction, you'll receive your payment in full. Until then, I can't have you sneaking off in the dead of night and leaving me to my own devices."

They gazed at each other in silence. They both knew he now had the legal right to not only his half of the dowry, but hers as well. According to the courts, every one of her pennies, every stitch of clothing she owned, every hair on her head had become his sole personal property in the moment they had signed the marriage register. He could steal from her, ravish her, even beat her with his fists, and no judge in England or Scotland would condemn him.

"Let me make sure I have this straight," he said softly, stealing a glance at the bed. "You were willing to trust me with your body, but you refuse to trust me with my own money."

She had no answer for that. Especially since he'd made it painfully clear that he was more interested in the money than her body.

"You disappoint me, Mrs. Wescott," he finally said. "I know I'm not a man of my word, but I thought you were a woman of yours."

He turned and strode toward the door.

"Where are you going?"

"Out," he said shortly without slowing his stride.

Catriona watched him walk away from her, her sense of helplessness growing. Even though their marriage was to be only a mock one, she couldn't bear the thought of him spending *their* wedding night in another woman's arms.

"No! You mustn't go!"

He turned on his heel, lifting one eyebrow in blatant challenge. "And why not? Can you give me a good reason to stay?"

For one desperate moment, Catriona considered marching over to him, throwing her arms around his neck, pressing her lips against his and doing just that. But if he refused her again, she didn't think her bruised pride would survive the blow.

She lifted her chin, squarely meeting his gaze.

"My uncle. I told you he was a canny man and I'm not sure he was entirely convinced by our charade. He may very well have hired a spy to follow us. Why, it could even be the coachman! John has been a devoted servant of Uncle Ross's for years."

Simon's eyes narrowed as he considered her words.

"If word gets back to him that my new husband didn't spend our wedding night in my bedchamber, he'll send men after us to bring me home. I'll never see my brother again and you'll never see a single penny of that dowry."

Simon raked a hand through his hair, then turned back to the door. Her spirits sank as she realized he had no intention of heeding her words.

"I'll leave you to your privacy to prepare for bed," he said, his words clipped. "I'll be back within the hour with some supper for the both of us."

"Thank you," she whispered, but he was already gone, leaving the echo of the door's slam ringing in her ears.

Simon stormed through the inn's common room, only too aware of the curious glances he was garnering from the handful of diners scattered among the long wooden tables. They probably didn't expect to see a groom fleeing his bride's bedchamber as if the devil himself had gotten there first.

He shoved open the front door and was halfway across the courtyard before he realized he had nowhere to go. Biting off an oath, he wheeled around and turned his face to the sky. A bashful moon peeped through the shredded veil of clouds, casting a lustrous glow over the courtyard. The rain had softened to a fine mist, but not even its soothing caress could completely melt the scowl from his brow.

He glared up at the lighted window of the second-story room he would share with his virgin bride on this night. At the moment he could think of any number of *creative perversions* he'd love to practice on her, starting with that beautiful mouth of hers.

He couldn't have said why he was in such a baleful temper. Catriona hadn't exactly double-crossed him. She had simply anticipated his next move and put him neatly in check, beating him at his own game. His exasperation was tempered by an even more dangerous thread of admiration. He didn't often encounter such a worthy opponent, either at the gaming tables or on the dueling field.

How could she have known he had every

intention of making off with his half of the money and leaving her stranded in Gretna Green? Could the blasted woman read his mind?

He slowly uncurled his fists, wondering when he had clenched them. He had never believed in responding to defeat with anger. That only gave your opponent the upper hand. He had always been able to deflect his father's taunts and bullying with a well-timed roll of his eyes or a flippant quip. And if that strategy occasionally backfired and earned him a vicious caning from one of his father's footmen, he would simply slip into the library after everyone was abed and steal one of the old man's wildly expensive bottles of port to take the ache out of his bruises and the dangerous edge off of his temper.

His lips curved in a lazy smile. He had allowed the new Mrs. Wescott to make him forget one of the most valuable and hard-earned lessons of his boyhood.

Catriona sat cross-legged in the middle of the narrow iron bedstead, hugging her faded plaid around her nightdress. Judging from the chill she'd glimpsed in her bridegroom's eyes before he'd slammed his way from their bridal chamber, she was going to need it. She'd made a halfhearted attempt to light the stingy bundle of kindling in the fireplace, but the meager flames had already subsided into embers.

Despite his promise, Simon had been gone for well over an hour. He was probably halfway to Edinburgh by now, she thought glumly, having decided that neither she nor her dowry were worth the bother.

She frowned as a cheerful scrap of melody came drifting through the door, at distinct odds with her mood:

> *Me bride, she is a bonny lass,*
> *As fair as she is fey.*
> *She stole a peek beneath me kilt,*
> *And fainted dead away.*

Catriona's eyes widened. Although the ditty was being bellowed out in a Scots burr thicker than the spring heather on a Highland hillside, the rich masculine baritone sounded alarmingly familiar.

> *When I asked her what distressed her so,*
> *She blushed and ducked her head.*
> *She dinna ken if she could take*
> *A stallion to her bed.*

Catriona's jaw dropped, then snapped shut as the door came crashing open. Simon stood in the doorway, gripping an open bottle of Scots whisky in one hand and an enormous sausage in the other.

He leaned against the doorframe and gave her a lopsided grin, charm practically oozing from his pores. "Hullo, darling. Miss me?"

Chapter 10

$\mathcal{S}$imon looked strikingly more cheerful and far more disheveled than when he'd stormed from the room. Somewhere during his travels, he'd managed to misplace both his coat and waistcoat. His rumpled cravat was draped carelessly around his neck and his shirt was open at the throat and half untucked. Oddly enough, the slovenly ensemble suited him, giving him a dashing flair usually reserved for pirates or long-lost princes.

His tawny hair was tossed as if he'd repeatedly run his fingers through it. Catriona's lips tightened. For his sake, she hoped it had been *his* fingers.

As if reading her mind, he waved the bottle in

the air. "I hope you don't mind, but I bought a few rounds for the lads down in the common room. Of course, you'll have to make good with the innkeeper tomorrow." He touched a finger to his lips as if to shield a shocking secret before whispering, "My purse is a wee bit light and my credit is none too good."

"I thought you were bringing supper."

"And so I did. This is your supper," he said, tossing the sausage at her.

Catriona awkwardly caught it, unsure how to properly handle the thing. It was a good ten inches long and three inches thick and looked more menacing than appetizing. If an intruder broke into their room, she could probably use it to club him insensible.

"And this is my supper," Simon finished, tipping the whisky bottle to his lips and taking a deep swig of the amber liquor.

"I believe you've had more than enough *supper* for one night," Catriona noted.

As if to prove her point, Simon took one steady step toward the bed, then began to stagger to the right.

He frowned. "Is it just me, or is this cabin listing to starboard?"

Tossing the sausage away, Catriona scrambled to her feet and rushed to his side. She wrapped one arm around his upper back, bracing her shoulder beneath his to keep him from falling.

Leaning heavily on her, he buried his face in her unbound curls and inhaled deeply. "You're certainly the prettiest cabin boy I've ever seen."

"Well, at least I haven't a mustache," she replied dryly, plucking the whisky bottle from his hand and setting it on the table before half tugging, half dragging him toward the bed. His lips found the back of her neck and began to nuzzle it in a most distracting manner.

By the time she shrugged him off of her shoulder and dumped him unceremoniously into the bed, she was starting to feel a little tipsy herself.

Before she could back out of his reach, he caught her hand in a strong grip and tugged her down on top of him, giving her a clear view of the golden haze of beard shadow that had begun to darken his jaw.

"The ship is spinning," he said solemnly. "Go tell the captain that we must be caught in a whirlpool."

"The ship's not spinning. Your fool head is. Close your eyes and it will stop."

He obeyed. "Mmmm . . . you're right. That feels much better."

Catriona had been right about something else

as well. The bed wasn't nearly large enough for two occupants to lie side by side. But it was the perfect size for her to stretch out on top of Simon, her thighs straddling his hips and the softness of her breasts molded to the muscular contours of his chest.

She might have protested when he wrapped one arm around her waist, but for once he didn't betray even a hint of lecherous intent. He seemed perfectly content to cuddle. She hesitated for a moment, then cautiously rested her cheek against his breastbone, secretly savoring the novelty of being held. Especially by him.

"When I was just a lad," he murmured, rubbing lazy circles on the small of her back, "my mother used to tell me that my bed was a tall ship and the night was the sea. She promised that if I'd close my eyes, I'd soon be sailing away on all sorts of magnificent adventures."

Catriona lifted her head, gazing intently at his face. A faint smile curved his lips, but his eyes were still closed.

She knew it was wrong to take advantage of his drunken state. But what could be the harm of engaging him in a conversation he probably wouldn't even remember on the morrow?

"What was she like?" she asked softly. "Your mother?"

He sighed. "Kind and beautiful, with a wicked wit and a generous heart. She had several lovers, of course. There will always be men who consider opera dancers to be little more than whores. Unfortunately, my father was one of them. But he underestimated her. She might have been beautiful, but she was savvy too. Savvy enough to leave a signet ring he had given her in a moment of passion with a solicitor so that upon her death he had no choice but to acknowledge me as his spawn."

"How did she die?"

Simon shrugged without opening his eyes. "A lingering cough. A stormy night. No money for a doctor. For a tragedy, it had all of the elements of a classic farce."

"You must have missed her terribly."

He nodded. "Whatever her other failings, she was a good mother. No matter how many men she took to her bed, she made it clear that I was the love of her life." A winsome smile quirked one corner of his mouth. "I suppose I inherited my 'passion for passion' from her."

Catriona pondered his words for a moment. "Do you believe she was looking for passion in the arms of all those men . . . or for love?"

Simon opened his eyes, his sleepy green gaze devoid of mockery. "Aren't they one and the same?"

"Only if you're very lucky," Catriona whispered, realizing too late that his lips were only a scant breath away from her own.

He slid his big warm hand beneath her curls, cradling her nape in his palm. Her eyes fluttered shut as he drew her mouth down to his, sending his seeking lips on a quest all their own. His tongue gently played over the seam of her lips before delving deep enough to sweep away all of her inhibitions. His kiss tasted of whisky and sin and all of the dark delights a man and a woman might experience in the lonely watches of the night.

Reminding herself that this was an encounter he also would not remember on the morrow, she kissed him back with all of the pent-up longing in her soul. In that moment she didn't care if he was looking for passion or love or just a fleeting thrill, as long as he was looking for it in her arms.

She sprawled on top of him with inelegant abandon, straddling not only his hips but also the unyielding ridge of flesh straining the buttery-soft fabric of his trousers. Breathing a tender oath into her mouth, Simon arched his hips off the bed, forcing her to ride him in a rhythm that echoed the sweet, slow slide of his tongue in her mouth. The motion sent shivers of delight cascading deep into her womb. The starched linen of her nightdress and the doeskin of his trousers only heightened the delicious friction between them.

The bed was a tall ship, the night was the sea, and he was the magnificent adventure drawing her deep into a whirlpool of sensation she had no desire to escape.

As those tremors of pleasure mounted, threatening to spill over into rapture, Catriona heard a heartrending groan she would have sworn was her own. Until it was followed by a rhythmic banging that made the entire wall next to the bed shudder and a caterwauling screech that made the tiny hairs on the back of her nape stand straight up.

Still straddling Simon, she sat up on her knees, alarm dousing her desire like a bucketful of icy water. "What in the name of heaven is that? Do you think someone is being murdered? Should we alert the innkeeper?"

"Only if inciting *le petit mort* is a crime." Wrapping an arm around her hips to steady her, Simon sat up, pressing his ear to the wall. "If I'm not mistaken, I do believe it's our eager young friends from the forge."

"How do you know?"

He cocked his head toward the wall. "Listen."

Catriona didn't even have to press her ear to the wall to hear the impassioned wail of "Oh, Bess!" followed by a piercing cry of "Oh, Jem!"

"Oh, hell," Simon snapped. "How in the devil are we supposed to get any sleep with that racket going on all night?"

It turned out that *all night* was an optimistic estimate. Just a few seconds later, Jem roared like a bull while Bess hit a trilling note worthy of an operatic aria. Blissful silence followed. Apparently the newlyweds had expired simultaneously.

Simon and Catriona had just breathed a mutual sigh of relief when the banging and moaning resumed, even more vigorously than before.

Simon collapsed onto his back with a groan of his own. "Oh, to be two-and-twenty again!"

Catriona shook her head in dismay. "I can't believe how thin these walls are." An even more terrible thought struck her. "So if we had . . . would they have . . . ?"

He nodded, eyeing her from beneath the decadent length of his lashes. "Every moan. Every sigh. Every syllable as you cried out my name and begged me to—"

She clapped a hand over his mouth. "What makes you think *I* would have been the one doing the begging?"

She felt him smile beneath her hand. Then he

rolled, neatly reversing their positions so that she was imprisoned beneath the muscled length of his body. Lacing his fingers through hers, he pinned her hands on either side of her head. "Give me ten minutes of your time and I'll show you."

With his eyes glittering down at her like shards of emerald and the hard, hungry weight of his hips still nestled between her thighs, it was a challenge that was nearly impossible to resist. But he was deep in his cups, she reminded herself. When he was sober he had walked away from her bed without a backward glance.

"As you were so quick to remind me earlier," she said softly, "I hired you to marry me, not bed me."

His eyes darkened, warning her that she was hardly in any position to bait him. He could just as easily restrain her with one hand while he unfastened the front of his trousers and shoved her nightdress up and out of his way. It pricked her pride to know that in some dark, wicked corner of her heart, she almost wished he would. He wouldn't even have to be rough with her. A few artful strokes with those deft fingers of his and she would be singing an aria that would make young Bess next door sound like a fishwife hawking her wares on the docks.

"You're absolutely right," he finally said, loosening his grip on her hands and rolling to his side. He propped himself up on one elbow and gazed down at her. "And since it seems I'm not to be compensated for either service, I should stop trying to ply my wares where they're not wanted."

Catriona rolled away from him before he could see just how badly she did want him. She was fully prepared to spend a miserable night wrapped in her plaid in one of the straight-backed chairs, listening to Jem and Bess noisily proclaim their undying love for one another. But before she could scramble off the bed, Simon's arm snaked around her waist. He tugged her against him, molding his chest to her back.

"Good night, Mrs. Wescott," he whispered into her hair. "I hope all your dreams are of me."

As she succumbed to the temptation and settled into the warm cup of his body, Catriona discovered that she had been wrong after all. There *was* room for two in the narrow bedstead—as long as they nestled together like two spoons in a cupboard drawer. She could still feel Simon's rigid arousal pressed to the softness of her rump, could still hear Jem and Bess rutting like livestock in the next room. But being wrapped in Simon's arms seemed to soothe

the tension from her body, making it possible to sleep.

And dream of him.

Simon awoke the next morning with empty arms and an aching head. He was no stranger to the aching head and he was usually relieved to find his arms and bed empty after a night of drunken revelry. It staved off the awkward parting kisses and the pouting demands for pretty promises he had no intention of making or keeping. But on this morning his arms felt emptier than usual— as if he'd been robbed of something precious through no fault of his own.

He swung his legs over the edge of the bed and pried open his eyes, groaning aloud when a bright blaze of sunlight struck them. Gripping his throbbing temples, he slammed his eyes shut and waited several minutes before gingerly try-ing again. This time the sunlight streaming through the dormer window under the east eave winked off of the open whisky bottle sitting on the table. There was only a thimbleful of liquor left in it, which certainly explained the aching head, if not his empty arms.

He glanced down. His clothes were much the worse for wear, but he was still wearing his shirt, his trousers, even his boots. He examined the bed, half dreading what he might find. The sheets were rumpled, but there was no coppery stain of any kind and no lingering musk of sex in the air.

He dropped his head into his hands as images from the night came flooding back to him. Usually liquor dulled his memory, making it foggy and unreliable, but these images came to him like the distant echo of a well-loved song—haunting and unforgettable. Catriona in his arms—beside him, on top of him . . . beneath him.

He also remembered a dark moment of temptation when he had come as close to ravishing a woman as he ever had in his sordid career as a libertine.

And not just any woman, but his wife.

Simon lifted his head, blinking away the glare until the humble bedchamber came clearly into focus. His arms and bed weren't the only things that were empty.

Catriona and all of her belongings were gone.

Chapter 11 🌿

The clever little baggage had double-crossed him.

Simon took the inn stairs two at a time, jerking a knot in his cravat as he went. He had been so busy plotting his own treachery that it had never occurred to him that his bride might betray him. No wonder she had anticipated his plan. It had been but a dull-witted echo of her own nefarious scheme.

He was at least going to have the decency to leave her with her half of the dowry. She had apparently absconded with the whole of it, abandoning him to the dubious mercy of his creditors. Since he had no money to flee to the Continent, it was only a matter of time before they caught up with him. That is, if the inn-keeper didn't summon the local constable first and have him tossed into jail for failing to settle their account. He wondered if she would weep prettily into her handkerchief when she heard he had been cast into debtor's prison or marched to the gallows by the same vengeful magistrate whose daughter he had seduced.

The irony of his predicament was not wasted on him. Usually it was the bride who woke in the harsh light of morning to discover her groom had deserted her. Many never even made it as far as Gretna Green, but were abandoned along the way after being robbed of both their pride and their virtue by some rapscallion who had never had any intention of marrying them in the first place.

Simon felt doubly ill-used. Catriona hadn't even bothered to rob him of his virtue, just his money and his pride. He knew a moment of sav-age regret that he hadn't taken her up on her of-fer to consummate their union. At least then she'd have something to remember him by, even if it was only a thorough—

Rounding the corner at the bottom of the stairs, he ran right into Jem.

Oblivious to his ill temper, the young man staggered backward and gave him a snaggletoothed grin. "Good morning, sir. I hope you and your lovely bride spent as pleasant a night as me and my Bess."

Simon snatched the lad up by the collar, bringing them eye to eye. "You'd have to be stone deaf not to know what a pleasant night you and your precious Bess spent. They probably heard the two of you moaning and screaming all the way to Edinburgh."

Jem's grin only deepened. "Do you really think so, sir?"

Shaking his head in disgust, Simon let him go. As Simon went striding toward the door, Jem continued up the stairs, a jaunty whistle on his lips and an extra strut in his step.

The encounter hardly improved Simon's temper. He was betrayed and abandoned, while Jem was returning to his adoring bride's bed for another earsplitting round of the blanket hornpipe.

How dare Catriona! he thought. Women didn't leave him. Women *never* left him. It simply wasn't done. If there was any leaving to be done, then *he* was the one who would do it. She was the one who was supposed to spend the rest of her days pining for his touch and mooning over the one grand passion of her life. Yet here he was, stranded at some ramshackle inn in some grubby little Scottish village while she and her ridiculously obese cat made a mad dash for the Highlands with *his* half of her dowry.

He threw open the front door of the inn, nearly knocking over another hapless bridegroom. She was a fool to believe she could escape him that easily. Why, he would steal a horse and risk hanging to go after her if he had to! He would find her and make her pay back every last half-penny of what she owed him. He would hunt her to the very gates of hell itself and make her sorry she had ever dared to double-cross . . .

Simon halted in midstride, his heart turning over in his chest. His bride stood in the middle of the courtyard next to a rickety farm cart. As if divining his presence with some miraculous sense beyond hearing or sight, she turned and spotted him. Reaching up to secure her wide-brimmed hat from the brisk breeze dancing through the courtyard, she gave him a smile every bit as radiant as the one Bess was probably giving Jem right now.

Relief and rage coursed through him in equal measure. He didn't know whether to sweep her into his arms or strangle her with his cravat.

Oblivious to the tumult of unfamiliar emotions making his heart feel heavy and his head light, she strode toward him, the sprigged muslin of her bottle-green skirts foaming around her trim ankles.

She opened her mouth, but before she could greet him, he blurted out, "Where in the bloody hell have you been?"

She looked taken aback, but only briefly. "Oh, I met young Jem in the stables for an assignation," she informed him cheerfully. "After last night, I was curious to see what all the screaming was about."

Simon narrowed his eyes at her, his earlier inclinations rapidly being replaced by an even more unacceptable urge—to snatch her up into his arms and kiss her insensible.

He folded his arms over his chest to help him resist the temptation. "And was he able to *satisfy* your curiosity?"

She lifted her shoulders in an airy shrug. "I've had better."

"Not yet," he replied smoothly. "But you will." He continued to glower at her, secretly admiring the fresh bloom of roses in her cheeks. "You can hardly fault me for being alarmed when I rolled over to bid my bride a good morning, only to discover she'd vanished without a trace."

Catriona snorted. "A good afternoon, you mean."

Simon squinted through bleary eyes at the

cobalt-blue sky, only to discover that she was right. The sun had passed its peak and was already inching toward the horizon.

"I tried to rouse you earlier, with no success," she said. "When I realized you were going to languish in bed for half the day, I took it upon myself to prepare for our departure."

He glanced around the courtyard, but the only vehicle in evidence was the farm cart. It was so loaded down with goods that the splintery bed sagged. "So where is our carriage?"

She slapped a hand on her head as another gust of wind threatened to dislodge her hat and gave him a nervous smile. "On its way back to London, I fear."

"Pardon?" he asked, hoping the aftereffects of the liquor had dulled his hearing as well as his sight.

"Well, when I told John we would be proceeding to the Highlands today, he insisted that he was only ordered to convey us as far as Gretna Green. He said he knew my uncle wouldn't approve of such a venture and would probably sack him as soon as he returned to London—that is, if he didn't get his throat cut by some highwayman or Highland savage first."

"And you let him go?" Simon asked incredulously, rethinking his decision not to strangle her.

"I hardly had a choice. He outweighs me by at least eight stone." She beamed at him. "But you needn't worry about our journey. I've taken care of everything."

"That's what I'm afraid of," he muttered.

She swept a hand toward the cart as if it were one of the king's crested coaches hitched to a team of prancing white stallions. "I had hoped to purchase a more *hospitable* conveyance, but I'm rather pleased to have found this one on such short notice."

Simon circled the monstrosity, studying it with a jaundiced eye. A pair of swaybacked nags had been hitched to the rig. Judging from its piteous condition, a pair of goats would have done just as well and probably would have been hardier. "Did they throw in the horses for free or pay you to take them? If the cart breaks down, at least we'll have something to eat."

Catriona tenderly patted the mangy withers on one of the beasts. "The blacksmith assured me they were sturdier than they looked."

"I certainly hope so. If not, they won't make it out of the courtyard." He circled around to the back of the cart, where several mysterious lumps, bumps and bulges lurked beneath a waterproof oilskin. "And what's all this? More hats?"

Catriona bit her lower lip, looking decidedly

guilty, which set off warning bells in his brain.

"While you were sleeping I took the liberty of purchasing a few gifts for my brother." When he cocked a brow at her, she rolled her eyes. "You needn't worry. I spent *my* money, not yours."

He lifted a corner of the oilskin to steal a look beneath it, but she danced in front of him, breaking the contact. "I have everything packed exactly the way I want it. I'd rather you not fiddle with anything."

He sighed. "And just where exactly are we supposed to be meeting this dear, sainted brother of yours?"

She turned to tuck the corner of the oilskin beneath its confining ropes, avoiding his eyes. "Near Balquhidder. I also purchased a map and enough food to last for nearly a week."

"Then as I see it, all we require is a driver. Did the blacksmith provide one of those as well?"

"No, I did. I thought you could do the honors."

"*Me?*"

"Well, you can drive, can't you? Isn't that one of the skills prized by libertines, rakes and hell-born babes?"

"Racing a prize gelding at Newmarket or tooling a phaeton down Rotten Row on a Sunday afternoon so you can flirt with the belles and their mamas is a bit different from coaxing a pair of broken-down nags up a steep mountainside with a cliff on one side and a sheer drop on the other."

"I'm sure you'll manage." She batted her silky eyelashes at him. "After all, you've had ample experience using your charms to coax nags into doing your bidding."

"It's a pity they never work on you." Simon gazed woefully at the sagging driver's bench, imagining how his bum was going to feel after only a few hours of being bounced around on it. A good third of the seat was already occupied by a cage constructed of narrow wooden slats.

He frowned. "And just what is that contraption?"

"A chicken crate."

He leaned closer to peer inside. The cage's occupant let out a low-pitched growl. "I hate to be the one to point this out, but that's not a chicken."

"Of course it's not a chicken! I couldn't very well let Robert the Bruce roam free as he did in the carriage. If he decided to go dashing off into the woods after a pine marten or a grouse, we might never find him."

Simon muttered something beneath his breath that earned him a reproachful look from Catriona.

He straightened. "I suppose there's only one more thing I need to know."

"Yes?"

"When do we leave?"

After three endless, grueling days on the road, Simon was beginning to wish he *was* the sort of villain who could strangle a woman with his cravat, leave her body moldering in the forest, and waltz merrily away with all of her money. The looks he shot Catriona were growing increasingly murderous with each jolting, grinding turn of the cart's wheels over the stony roads.

To add to his torture, it seemed that every dip and jerk of the wagon brought some part of his body into tantalizing contact with hers. Their knees and thighs collided with every bump, and with each flick of the reins his elbow would brush the beguiling softness of her breast.

As if to mock his surly temper, Catriona's demeanor only grew sunnier with every passing league. Most women of his acquaintance would have long ago succumbed to a fit of tears or the vapors at being forced to endure such primitive traveling conditions. But not Catriona. She chattered on cheerfully and at great length about every crested tit, red squirrel and patch of early-blooming wood sorrel they encountered.

One would have thought God had designed them purely for her pleasure. As the rolling pastures of the Lowlands gave way to the craggy peaks and brooding moors of the Highlands, that enchanting lilt he remembered from the barn began to creep back into her speech.

"I feel as if I can truly breathe for the first time in ten years," she said as the cart lumbered its way up a narrow, twisting path more suited for sheep than humans. "I don't think I ever realized how much soot I'd sucked into my lungs." She closed her eyes and took a deep breath of the crisp mountain air, her blissful expression making Simon wish he was the cause of it. "Doesn't it make you feel almost drunk with delight?"

"No, but this will," he replied shortly, drawing a fresh bottle of Scots whisky out from under the bench and uncorking it with his teeth.

The dilapidated inn they had stayed at the night before had provided very few comforts, but the copper still bubbling out back had almost made up for that. If the Scots could do one thing right, it was make whisky. Simon had cajoled a reluctant Catriona into purchasing three bottles of the stuff, hoping it would make both the journey and her company more tolerable.

He groaned as the cart jolted through a

particularly nasty hole. "I can't decide which aches more. My head or my arse."

Catriona gave the bottle a disapproving look. "Your head might ache less if you wouldn't drink so much."

"My head might ache less if you wouldn't talk so much." Eyeing her defiantly, he brought the bottle to his lips and took a long, deep draw of the whisky.

She pulled her plaid around her shoulders and turned her profile to him, a hint of a tantalizing pout playing around her full lips. But Simon wasn't destined to enjoy the peace and quiet of her sulk. As the wagon rounded a bend, emerging on a broad shelf of rock that overlooked the valley below, a sharp cry spilled from her lips.

Simon tugged the horses to a halt, afraid they were about to be set upon by a horde of marauding Highlanders. Before the cart could come to a complete stop, Catriona had scrambled to the ground and run to the very edge of the cliff.

Her slight figure was framed by a distant range of snowcapped peaks. The wind whipped across their majestic crags, sending billows of fresh snow gusting across the valley. Golden beams of sunlight slanted down from the west, polishing the shards of ice into glittering flecks of gold. They waltzed on the wind, twirling like lovers to the strains of a symphony inaudible to human ears.

Even to Simon's jaded eyes, it was a spectacular sight. But no more spectacular than the sight of Catriona standing there on the edge of that cliff, her face tilted skyward to welcome the arrival of the snow, her expression rapturous. The lusty fingers of the wind made short work of her chignon, tearing away the pins and sending gleaming tendrils of hair fluttering about her face and shoulders. But the wind couldn't sway her noble bearing or the proud set of her slender shoulders. It was if his bedraggled little Celtic princess from the barn had finally found a kingdom worthy of her.

Hugging her moth-eaten plaid around her shoulders as if it were an ermine stole, she turned to him, her smile heartbreakingly earnest. "Oh, Simon, isn't it just the most glorious thing you've ever seen?"

"No," he whispered, too low for her to hear.

His lack of enthusiasm did not discourage her. Laughing aloud, she turned back to the cliff and spread her arms wide as if to embrace the whole world and everyone in it.

Except for him.

Despite the crisp mountain air pouring into his lungs, Simon suddenly felt short of breath.

He feared it wasn't the dizzying height of their perch making him feel light-headed, but some profound shift in the balance between the earth, the sky and his heart.

"If you're done admiring the view, I'm just about done freezing my arse off," he called to her, sounding even gruffer than he intended.

Giving the snow-and-sunswept sky one last lingering look, she reluctantly turned back toward the wagon. She clambered awkwardly back up on the bench, looking at him askance when he didn't even offer her a hand. As she settled herself beside him, her slender body radiating warmth, Simon stared straight ahead and clutched the neck of the whisky bottle, terrified that he had finally fallen victim to a thirst so powerful even the finest of whiskys could not quench it.

By nightfall the spring snow had thickened, settling like downy white feathers in Catriona's hair. More chilled by Simon's inexplicably icy mood than by the frosty wind, she drew her faded plaid up over her head and huddled on the far corner of the driver's bench. Without the heat of Simon's body or his effortless charm to warm her, she was soon wracked by uncontrollable shivers.

The darkness deepened, but there was no sign of an inn, a cottage, or even a barn where they might seek shelter. Simon stole a glance at her, then swore beneath his breath and snapped the reins on the horses' backs, driving the wagon off the road and into a forest clearing.

Without breaking the awkward silence, he gathered several armfuls of kindling and built a crackling fire. While he tethered the nags to a nearby tree so they could graze through the thin crust of snow, Catriona roasted potatoes in their crusty jackets and fed bits of dried beef to Robert the Bruce.

They were eating the steaming bits of potato with their fingers when Simon finally spoke. "So tell me about this sainted brother of yours."

Torn between relief that he was speaking to her again and dismay at his choice of topics, Catriona laughed nervously. "Oh, I can assure you that Connor is no saint. At least he wasn't when he was a lad. He was five years older than I and never missed an opportunity to tug on my braids, use my dolls for archery practice or put a mouse in my bed."

"So you adored him, then?"

"With all my heart," she admitted with a wistful smile. "He might tease me mercilessly, but if anyone else so much as looked at me crooked, they could expect a bloody nose or a black eye for their trouble."

Simon stretched out his legs and leaned back on one elbow, his shadowed eyes unreadable. "It must have been hard for him to let you go."

"I don't think he believed he had a choice. After our parents were . . . murdered by the red-coats, I cried and begged him not to send me away. But he wiped away my tears and told me I had to be brave. That the Kincaids never cried when they could fight. He promised to come for me as soon as it was safe and bring me home."

Simon frowned. "But he sent for you instead? Rather than coming to fetch you as he'd promised?"

She suddenly took a keen interest in digging the last crumb of potato from its charred skin. "So what was *your* brother like?"

He shrugged. "Fairly insufferable. Our father could barely stand the sight of me, but I suppose Richard still saw me as some sort of rival for the old man's affections. He never missed an opportunity to remind me that he was the true heir and I was nothing but a bastard. Richard was twelve when my father took me in. When I first arrived at the ducal estate, his favorite game was to take me to some remote corner of the house and leave me there, knowing I couldn't find my way back."

Catriona's heart ached at the image of Simon as a small boy, wandering a bewildering maze of corridors while his brother mocked him. "You must have hated him," she said softly.

"Almost as much as I idolized him." Simon used the tip of his knife to flip his potato skin into the fire. "But I suppose the final joke was on him, because now he's dead and I'm our father's only son." He dug the half-empty whisky bottle out from under his bedroll and raised it in a toast. "To absent brothers everywhere."

"To absent brothers," Catriona echoed. "Wherever they may be," she added, lowering her eyes.

Simon stretched one leg out in front of him and tipped back his head to study the sky. The snow had stopped and the curtain of clouds had parted to reveal a scattering of stars. Their twinkling edges looked sharp enough to draw blood.

He'd already polished off the first bottle of whisky and started on the second, but the familiar numbness had failed to dull the fresh ache in his heart. His body was drunk, but his mind was painfully sober.

He shifted his gaze to Catriona. She had retreated to her nest of blankets on the other side of the fire and fallen asleep almost instantly. Perhaps it wasn't too late to convince himself that what he felt for her was simply lust—a cruel trick being played on his heart by his body to protest being denied what it so desperately wanted.

He shook his head. He should have known better than to take a wife, even a mock one. He would have been better off squandering his charms on other men's wives.

Catriona rolled to her side, throwing one arm over the brocaded portmanteau she guarded with more care than her virtue or her heart.

Setting aside the open bottle of whisky, he rose as silently as an assassin and padded around the fire to stand over her. Despite its crackling flames, her delicate nose was still pink from the cold. He would have liked nothing more than to strip off his clothes, slip beneath those blankets, and warm her with the heat of his body. He ached to make her flush with passion . . . with pleasure . . . with desire. He could almost feel the sweet and timeless slide as they danced together beneath the blankets, skin to skin and heart to heart . . .

He ran a shaking hand over his jaw, feeling feverish despite the chill breeze.

Kneeling beside her, he gently slipped the portmanteau from her grip. He hesitated for a moment, then drew off his coat and laid it over her, adding one more layer of warmth to her nest.

* * *

Catriona breathed in the intoxicating masculine scent of warm toffee and sea breezes, then sighed with pleasure. She opened her eyes to find Simon crouched on the other side of the fire in his shirtsleeves, his hair gleaming like freshly minted gold in the firelight. She glanced down to find his wool coat tucked around her.

A sleepy smile curved her lips. Although he would deny it to his last whisky-scented breath, somewhere within that lean and muscled rogue's body of his beat the noble heart of a gentleman. She blinked drowsily as she returned her adoring gaze to him.

A gentleman who was kneeling over her gaping portmanteau. A gentleman who was rifling through its contents with the icy efficiency of a Covent Garden cutpurse. A gentleman who was cocking a lascivious eyebrow as he held the most unmentionable of her unmentionables up to the firelight. A gentleman who was tossing that delicate garment carelessly aside so he could draw her most prized and private possession into his sneaky, greedy, thieving hands.

Chapter 12 🌿

Catriona shot up out of her nest of blankets as if a stray spark had ignited them. "Don't!" she shouted, shattering the tranquil hush that had fallen over the forest.

Simon froze, his hand poised over the lid of the delicate rosewood box. Cradling the bottom of the box in his other hand, he slowly rose to his feet, eyeing her warily.

"Don't," she repeated, more softly this time. "Please."

He studied her through narrowed eyes just glazed enough to warn her he had imbibed more of his supper than he had eaten. "Just what are you hiding, my clever little Cat? A sapphire necklace worth more than your dowry? Letters from an admirer? Is it really your brother waiting for you at the end of this road or someone else? A lover, perhaps?"

She took one step toward him, then another, approaching him with the same caution she might have used to corner a wild animal in its den. "Just give it to me, please. It's mine." She made a sudden grab for the box, but he easily lifted it just out of her reach.

"Not at the moment. At the moment, it happens to be mine."

Realizing that she had no hope of wresting the box from him by virtue of her height or physical strength, she folded her arms over her chest and glared daggers at him. "You have no right."

"That's where you're wrong, my dear." He gave her a lopsided grin she might have found charming if he hadn't been holding her heart in his big, clumsy hands. "I have every right. Have you forgotten that we're married now? What's yours *is* mine."

She watched with helpless dread as he began to lift the lid of the box one agonizing inch at a time, watching her reaction from beneath the decadent length of his lashes.

She realized too late that he was only teasing her. By the time he let the lid fall shut and offered the box to her, she had already made another frantic lunge for it. The back of her hand struck the edge of the box, tipping it sideways and sending it crashing to the ground. The lid flew open and its contents went spilling across the ground—not jewels or pound notes or love letters but fragile newspaper clippings, faded and yellowed with age.

Before she could react, Simon had squatted and swept the nearest one into his hands. He unfolded it, paying little heed to the careful creases she had smoothed into the paper when she had lovingly tucked it away.

As he gazed down at the faded newsprint, Catriona bowed her head, already knowing what he would find. It was a sketch done by an artist with a sure and gifted hand. A sketch of a young man standing at the top of the gangplank of a mighty warship. He was lifting his hand to greet the throng of adoring onlookers who had come to the docks to welcome home their conquering hero. A gracious smile played around his lips and there was no trace of mockery or cynicism in his clear-eyed gaze.

Simon studied the sketch and accompanying article for several seconds, then reached for another handful of the fallen papers. He thumbed through them one by one, his eyes growing ever more unreadable and his jaw more set.

These weren't the sordid scandal sheets detailing his gleeful plunge into debauchery. These were respectable articles from the *Times* and the *Morning Post*, their gushing prose lauding his heroic actions at the Battle of Trafalgar. Catriona could have quoted most of them word for word.

Letting the last of them drift from his fingers, Simon slowly straightened. She could almost feel the weight of his accusing gaze.

"You lied to me, didn't you?" he asked softly, the words barely a question. "You told me that you sought me out because I was a rogue, a mercenary who 'couldn't resist turning a tidy profit for a minimal amount of effort.' "

She lifted her chin, forcing herself to meet his gaze. "It's true, is it not?"

"Yes, it is. But that's not why you came to the jail that day. You came because you were looking for this man." He stabbed a finger toward the sketch of his own handsome visage, now lying abandoned on the cold ground. "This . . . this . . . imposter!"

"He wasn't an imposter!" Catriona cried. "He was you!"

Simon shook his head. "Oh, no. He was never me. He doesn't even exist."

"He did. Once." Both Catriona's voice and her hands were beginning to tremble with passion.

"He was the man who risked life and limb to defend his country against the French. He boarded the *Belleisle* knowing he might never return alive to England's shores. When he realized his captain was in dire peril from a sniper's musket ball, he threw himself in front of him with no thought for his own well-being. He was willing to sacrifice himself to save his fellow—"

"I tripped!"

Simon's shout cracked through the clearing like a pistol shot. When its echo faded, the only sound was the popping and crackling of the campfire.

"You what?" Catriona whispered.

"I tripped," Simon repeated, a sneer curling his upper lip. "I wasn't trying to nobly sacrifice myself to save my captain's life. I was trying to get the bloody hell out of the way before I got my fool head blown off by a cannonball. It was pure bad luck or perhaps a cruel joke of fate that I went dashing for cover at the precise moment a marksman fired at my captain from the rigging of a French ship." He rubbed his fingers over the jagged scar on his brow as if it still pained him. "If I hadn't tripped over a fallen lanyard and stumbled into the path of that musket ball, he'd be dead right now and I'd never have been hailed as a hero."

"You tripped?" Catriona repeated stupidly.

"That's right. I didn't regain consciousness for over a week after the battle, and by the time I woke up, word of my so-called *sacrifice* had already spread through the entire fleet. When I opened my eyes, my captain was standing at the foot of my hammock beaming at me. He said that if not for me, he would have met the same fate as Nelson on the *Victory*. He was the one who informed me that the King himself would be waiting to knight me for valor the minute I set foot on English soil."

"I was there," Catriona whispered, more to herself than to him. "I was there that day on the docks. I begged Uncle Ross to take the whole family on an outing so we could watch the *Belleisle* sail into port. Georgina napped the entire time and Alice did nothing but complain because she loathed being crammed into the carriage with the rest of us. She accused me of dirtying the hem of her petticoat with my big, clumsy feet. But I didn't care."

Simon was gazing at her as if her confession pained him more than his own.

A ghost of a smile curved her lips. "I'll never forget how handsome you looked in your uniform when you came striding down that gangplank—like a young prince who had just saved his kingdom from some terrible villain. The crowd was calling your name and all the pretty young girls were throwing roses in your path.

"Uncle Ross tried to stop me, but I scrambled out of the carriage and snatched up a rose from the boardwalk. When you passed by me, I held it out to you and you took it. You smiled at me, but I knew you hadn't seen me. Not really. I was just another face in the crowd."

"Another fool, you mean," he said harshly. "There were a hundred heroes in that battle—most of them genuine. Why in the bloody hell did you have to choose me?"

"I don't know! You looked so handsome and noble in your uniform that day in the barn, especially when you stood up to Alice on my behalf. I suppose I convinced myself that if I'd had a champion like you five years before . . ." She trailed off, unable to voice her most secret conviction.

"What?" he snapped without an ounce of mercy. "Your parents wouldn't have been slaughtered? Your brother wouldn't have had to send you away? Do you think I would have battled the redcoats on your behalf? Come thundering up on my white charger and whisked you away to a place where no one could ever hurt you or belittle you or break your heart?" He leaned his shoulder against a tree, looking as beautiful and heartless as she had ever seen him. "Don't you see, darling? I'm no noble hero from some ridiculous Scottish fairy tale, and I never was. I'm no Robert the Bruce or Bonnie Prince Charlie. I'm the worst sort of coward, and now you know it, so you can stop sleeping with that silly box of clippings under your pillow when what you really need in your bed is a man."

Unable to bear the cynical glint in his eye, Catriona dropped to her knees and began to gather up the remainder of the fallen articles, her hands painstakingly gentle as she handled the fragile newsprint.

Simon covered the distance between them in two steps, grabbed her by the shoulders and snatched her to her feet. His eyes were no longer mocking, but blazing with passion. "Damn it to hell, Catriona! It doesn't matter what those silly scraps of paper say. I'm no hero!" Reversing their positions, he backed her against the tree, imprisoning her there with the unyielding length of his body. The scent of danger roiled off of him, even stronger than the whisky on his breath.

"What are you going to do, Simon?" she whispered, meeting his challenging gaze with one of her own. "Ravish your own wife just to prove you're a villain?"

Catriona had only the space of a ragged breath, a shuddering heartbeat, to gaze into the fierce depths of his eyes before his mouth descended on hers. Simon Wescott the legendary lover, the quicksilver-tongued seducer of women, had vanished, leaving behind a savage more suited to this wilderness than to a London drawing room.

If he'd thought to frighten her away with his kiss, he was doomed to disappointment. She was no longer the starry-eyed child who had tenderly tucked those clippings into that box. Instead of shoving him away with a maidenly shriek of horror, she twined her hands through the silken strands of hair at his nape and welcomed the hungry thrust of his tongue even deeper into her mouth. She countered his fierce assault on her senses with tenderness, offering up her mouth, her heart, her very soul for the taking.

He responded to her invitation with a strangled groan. He kissed her again and again, drinking from the chalice of her mouth as if he were Percival and she the Holy Grail. Without missing a stroke of his kiss, he slipped one arm beneath her hips, lifting her, spreading her, until he could stand between her legs and press the rigid heat between his to her tender core.

Catriona gasped into his mouth. That demanding pressure—so foreign, and yet so enticing—warned her that he wanted more from her than just a kiss. Much more. She had always known he was stronger than her. She just hadn't realized he was strong enough to balance her weight with one arm while he bunched her skirt up in his other hand so he could slip his hand beneath it. The blistering heat of his palm glided up the cool satin of her thigh but did not linger. It was not her pleasure he sought on this night but his own. This wasn't the elegant bedchamber at her uncle's house or even that narrow bedstead in the Gretna Green inn. He hadn't come to give, but to take.

When his fingers reached their destination, she was already swollen, already open, already wet with desire for him. The temptation was too great. Without a trace of the grace or finesse that had earned him his reputation, he thrust two fingers roughly into her. When he heard her breathless cry and felt her silken flesh convulse around his fingers, he was as shocked as she was.

Biting off an oath, he released her so abruptly she had to cling to the trunk of the tree behind her to keep from falling.

He backed away from her as if she were the one who had sought to trap him with some honey-baited pot, his chest heaving with reaction.

"What do I have to do, Catriona? How far do I have to go to prove to you that you can't make me a better man just by believing I am?"

With that, he bent to scoop up a thick handful of the fallen clippings and hurled them into the fire.

"No!" Catriona rushed forward with a broken little cry.

But it was too late. The clippings and sketches were already beginning to smolder and curl up around the edges.

Catriona stood there for a long time, watching all of her girlhood dreams go up in smoke. When she finally lifted her head to gaze at him, it was through a stinging haze of tears. "You're right, Simon. You are the worst sort of coward. I just don't know who you're more afraid of— yourself . . . or me."

Biting back a choked sob, she turned and fled into the forest.

Simon stood with his hands clenched into fists as the sounds of Catriona crashing through the underbrush slowly faded. He knew he ought to go after her. That's what any decent man would do.

He sank down next to the fire and brought the half-empty bottle of whisky to his lips. With enough whisky and any luck at all, he might not even remember the cursed events of this night. Might be able to forget the stricken look in Catriona's eyes and the tears that had spilled down her cheeks as she watched him destroy her sentimental treasures.

But he didn't think any amount of liquor would drown out the echo of her breathless cry as she shuddered to completion beneath his hand—that one pure shining moment of grace when he had deserved nothing but her condemnation and contempt.

He reached into the fire and plucked out a charred scrap of newsprint, singeing the tips of his fingers but not caring. It was another sketch of that handsome young officer arriving at the docks in London, a plaster bandage adorning his brow like the laurel wreath of a conquering warrior.

Catriona hadn't been the only woman waiting to greet him on the docks that day. He had never told a single soul about seeing that other ghost from his past. He might have recognized Catriona if he hadn't already been numb with shock, his gracious smile frozen on his lips.

No matter how long or how intently Simon studied his face, the man in the clipping was still a stranger. He finally crumpled up the sketch and tossed it back in the fire. He took another searing gulp of the whisky, watching it burn to ash.

He hadn't been completely honest with Catriona. He had wanted to believe the lies the paper had printed about him nearly as badly as she did. He had wanted to believe he could be a man of honor. The sort of man who would lay down his own life to protect his commanding officer. The sort of man who could make his father proud. The sort of man who deserved to have roses strewn in his path by pretty young girls who dreamed of noble princes and conquering heroes.

When he had first returned to London, he had even tried to convince himself that perhaps his own memory was faulty. That perhaps somewhere on the heaving decks of that ship, with the choking stench of gunpowder scorching his nostrils and the thunder of the cannons booming in his ears, he had made a split-second choice between his life and his captain's. But when he had tried to live up to that legend, he had discovered that the one person he could not deceive was himself.

He was no hero. He was a bastard and a coward who would never be worthy of so much as a rose petal from a woman like Catriona.

He sank back on one elbow, determined to drink until he couldn't see, couldn't think, couldn't remember what he was drinking to forget.

Catriona couldn't run far or fast enough to escape her own folly. A strangled sob caught in her throat. She didn't even care where she was going, as long as it was away from *him*.

She had wasted five years of her life loving the ghost of a man who had never even existed. She had fallen in love with a pretty boy in a starched uniform, only to discover that the boy was nothing but an illusion and the uniform might as well have been hanging on a dressmaker's dummy. She had been blinded by both the teasing sparkle in his eyes and the shiny braid on his shoulders and now she was left with nothing to blind her but her tears.

It was incredibly mortifying to remember how she had entertained any number of fantasies that involved dabbing a cool cloth on his wounded brow and spooning broth between his lips while he recovered from his injury and fell deeply and irrevocably in love with her. And what about all of the hours she had wasted kissing her hand and pretending it was his lips and practicing her penmanship by copying

Catriona Wescott and *Mrs. Simon Wescott* into the pages of her journal?

She could have easily forgiven him for not intentionally saving his captain from that musket ball. But she didn't think she could ever forgive him for deliberately trying to break her heart. For denying the truth she tasted on his lips every time he kissed her.

Stray twigs lashed painfully at her cheeks as she raced through the forest, her half boots crunching over the thin crust of snow. She dodged the outstretched claws of a hazel tree and plunged down a long, stony hill furred with moss and mottled lichen. She might have run all the way to the highest peak of the Highlands if she hadn't been forced to stop and catch her breath.

Clinging to the smooth trunk of an aspen, she sucked frigid gasps of air into her starving lungs. Somewhere in the distance she could hear a burn rushing over the rocks of a creek bed. After only a few seconds of inactivity, she began to shiver with both exhaustion and cold. It was far too easy to wish she had Simon's coat wrapped around her. And easier yet to wish she had his strong, warm arms wrapped around her.

She took off again, scrambling up a steep hillside. Her nails dug into the exposed roots that jutted from the rocky soil.

She burst over the top of the hill, only to find herself teetering on the brink of a dizzying precipice. Her arms cartwheeled wildly, snatching at the air for tree limbs that were just out of her reach. A shrill scream tore from her throat as her momentum sent her plunging over the edge of the cliff and into the icy waters of the burn below.

The cold dug its razor-sharp claws into her with brutal force. For a terrifying flash of time, she couldn't scream, breathe or think.

The creek would probably shrink to a lazy trickle during the summer, but at the moment its banks were swollen with the melting snows pouring down from the mountains. By the time Catriona surfaced, sputtering and coughing and gasping for breath, she had traveled a good ways downstream.

Bobbing like a cork on the open seas, she tipped back her head and screamed, *"Simon!"*

He might not want to be her hero, but he was all she had. And hadn't he held her when she was lonely? Covered her when she was cold? Stood up to her uncle and Alice and Eddingham on her behalf?

She opened her mouth to scream again but was only able to drag in a single desperate gulp of air before the weight of her skirts dragged her beneath the water and into the merciless arms of the current.

Chapter 13

Simon! Help me, Simon! Please!

Simon sat bolt upright, his heart thundering like a cannon and that beseeching cry still ringing in his ears. He cocked his head to listen, but all he could hear was the merry chittering of a red squirrel and the hoarse rasp of his own breathing. He ran an unsteady hand over his jaw, haunted by that hollow echo.

He must have been dreaming.

God knows his dreams had been vivid enough. He had been roaming the bewildering labyrinth of his father's house—one minute a small boy, the next a man. He would catch a glimpse of flowing skirt down a shadowy corridor and hear a haunting echo of his mother's laughter. But when he tried to follow her, his legs would grow shorter with each step and he would soon find himself all alone again.

Somewhere in the wee hours of the morning, he had finally turned a corner, only to come face to face with a chilling apparition of Catriona holding out her hands to him in supplication, rose petals streaming like blood from her pale fingers.

Shrugging away a shudder, he slowly climbed to his feet, his limbs so stiff with cold he was surprised they didn't creak. The fire had died sometime during the night and his mouth tasted like ashes. The empty whisky bottle lay on the ground a few feet away, as if it had been flung there in a fit of pique. As the watery sunshine struck him full in the face, the pounding of his heart was supplanted by the pounding in his head.

Burying his head in his hands, he groaned.

He was answered by a plaintive meow.

Simon lifted his head to find Robert the Bruce's chicken crate sitting next to an empty nest of blankets. A chill traveled down his spine. Catriona might abandon him without a backward glance, but she would never abandon that damn cat of hers. If he had been in full possession of his wits last night, he never would have let her go running off into the forest by herself.

He swung around, his bleary eyes scanning the underbrush. "Catriona!" he called. "Where are you, sweetheart?"

The wind whispered through the swaying boughs of the pines, but its secrets were not meant for his ears. He started toward the direction where he had a vague recollection of her disappearing, but a doleful "Mrrrwww" stopped him in his tracks.

He swore but turned back anyway, knowing what Catriona would want him to do. He soon had Robert the Bruce tethered to a tree by the generous length of leather designed to allow him a bit of freedom during their travels. It was also long enough to allow him to climb the tree if a predator approached. The cat glared at him accusingly over a mouthful of dried beef.

"Stop looking at me like that," Simon ordered, glaring back at him. "I'll soon find your mistress and she can go back to pampering you like the fat little brat you are."

Leaving the cat to his breakfast, Simon plunged into the woods. Although he felt as if his skull were going to crack wide open each time he did it, he paused every few steps to call Catriona's name. She was probably ignoring him just to punish him. It wasn't as if he didn't deserve it. For a man who had always prided himself on treating the fair sex with the tenderest of consideration, he had certainly behaved like the bastard he was last night.

As if to atone for yesterday's flirtation with winter, the morning had brought with it a tantalizing promise of spring. A warming breeze wafted in from the west, caressing the tightly coiled buds on the naked tree branches and stirring Simon's hair. He hesitated at the top of a steep hill, the back of his neck prickling. Haunted by the sensation that he was being watched by eyes even more ancient than the towering evergreens, he glanced behind him. Despite the feeling that he was being followed, he had never felt more alone in his life.

He was beginning to feel as if his nightmare had pursued him into his waking hours. He half expected to catch a glimpse of flowing skirt in the distance or hear the haunting echo of a woman's laughter. Growing ever more fearful that his path was carrying him farther away from Catriona instead of closer, he swung around to circle back to their camp. But the faint murmur of water lapping at rock lured him into a spacious glade occupied by a deep, dark pool. Its serene waters were fed by a natural waterfall that burbled over a jagged shelf of rock on the far side of the pool.

Simon staggered to his knees along its bank, promising himself he would linger just long enough to rinse his mouth and splash the remaining fog from his head.

He dashed handfuls of water over his face, welcoming its icy sting. The man gazing back at him from the pool with the beard-stubbled jaw, haggard cheeks and desperate, bloodshot eyes suddenly seemed as much of a stranger to him as the handsome young officer in Catriona's clippings.

He plunged his whole head beneath the water, obliterating his reflection, then jerked it back out, flinging his sopping wet hair out of his eyes. Only then did he notice the large flat rock crouching in the sun-dappled shadows on the other side of the pool.

And the reddish-gold tendrils of hair floating lazily on the surface of the water.

Just like that, his heart stopped. And for one agonizing moment, he wasn't sure it was ever going to beat again.

But then he saw the small, pale hand curled up at the rock's edge and realized the tendrils of hair were cascading over the rim of the rock and into the water.

"Sweet mother of God," he breathed, the words more prayer than oath.

Without a thought for his clothes or his comfort, he plunged into the water and splashed his way over to the rock. He hauled himself on top of it to find Catriona stretched out on her back with her eyes closed, so still and pale that for one terrible moment he feared it would take more than a prince's enchanted kiss to rouse her.

But the sodden bodice of her gown clung to a chest that was gently rising and falling with each shallow breath. Simon gathered her into his arms, shuddering to think what might have happened if she hadn't found the strength to drag herself out of that frigid water. Her flesh was damp and clammy, but he could feel the precious warmth radiating from her body's core.

He gazed down into her face, desperately missing the roses that usually bloomed in her cheeks. "Catriona? Sweetheart? Can you hear me?"

"Of course I can hear you," she murmured, her voice weak but clearly audible. "I'm not deaf like *some* people." She slowly opened her eyes and glared at him, looking even more disgruntled than Robert the Bruce. "I've been calling for you for hours. What took you so long to rescue me? Did you *trip*?"

A raw bark of laughter escaped him as he

tightened his arms around her and buried his face in the damp ropes of her hair, humbled by a grace he did not deserve. "That's right, angel. I tripped. And I don't think I've ever fallen quite so hard or so far before."

Catriona had to be dead. It was the only explanation for what she saw when she finally managed to shake off her exhausted stupor long enough to pry open her eyes.

She sighed, feeling a vague pang of disappointment. She had fought so hard to survive tumbling into that burn. She had spit and sputtered and struggled and snatched at the passing branches, never dreaming her deliverance would come in the form of being swept over a waterfall. When the still, cold waters of the pool had sought to lure her into their seductive embrace, she had even managed to claw her way out of them and collapse on top of the rock. But apparently all of her efforts had been in vain.

Because if she wasn't dead, then why was the ghost of all of her girlhood passions kneeling a few feet away, pouring the contents of a full whisky bottle into the rocky soil?

His cheeks and jaw were freshly shaven, his tawny hair bound neatly at the nape in a leather queue, his profile classically handsome enough to be minted on a Roman coin. He still had the shiny black Hessians and dazzling white shirtsleeves. All he lacked was the dark blue dress coat and white breeches of a Royal Navy officer and he would have been one wicked grin away from seducing her cousin and stealing her heart.

Sunlight winked off the bottle as he held it up, shaking the last few drops from it. Catriona frowned, growing even more bewildered. If she wasn't dead, then she was definitely delirious with fever, because the Simon Wescott she knew would never waste fine Scots whisky that way. The only place he'd be pouring it was down his throat.

Tossing the empty bottle away, he glanced in her direction and their eyes met. That's when she saw the jagged scar that bisected his left eyebrow and gave the boyish purity of his looks its compelling masculine edge.

Her sense of reality was knocked even further askew when Robert the Bruce butted his furry head against Simon's thigh, his adoring purr audible all the way across the clearing.

"Traitor," she muttered, turning her face away and closing her eyes.

When she opened them again, Simon was standing over her, his golden hair haloed by sunlight.

"If you're an angel," she said crossly, "then God has a remarkably wicked sense of humor."

"Oh, I'm no angel, sweeting." He knelt beside her, bringing his devilish grin into crisp focus. "I'm Lieutenant Simon Wescott, at your service, miss."

She pressed the back of her hand to her brow, striving to be brave but failing miserably. "I knew it! I'm dying, aren't I? I must be delirious with fever."

He gently tugged her hand into his own, forcing her to look at him. "On the contrary, there's no trace of fever, no chills, no congestion in your lungs. You've been sleeping like the dead all morning, but I think you just might survive." The teasing sparkle in his eyes faded to a somber glow. "I have to confess that when I first saw you lying on that rock, I thought—"

"You would have need of a new situation. And a new wife," she finished softly, the word sending an absurdly pleasurable little shiver down her spine. "Ah, but there was a bright spot. My entire dowry would have been yours." As Robert the Bruce sought to shove his way between them, rubbing against Simon and shooting her a resentful glance, Catriona scowled. "As well as the fickle affections of my cat."

Simon gave the cat a gentle shove, but Robert

failed to budge and only purred louder. "I can promise you that I've done nothing underhanded to court the rascal's favor. He's shadowed my every step ever since I roasted a fresh fish I caught in the pool so you'd have something to eat when you woke up."

She sighed. "If he were Roberta the Bruce, I could understand his defection."

As she struggled to a sitting position, Simon slipped one arm around her shoulders. She wanted nothing more than to sink into his embrace, but she forced herself to wiggle around until she was supporting her own weight. Only then did she realize that the gown and shift she'd been wearing the previous night were draped over a nearby branch. She glanced down, half afraid of what she would find, but she was comfortably enveloped in one of Simon's crisp dry shirts.

As she tugged down the hem to cover an alarming expanse of pale thigh, Simon held up one hand as if to forestall a lecture. "I know what you're thinking, and I can't say that I blame you, but I can promise you that I was—"

"A perfect gentleman," she finished for him. "That's what I was afraid of." She eyed him thoughtfully. "You did say you were at my service, didn't you, Lieutenant? Just what services do you provide?"

He opened his mouth, then closed it again. "Sorry. Old habit." His sheepish smile faded. "You hired me to look after you, but I'm afraid I've been woefully remiss in my duties."

She shrugged. "You didn't push me into the burn."

"But I did fail to pull you out of it. If I hadn't been so drunk, I might have heard your cries for help long before I did."

"And come rushing to my rescue, just like the hero of my dreams?" she asked, mocking herself as much as him.

He cocked one eyebrow. "If nothing else, I could have tossed you a rope while I polished off the last of the whisky."

Catriona glanced across the clearing to where the empty bottle lay glinting in the sun. "If I'm not mistaken, you just polished off the last of the whisky." She frowned at him in puzzlement. "Why did you pour it out? Was there something wrong with it? Was it bad?"

He rested one elbow on his bent knee, gazing off into the distance as if he could see something she would never be privy to. "No. But it made me that way."

Noting for the first time that his hands weren't completely steady, Catriona couldn't resist capturing one of them in her own. "You've never been truly bad. Only a trifle bit naughty on some occasions and a wee bit wicked on others."

Simon lifted his hand to her cheek. His fingers gently cupped her jaw while his thumb feathered gentle strokes over her lips, coaxing them to part of their own accord. As she gazed into the fathomless green depths of his eyes, a sweet shiver cascaded through her. He had been wrong. She was suffering from a fever. A fever that raced through her veins and burned away all traces of common sense, leaving only an unbearable yearning for this man.

She closed her eyes, already anticipating the tantalizing caress of his lips against hers. Which left her feeling rather ridiculous when it didn't come. She opened her eyes to find him standing a few feet away, his hands on his hips and his back to her. Something in his stance made her climb to her feet as well.

"You hired me to escort you to your brother," he said, "not seduce you."

"And what's this? A sudden attack of scruples? If you lie down for a while and put a cool cloth on your head, I'm sure it will pass."

He turned to look at her then, his expression grim. "My lack of scruples nearly cost you your life last night. Among other things," he added pointedly.

"Yes, that's why I really threw myself into that burn," she said cheerfully. "I was playing at Ophelia because I couldn't bear the shame of nearly being ravished by my own husband."

He stabbed a finger at her. "Don't call me that!"

"What should I call you?" She took one step toward him, then another, her long legs exulting in their freedom from stockings, petticoats and cumbersome skirts. "Darling? Sweetheart? My lord and master?"

He took a step backward. "You are the most infuriating woman. I don't even know who I am anymore. You make me a stranger to myself!"

"Oh, I know exactly who you are. You're Simon Wescott—notorious libertine."

"That's bloody well right! I may not be a gentleman, but I don't lose my temper, I don't get mean when I drink, and I seduce women, not ravish them." He shook his head helplessly, his voice both deepening and softening. "I've never touched a woman the way I touched you last night."

She drew another step closer to him. "As if you'd been waiting your whole life to taste her kiss? As if you'd die if you couldn't have her?"

"In case you've forgotten, you were the one who nearly died."

"That's only because I forgot what my brother told me all those years ago. That the Kincaids never cry when they can fight. I shouldn't have run away last night. I should have stayed and fought for what I wanted."

"And what was that?"

"You. Not Simon Wescott the legendary hero, but Simon Wescott the man."

Simon didn't exhale for a long moment and when he finally did, his exhalation was as fierce as his expression. "If you truly know what sort of man I am, then you also know I'm perfectly capable of making love to you without loving you."

Another step and she would be close enough to touch him. "I'm not asking you to love me."

He was the one who closed the distance between them then, drawing her into his arms and brushing the smooth, firm warmth of his lips over hers again and again, as if to savor their plump sweetness before delving deeper with his tongue.

If last night's kiss had sought to take, this one sought only to give. To give pleasure, to give bliss, to give a tantalizing taste of the *services* he was only too capable of providing. As his tongue danced over hers in the most compelling of rhythms, she felt like she was drowning all over again. Only this time she wasn't sure she could survive without the life-giving sweetness of his breath in her mouth.

A life that was nearly ended by the arrow that came whizzing past them, burying itself with a deadly *thunk* in the trunk of a nearby birch.

Yelping with alarm, Catriona threw her arms around Simon's neck. "What was that?"

His arms tightened around her waist, drawing her against the shield of his body. "If I remember my navy cant correctly," he whispered into her hair, "I believe that was a warning shot fired across our bow."

Simon's words proved prophetic because a heartbeat later more than a dozen gray-and-green-garbed figures came melting out of the forest, bows drawn.

Simon tried to tuck her behind him, no easy feat since they were surrounded on all sides. As he pivoted in a wary circle, Catriona danced on her tiptoes, struggling to see over his shoulder.

Dark hair hung in greasy braids around their attackers' faces. They'd painted their cheeks with some sort of dried mud, which made their narrowed eyes stand out in stark contrast.

Gray, dark-lashed eyes the color of the morning mist hanging over the moors.

Catriona popped out from behind Simon, an astonished smile breaking over her face. "Why, I know who you are! You must be my brother's band of merry men!"

Simon snatched her back into his embrace, wrapping an arm firmly around her waist. "I hate to be the one to point this out, darling," he murmured, eyeing the deadly tips of the arrows aimed directly at her heart, "but they don't look particularly merry at the moment."

Chapter 14

atriona could only imagine what a sight she must make, stripped down to Simon's shirt with her long legs exposed and her hair hanging in tangled elflocks around her face. Even so, she could not bring herself to cower in mortification before these men. She held her head high as she scanned their forbidding faces, Simon's arm still locked like an iron bar around her waist.

"You're the band of men led by the outlaw who calls himself the Kincaid, are you not?" she called out boldly. Unable to hide her eagerness, she studied each face in turn. "Is he here? Is he among you?"

The men exchanged uncertain glances. One of

them—a head taller than the others—stepped forward, his deadly grip on his bow never wavering. His rawboned face might have been handsome had it not been stripped of every last trace of humor and hope. "Why don't we discuss that after ye hand o'er yer money and jewelry, lass?"

She tried, but could not quite stifle her laugh. "Don't be ridiculous. There's no need for you to rob us. Why, I've brought you all gifts!"

One of the other men snorted. "Did ye hear that, Kieran? The lass has brought us gifts. What does she think this is? Christmas morn?"

"I've allus wanted a spinning top and a set of tin soldiers," one of his companions quipped, earning a rumble of laughter from the rest of the men.

"Hush!" Kieran snapped, stifling them in mid-chuckle. "There's no need to mock. The puir wee lass is plainly daft."

"That's right, gentlemen," Simon inserted smoothly. "The puir wee lass is indeed quite daft, and if you'll give us leave to go, I promise to cart her right back to Bedlam where she belongs."

Catriona trod firmly on his toes, earning a pained grunt. "I'm not going anywhere until I find what I came for, and that's a man who calls himself the Kincaid. But you might know him as Connor Kincaid—my brother."

Again those uncomfortable glances. A knot began to form low in Catriona's belly.

"Connor never mentioned no sister," one of the men called out.

She shrugged to hide how much his words stung. "That doesn't surprise me. After he sent me back to London to save me from the redcoats, he probably thought I'd be safer if everyone forgot I existed."

The Kieran fellow who seemed to be their leader lowered his bow and sauntered forward, jerking his head toward Simon. "If ye're Connor's sister, then who is he?"

She and Simon spoke at the exact same time.

"He's my husband."

"I'm her bodyguard."

Catriona felt Simon tense as Kieran looked her up and down, his lascivious gaze taking in every inch of her, from the crown of her disheveled hair to her pink little toes. "Husband or bodyguard, it looks like he's been performin' his job with great enthusiasm."

Suddenly it was no longer Catriona in Simon's arms but the insolent Highlander. The man made a strangled sound as his bow tumbled to the ground and Simon rammed the muzzle of a small but quite deadly pistol against his jaw.

Catriona could only gape at him, dizzied by

the swiftness and grace of the move. She hadn't even known he *owned* a pistol, much less carried it on his person.

Using his captive as a shield, Simon swung in a tight circle, making sure every man in that clearing saw the weapon pressed to their leader's bobbing Adam's apple. "This pistol only carries one shot, but I can assure you that's all I'll need. Now toss your bows to the ground or you'll be one man short." The brisk note in his voice warned that he would brook no disobedience. "Or should I say one head short."

After a round of hostile mutters and surly glances, the Highlanders reluctantly complied.

"Your knives as well," he demanded, watching with grim satisfaction as a host of blades emerged from grimy sleeves and secret pockets to clatter into the growing pile of weapons on the ground.

"Nicely done. Now, if one of you is Connor Kincaid, I suggest you step forward and apologize to your sister for allowing these mannerless ruffians to insult her."

The men shuffled their feet for a minute or two before a squat fellow with jug ears and two front teeth missing finally stepped forward. Simon frowned. He certainly couldn't see a family resemblance.

The man scuffed one rag-wrapped foot on the

ground, the mud streaking his cheeks only making his broad, homely face look more doleful. "Conner isna with us no more."

The blood drained from Catriona's face, leaving it as pale as an alabaster mask. As she swayed, Simon swore beneath his breath, wondering if he was going to have to free Kieran so he could catch her.

But she bit her bottom lip, visibly composing herself, and asked softly, "How long?"

Before the man could reply, Kieran spat, "The bastard ducked out on us before the winter snows. Said he was sick of our drinkin' and our wenchin' and our thievin' ways. Said we could end up dancin' a fling at the end of a hangman's noose if we wanted, but he'd had his fill o' this life and the cursed Kincaids."

Catriona didn't say a word. She simply turned, walked over to the wagon and stood with her back to them all.

Kieran squirmed violently in Simon's grip. Sensing that the man was no longer a threat to them, Simon shoved him to his knees and slid the pistol into the waist of his trousers.

He moved toward the wagon. Catriona's shoulders were bowed. Her slender white hands gripped the wagon's bed as if it were the side of a rapidly sinking dinghy.

Simon rested a hand on her shoulder, murmuring, "I'm so sorry, darling."

She turned to look up at him, but it was fierce
joy that lit her face, not sorrow. "Why are you
sorry? Don't you see? My brother is still alive!"

Simon gazed down at her, waiting for her
words to make sense. When they finally did, he
almost regretted it. "Do you mean to say that
you dragged me all the way up to this godforsaken wilderness without even knowing if this
brother of yours was dead or alive?"

"Uncle Ross tried to convince me that he was
dead. I haven't received so much as a note from
him in the past ten years. When Eddingham
came to my uncle's house, he told us that the outlaw they called the Kincaid had vanished several months ago. Naturally, I feared the worst."

"Eddingham? What does Eddingham have to
do with all this?"

She sighed. "I'm afraid the marquess just
bought this parcel of land from the Crown. He's
planning to use English soldiers to hunt down
the last of the Kincaids so he can use the land for
grazing Cheviot sheep."

Simon's ears were beginning to feel curiously
hot. "And just when were you planning to tell
me all this? Before or after the redcoats ran me
through with a bayonet?"

"I was afraid you'd back out of our arrangement. I know you don't care for . . ."—she inclined her head, the first flicker of guilt dancing over her delicate features—"complications."

"Oh, my life has become very complicated indeed since that unfortunate moment when you strolled into my jail cell." He paced a few feet away from her and then back, raking a hand through his hair. "Just when is Eddingham planning to carry out this plan of his?"

Catriona swallowed. "As soon as the winter snows thaw."

Simon glanced down. They were standing in a puddle of mud. The bright spring sun and westerly breeze had melted away every trace of the snow that had fallen the night before.

Grabbing Catriona by the hand, he yanked her toward the front of the wagon.

"What do you think you're doing?" she cried, stumbling after him.

"Taking you back to your uncle in London. That Kieran fellow was right. You're a puir daft lass and you ought to be locked away."

She planted her feet in the mud but could find no purchase against his determined momentum. "We can't leave now! Just look at the unfortunate creatures!" She swept a hand toward the motley crew of bandits who were gathering their weapons, muttering among themselves, and shooting her and Simon murderous looks. "They're the last of the Kincaids. Even Connor has deserted them. They need me now more than ever!"

"If you had been standing downwind of them, you'd know that what they need is a nice hot bath. Preferably in a jail cell."

Digging her sharp little fingernails into Simon's palm, Catriona broke away from him. She snatched up her tattered plaid from her pile of blankets, wrapped it around her shoulders and marched resolutely over to the milling band of thieves.

"My brother was right," she shouted, winning back their reluctant attention. "You *are* cursed. I know you've all heard the words that were spoken by my great-grandfather as he lay on that battlefield at Culloden with his life's blood seeping into the dirt after being betrayed by his own son for thirty pieces of silver and an earldom. 'The Kincaids are doomed to wander the earth until they're united once again beneath the banner of their one true chieftain.'" She straightened to her full height, her gray eyes glittering like polished moonstones. "Like it or not, with my brother gone, I *am* that chieftain. I *am* the Kincaid."

Kieran shook his head and laughed aloud. "Och, lass, what ye are is out o' yer bluidy mind."

Still shaking his head, he slapped one of the other chuckling men on the back and started toward the forest.

As the men began to melt back into the trees, Catriona felt a flare of panic. She'd waited ten long years for this moment. Ten years of enduring Alice's taunts and pinches, ten years of feeling like an unwelcome stranger in her uncle's house, ten years of longing for a home she could barely remember.

"Wait!" she cried. "You can't go! I brought you gifts, remember?"

The men froze, then turned back as one, unable to hide the greedy gleam in their eyes. Catriona marched boldly over to Kieran, jerked the dagger out of his belt and strode back over to the wagon.

Simon watched through narrowed eyes as she sawed at the ropes binding the oilcloth. It took her several minutes of struggle, but they finally fell away, allowing her to throw back the oilcloth with a theatrical flourish.

The men inched nearer, their curiosity outweighing their caution. Catriona beckoned them forward, eager to reveal her treasures.

"I know the English have outlawed most of these things to rob you of your heritage and your pride. We could have been hanged for smuggling them into your hands, but I thought it well worth the risk."

"How very noble of you," Simon said dryly, folding his arms over his chest. "I'm glad to know it was worth risking my neck as well."

She shot him a quelling glance. Reaching into the bed of the wagon, she dragged out a heavy bolt of green and black tartan. "This isn't precisely the pattern of the Kincaid plaid, but it's as close as I could come. I bought two dozen bolts of the wool. You can use it to make kilts and plaids for yourselves, gowns for your wives, and blankets for your horses."

"What horses?" asked the homely fellow who had stepped forward earlier, scratching one of his enormous ears.

"What wives?" asked another man, spitting a fat wad of tobacco on the ground.

"Well . . ." Catriona said, at a sudden loss for words. She awkwardly heaved the bolt of wool back into the wagon, then dusted off her hands. "I'm sure you'll appreciate my next purchase. I've brought you several volumes of poetry by your esteemed countryman Robert Burns. I couldn't believe my good fortune when I stumbled upon them in a tiny bookshop in Gretna Green." She drew out one of the cloth-bound volumes, leafing through its faded, gilt-edged pages with reverent hands. "They're a bit the worse for wear, but that won't stop you from reading them by the fire on a cold winter's night."

"If we could read, that is," Kieran said with such gentle sarcasm that even Simon winced.

"Oh." Both her face and her spirits falling, Catriona tucked the book back into the wagon. She could not help but brighten when she saw her next treasure. "I suppose that brings us to the crown jewel of our little collection." Reaching back into the wagon, she dragged out a tangled nest of pipes. "Aye, it's just what you'd hoped for—a genuine set of bagpipes!"

She stroked the instrument, feeling tears well up in her eyes. "They've been banned in the Highlands since old Ewan Kincaid died at Culloden. The English thought that if you could rob a man of his music, you could crush his spirit as well. Without the triumphant wail of this exquisite instrument calling him to battle, they believed he would be too disheartened to fight." She lifted the bagpipes to her shoulder, sweeping each of her kinsmen in turn with her shining gaze. "But they didn't take into account the song that still echoes in the heart of every Highlander. The stirring drumbeat that demands freedom—freedom from oppression, freedom from tyranny, freedom from—"

"Have ye any whisky in there?" Kieran interrupted impatiently, peering over her shoulder. "Any gold? Any food?"

Catriona blinked at him, taken aback. "We have a few extra potatoes and a loaf of bread."

"Have ye any boots to keep our feet from crackin' and bleedin' durin' the long winter months? Or guns to fight the English who've spent the last fifty years tryin' to drive us off our own lands?" He plucked the bagpipes from her hands and held them aloft. "What do ye expect us to do with these, lass? Pipe them to death?"

His men responded with an ugly swell of laughter. Catriona felt something deep inside of her begin to shrivel.

Kieran carelessly tossed the bagpipes into the back of the wagon and plucked out one of the books. "Or maybe we could read 'em a poem from one o' these fancy books o' yers. If we're lucky, they might doze off before they could find a rope and string us up from the nearest tree."

"I d-didn't . . ." Catriona stammered, mortified that she had been so painfully naïve. "I never meant to . . ."

She flinched as Kieran used his wiry hands to break the spine of the book and rip it clean in two. "Ye can take yer gifts back where they came from. We don't need yer bluidy charity and we sure as hell don't need ye. We've done just fine without a chieftain for all these years. We're free men and we'd just as soon stay that way—free o' the English and free o' the likes o' ye!"

Tossing the book at Catriona's feet, Kieran turned on his heel and strode toward the forest with his men falling into step behind him.

Catriona stood there, looking much as she had the first time Simon had seen her—barefoot, wrapped in her beloved plaid, her sun-kissed hair tumbling around her face, her slender shoulders painfully rigid. But then her pride had been a shining mantle and now it lay in tatters around her feet.

Simon tore his gaze away from her stricken face, wishing he could turn his back on her as easily as her kinsmen had.

"I wouldn't be so quick to dismiss the lass if I were you," he called after Kieran, his ringing words stopping the men in their tracks.

The Highlander slowly turned, eyeing him warily. His hand tightened on his bow, but he made no move to raise it.

"You may believe you have some God-given

right to this land, but there's a man called the Marquess of Eddingham who thinks differently."

"Go on," Kieran reluctantly urged.

"Your time is running out," Simon said. "Eddingham is coming for you and your men and he's bringing a battalion of English soldiers with him. Catriona risked her life and her reputation to come here and warn you. So if I were you, I'd pay more heed to her words and less to your own foolish pride."

Kieran studied him, his lips thinned to a taut line, his gray eyes as hard as polished flint. "We can offer ye and yer woman shelter for the night but not much more," he finally said. "And ye'd best bring those taters o' yers if ye want anythin' to fill yer bellies."

As the men melted back into the forest, Simon began to pack up their belongings without a word.

He could feel Catriona hovering behind him but managed to ignore her until he felt her hand brush his sleeve. "Simon, I—"

He wheeled around to face her, something in his eyes making her take a step backward. "I'm your hired gun, Miss Kincaid, nothing more. When I've completed the job to your satisfaction, I'll expect my money. I might be willing to take a bayonet through the heart as part of my duties, but if you want me to perform any other *services* for you, it will cost you extra."

He scooped up Robert the Bruce and thrust the cat into her arms, then turned away from her, stepping neatly over the shredded volume of love poetry.

Chapter 15

Catriona sat atop the highest point of the crumbling ruin that had once been the home and pride of Clan Kincaid, watching the moon rise over the jagged crest of the mountains. As the sky slowly deepened from lavender to purple to indigo, she leaned against the stone merlon behind her and wrapped one arm around her bent knee.

The rest of the towers that had once crowned the castle had been smashed to rubble by English cannonballs over sixty years ago, leaving only this one monument to the clan's former grandeur. Her grandfather had fled its shattered walls and never looked back, having set his ambitious sights on an earldom and a fine estate in London.

She heard a footfall on the parapet walk behind her. "If you've come to push me off the tower before I make any more embarrassing speeches about the triumph of the Highland spirit and freedom from tyranny," she said without turning around, "you'll probably have to stand in line."

"I'm willing to wait my turn," Simon said, propping one foot on the parapet next to her and gazing up at the milky swath of stars that frosted the northern sky.

"My father used to bring us here when we were children," she said. "Connor would be clinging to his hand and I'd be riding high on his shoulders. The place was a ruin even then, of course, but all Papa saw was the palace it had once been." A wistful smile touched her lips. "He would spend hours telling us thrilling stories about the lords and ladies dancing in the great hall, the wild skirl of the bagpipes calling the warriors to battle, the Kincaid banner flying proudly from the castle ramparts. He'd describe it so clearly we could almost hear the banner snapping in the wind, heralding the splendor of days gone by and the glory of days to come."

"He was a dreamer," Simon said softly.

"He was a fool," she said flatly. "Just like me." She spared him a brief glance. His hair was loose and rippling in the wind like corn silk. "You must find me even more ridiculous than they do."

He laughed, but the sound held little humor. "I've never been bold enough to believe in anything. Why would I mock your faith, however misguided?"

"It wasn't faith. It was folly. Kieran was right. I brought them bagpipes and books when what they needed was food and shoes."

"You tried to give them something more valuable and lasting than a fresh pigeon pie or a pair of new boots. Their pride."

"Pride won't fill their bellies or give them the weapons and resources they need to fight Eddingham." She swung around to face him, knowing he never would have sought out her company if he didn't have news to deliver. "They're going to run, aren't they?"

He nodded. "They believe they have no choice and I can't help but agree with them. If they scatter before Eddingham's men arrive, then at least they'll escape with their lives."

Catriona lifted her gaze to the shimmering opal of the moon. "I thought I was coming home. After all those years of living off of Uncle Ross's charity, of putting up with Alice's bullying and knowing I could never truly belong in their world, I thought I'd find a family here among my own people." She rested her cheek on her knee, the ache in her heart threatening to spill over into tears. "Now I feel as if there's no place in this world for me."

Once Simon might have stroked her hair or made a gentle joke to comfort her. Now he simply said, "Perhaps someday you'll learn not to put your faith in hopeless causes."

Offering her a curt bow, he turned and walked away, his clipped footsteps echoing all the way down the stone stairs.

The night wind seemed to blow several degrees colder. When Catriona heard footsteps behind her, she sprang up from her perch to face the stairs. "Oh, Simon, I—"

But it wasn't Simon who stood there. It was Kieran.

He'd washed the mud from his cheeks to reveal a face that was all hollow planes and sharp angles. Without the grimy mask obscuring his features, she realized he was much younger than she'd first believed, probably a year or two younger than Connor.

He moved toward her with the wary grace of a feral cat, his expression so resolute that she took an alarmed step backward. For all she knew, he really *had* come to fling her off the parapet.

"I remember ye," he said, stopping a scant two feet in front of her.

"You do?"

"Aye. Ye were a wee thing, all ribbons and braids and big gray eyes. Ye used to follow Connor wherever he went, tumbling after him like some sort o' vexsome kitten. Me mum and da lived in the village near yer cottage. We were friends even then, Connor and me."

She smiled, her own memory stirred by Kieran's confession. "He used to make Mama promise to stop me from following him. But the minute she turned her back to put a tray of cross buns in the oven, I'd sneak out of the cottage and be right back on his heels."

Kieran nodded. "I know I said some harsh things earlier, but I wanted ye to know Connor was like a brother to me."

"He was like a brother to me too. Once." Catriona swallowed around the lump in her throat so she could ask the one question that had been haunting her ever since Kieran had revealed her brother's fate. "If he was going to leave this place, going to give up on all of you and our father's dream of reuniting the clan, then why didn't he come to me? Why didn't he come *for* me?"

Kieran shook his head. "He wasn't the same

lad ye remembered. This life takes a harsh toll on a mon, lass. Too many days o' knowin' the only food ye'll have in yer belly is what ye can steal. Too many nights o' takin' yer pleasures wherever ye can pay for them 'cause no decent lass would ever look at ye twice. There's a reason there are no women among us, no bairns, and only a handful of auld men." He touched a hand to his neck. "Sometimes ye wake up chokin' in the middle o' the night 'cause ye can feel the hangman's noose already tightenin' 'round yer throat.

"Yer brother had seen things . . . done things just to survive that no mon should ever have to do. If I had a sister, I'd spit in her face before I'd let her be seen in the street with me."

"Then you'd be just as big of an arse as my brother, wouldn't you?"

Looking taken aback by her boldness, he cleared his throat, then reached into the pocket of his threadbare tunic and drew out a book. "Some o' the lads were wonderin' if ye'd be so kind as to read us a poem out o' one o' yer fancy books? They don't care much for kissin' and the like, but some swordplay or bloodshed might be just the thing. Preferably English blood, of course," he added, the ferocious glint in his eye deepening along with his shy grin.

Biting back a smile of her own, Catriona took the book from his hand. "I believe I know *just* the poem."

When Simon returned to the ruins of Castle Kincaid after hiking the surrounding hills for well over an hour, the last thing he expected to find was Catriona holding court in what had once been the great hall.

Since the English had blown off its roof and rafters decades before, leaving it open to the majestic sweep of the sky, the hall was now more courtyard than court. Nature had wasted no time in reclaiming what man had so briefly called his own. Thick clumps of grass sprouted through the cracks in the flagstones. Moss grew lush and green on the north walls, while nightjars flitted to and fro through the gaping wounds of the windows. A cheery bonfire burned among the crumbled bricks where a hearth used to be.

Catriona was reading aloud by the light from that fire, the Highlanders gathered around her like a flock of grubby, overgrown nursery children. She sat cross-legged on a broad stone with the Kincaid plaid tucked around her shoulders and Robert the Bruce draped across her lap like a fat, furry rug. She absently stroked his ruff as she read, earning an adoring blink from his drowsy golden eyes.

"Fickle beast," Simon murmured, hanging back in the shadows of a fallen rafter just outside that circle of light.

Judging from the beguiling hint of hoarseness in her voice, 'The Battle of Sherramuir' wasn't the first poem she had read them. Her Highland lilt had returned, melting away the crisp edges of the accent she had acquired during her years in London and making her every word sound like music.

Simon shook his head in disbelief. The motley band of thieves and cutthroats were hanging on her every syllable just as he was.

As he watched the firelight dance over her gleaming curls and delicate features, he fought to kindle the embers of the fury that had sent him stalking over those hills. He should have known better than to even consider trusting his heart into her hands. She wasn't the first woman to betray him. Or the first woman willing to sacrifice him for another man. But he was determined that she would be the last.

Her voice softened as she reached the final stanza of the poem:

> *They've lost some gallant gentlemen,*
> *Amang the Highland clans, man!*

> *Now wad ye sing this double flight,*
> *Some fell for wrang, and some for right,*
> *But mony bade the world guid-night.*

She finished with a melancholy sigh and gently closed the volume. A grizzled old Highlander fished a filthy kerchief out of his pocket and dabbed at his eyes.

The tender moment was spoiled by a rude bleat. Everyone, including Simon, winced and swung around to glare at the culprit.

A gangly lad of about fifteen was sitting on a nearby rock. He grinned sheepishly, nodding toward the bagpipes in his arms. "I thought ye might enjoy some after-dinner music."

Kieran snickered. "Hoot, Callum, I thought ye were slaughterin' a lamb."

"I thought he ate too much haggis," one of the other men said, referring to the notorious Scots delicacy that was usually boiled and served in a sheep's stomach.

The lad made another valiant effort to coax something resembling music from the instrument, his face growing more purple by the minute as he heaved and pumped and squeezed and puffed, all to no avail.

The man sitting next to Kieran tucked a blade of grass between his teeth and sighed. "Puts me in mind of a lass I once met in Glasgow. Why, she could blow the varnish right off a—"

Kieran elbowed him in the ribs hard enough to make him double over, nodding toward Catriona. "Mind yer tongue, Donel. We've a lady among us."

When a particularly tortured squeal sent Robert the Bruce darting off into the night, the grizzled old Highlander who had wept at the end of the poem marched over to the boy and snatched the bagpipes from his hands. "Give me those, lad. Ye should be ashamed o' yerself! Ye're a disgrace to the Kincaid name!"

As he went striding off into the darkness, removing both the bagpipes and their ears from harm's way, the men raised their mugs of ale in a toast and sent up a collective cheer.

Catriona laughed and lifted her own mug, joining in with a rousing huzzah of her own. As she lowered it, Simon stepped out of the shadows and their eyes met.

"Come join us, Wescott!" Kieran called out. "Yer wee wife here has been readin' us some poetry written by one o' the finest Scotsman who ever lived—Robbie Burns."

"Robbie Burns," his clansmen echoed reverently, lifting their mugs again.

"Oh, I'm familiar with his work." Still gazing

into Catriona's eyes, Simon softly recited with a flawless Scots burr:

> *As fair art thou, my bonnie lass,*
> *So deep in luve am I;*
> *And I will love thee still, my Dear*
> *Till a' the seas gang dry.*

For a timeless moment, Catriona continued to gaze at him, her eyes misty with longing, her lips parted, ripe for the kissing. Then she ducked her head with an awkward laugh. "My Mr. Wescott grew up in the theater. He can make even the most preposterous drivel sound convincing, can he not?"

Kieran's cool, assessing gaze traveled from one to the other of them. "Hell, if his tongue is as silver in bed as out of it, I just might marry him meself."

The men's rollicking laughter was cut short by a pure sweet note that seemed to pour from the throat of heaven itself. As that note soared into a full-blown tune, every hair on the back of Simon's neck stood straight up.

The men of Clan Kincaid exchanged stunned glances. Even Kieran couldn't quite hide the wonder in his eyes. Catriona came to her feet and, one by one, they all followed, drifting silently toward the lone remaining arch on the north wall to find the grizzled old Highlander silhouetted against the moonlit sky. He was standing at the edge of the steep cliff that overlooked the vale below, the bagpipes cradled against his shoulder.

The majestic strains hung in the air like the wailing ghost of days gone by, singing of battles won and loves lost, hopes fulfilled and regrets mourned, dreams forsaken but never forgotten. Simon felt those lofty notes pierce his own soul, calling him to a battle that wasn't his own, a woman he might love for the rest of his days, a home he'd never known. The melody seemed to carry with it the haunting echo of fife and drum and a thousand voices raised in one accord.

Every man on that hillside stood a little straighter, including him, and without knowing how they got there, he found his hands fiercely gripping Catriona's shoulders.

By the time the old man sent the last note of his tune winging its way across the vale to find its final resting place in the arms of the mountains, hers weren't the only cheeks wet with tears.

Kieran was the first to recover. "Ye can save yer bluidy dirges for me burial, auld mon," he called out. "Do ye not know any fine dance tunes?"

The old fellow glowered at him. "I didna want

to waste me breath, since it's likely the only place you'll be dancin' is on a gibbet, ye young fool." With that, he lifted the pipes to his lips and launched into a merry reel.

His eyes glittering with mischief, Kieran turned and offered Simon and Catriona a surprisingly courtly bow. "If ye'll excuse us, sir, I do believe the lady promised the first dance to me."

Before Simon could protest, Kieran had grabbed Catriona by the hand and snatched her from his arms. She threw him a helpless glance over her shoulder as Kieran whisked her into the reel, leading her down a double line of her hooting, clapping clansmen.

Simon watched her pass from hand to hand, from man to man, her cheeks growing pink with exertion, her grin blooming into full-blown laughter as she tossed back her head and kicked up her heels, sending her skirts whirling around them. He had danced with countless women in scores of ballrooms, almost always knowing the night would end with one of them in his bed. But he'd never been as hard or as hungry as he was in that moment.

Or as dangerous.

He wanted Catriona. So much that he was willing to risk everything to have her in his bed—his pride, his heart, even his life. Regretting that he could no longer dull both his wits and his longing with whisky, he turned on his heel and went stalking off into the darkness, never seeing Catriona's smile fade as she watched him go.

Chapter 16

Simon awoke the next morning feeling as if he had the weight of the world on his chest. But when he cautiously opened one eye, he discovered it was just Robert the Bruce. Giving him an insolent look, the cat cocked back on his rump and began to lick himself between his splayed hind legs.

Simon lifted one eyebrow. "If men could do that," he growled, "we'd have no need of women."

"Oh, I don't know. Without a woman or at least a decent valet, you still wouldn't be able to find your stockings or properly tie a cravat."

At that wry pronouncement, Simon sat up abruptly, dumping the cat from his chest. The beast gave him a malevolent look as he saun-tered away, his tail twitching in indignation.

Catriona was perched on a fallen stone that had once been part of an overhead arch in the mossy grotto he had claimed for his bedcham-ber. He was surprised to see her blankets spread out less than a foot away from his. It was proba-bly just as well that he had never known she was within arm's reach during the long, lonely hours of the night.

She had donned a gown the color of fresh straw-berries and twisted her curls atop her head in a careless knot, leaving several of the more unruly ones free to tumble over her cheeks and nape.

She eyed him warily, as if unsure of her wel-come. "I hated to send Robert to wake you, but I thought you were going to sleep until noon again. We've been summoned."

"By whom?" He yawned and raked his tou-sled hair out of his eyes. "The King?"

"No, the clan. It seems that Kieran has called a Council."

"Is that like Parliament? Will we have to wear long black robes and powdered wigs and listen to unbearably pretentious debates about the rag-ing inflation and whether or not the King is too balmy to rule?"

"The Council is an ancient custom of the clan and is only called when an important matter is to be decided or announced." She leaned forward, her eyes sparkling with excitement. "According to Callum and Donel, no one in Clan Kincaid has called a Council since the '45."

Simon sighed and tossed back his blankets. "Then by all means, let me find my robe and wig."

Simon and Catriona entered the ruins of the great hall a short while later to find her clansmen already gathered. The men were using the collapsed rafters as benches while Kieran stood in their midst, one foot propped on the same broad stone Catriona had occupied the night before. Their carefree merriment of the previous night seemed to have vanished, leaving their sun-leathered faces solemn and unreadable. Their mood seemed to be at odds with the cheerful wisps of clouds drifting across the dazzling blue swath of sky above.

Kieran wasted no time on pretension or formalities. As soon as Simon and Catriona entered their hallowed circle, he looked Catriona dead in the eye and said, "We want you to stay."

"Oh, we plan on it," she assured him. "We're very honored that you invited us to sit in on your Council."

"No," Kieran said. "I mean we want you to stay here. At Castle Kincaid. With us."

Catriona shook her head in wonder, hardly daring to believe that someone might actually want her. That she might have finally found the home and family she had been dreaming of for so long. "But Simon told me you were going to run away. That you were going to scatter and hide so Eddingham wouldn't find you."

"Most of us have been runnin' and hidin' since the day we were born. Connor used to say that sometimes a mon has to find a spot to make his stand, even if it turns out to be his last one." Kieran's gaze swept the ruins of the great hall. "Well, this looks to be as fine a spot as any to me."

His men nodded their agreement.

"Never cry when you can fight," Catriona murmured to herself, still hearing Connor's voice in her head.

"We have only one condition," Kieran said.

"Anything," Catriona replied, a joyful grin breaking over her face. "Anything at all."

He nodded toward Simon. "We want him to be our chieftain."

Catriona's grin faded. "Simon? You must be joking. Why, he can't be your chieftain! He's not even a Kincaid."

"And neither are ye, since ye married him," Kieran reminded her. He sighed. "Ye may be a descendant of auld Ewan Kincaid himself, but we canna have a lass leadin' the clan. We need a mon." He folded his wiry arms over his chest, shooting Simon a mocking look. "And this one's already proved himself handy with a pistol."

It wasn't until Simon took a step backward, holding up his hands as if to ward off a blow, that Catriona realized he looked nearly as horrified as she was feeling. "Oh, no, you don't! If you think I'm leading this motley band of thieves and pickpockets into battle against a battalion of English soldiers just so you can lay claim to this crumbling pile of rocks, then you're all bloody daft."

"He's right. You don't need him. You need me!" Catriona cried. "I've spent my whole life preparing for this moment! I know the history of the clan. I've spent hours studying famous battles fought in these very mountains. You need wits and ingenuity just as badly as you need swagger and muscle."

Kieran shook his head, the pity in his eyes even more damning than the determination. "What we need, lass, is a mon. If yers will agree to serve as our chieftain, then we'll stand and fight. If not, we'll be packed and gone by nightfall and this Eddingham fellow can help himself to this crumblin' pile o' rocks."

His face might have been carved from those same rocks. Catriona realized with a flash of despair that he was not to be swayed.

She turned to Simon, her desperation mounting. "May I have a word with you, please?" Feeling the curious eyes of her clansmen traveling from one of them to the other, she added, "In private."

Seizing his arm, she urged him through the arch at the north end of the great hall where they had stood only the night before and marveled together at the majestic song of the bagpipes.

Once she was sure they were out of earshot of the others, she turned away from Simon to gaze across the sunny vale. She couldn't bear to look at him in that moment, didn't want him to see how deeply Kieran's rejection had cut her. The gusty wind tore at her skirts and whipped stinging strands of hair across her cheeks.

"You heard Kieran," she said. "They don't want me, but they'll take you."

"I'm afraid my military services are no longer available. I've been reduced to playing nursery maid to women who have completely lost their wits."

She swung around to face him. "If you don't agree to be their chieftain, they're going to scatter to the four winds. The Kincaid name and clan will be lost forever."

"And just when did that become *my* problem?"

Catriona took a step forward and splayed her palms on his chest. The strong, steady beat of his heart beneath her hands felt like hope. "Don't you see, Simon? This could be your chance. It's not too late for you to be a hero."

To be my hero.

She didn't possess the courage to speak the words aloud, but they were there in the pleading way she gazed up at him, the nearly imperceptible tremble of her lower lip. She was offering him more than just the chance to lead her clan. She was offering him her heart.

Simon gazed down at her for a long moment, then caught her by the wrists and gently removed her hands from his chest. "My chance to be a hero came and went a long time ago, darling. And I've never been either fool or dreamer enough to ask for a second one."

Freeing her wrists, he turned and began to pick his way over the rocks and down the hillside, leaving both the castle and Catriona behind.

* * *

Simon didn't return to the castle until full dark had fallen and the moon had drifted halfway across the sky. There was no joyous skirl of bagpipes to call him home, no voices raised in drunken snatches of song, no merry ripple of feminine laughter to stir both his heart and his groin.

The castle crouched at the edge of the hill, a heap of crumbling stone fit only for the rats scampering through its roofless corridors and collapsed dungeons. Simon felt an odd catch in his heart as he gazed up at the parapet of its lone remaining tower.

He moved as silently as a ghost through the archway and into the ruins of the great hall to find Catriona sitting on the broad stone that had served as her stage only twenty-four hours before. She was sitting with her chin propped on her hand, searching the sky as if its twinkling stars held the answers to every question she had never dared to ask. As he drifted nearer, he could see that her cheeks were stained with grimy tear tracks but her eyes were dry.

"They've gone," he said.

Although it was not a question, she nodded.

"I'm sorry," he said, the words more heartfelt than she would ever know.

"Yes, you are," she said coolly. She rose to face him and he almost wished she hadn't. Her eyes were nearly as flinty as Kieran's. "You're a sorry excuse for a husband and an even sorrier excuse for a man."

His father had said far worse to him on many occasions and he had dismissed it with nothing more than a shrug and a mocking laugh, but Catriona's contempt slid like a rusty blade through his gut. "What did you want me to do, Catriona? Lead them and you to an almost certain destruction? To be willing to watch you all die in a hail of pistol balls or swing at the end of a hangman's noose, all for the sake of some ridiculous dream that should have been abandoned decades ago?"

"It was *my* dream!" she cried, fresh tears welling in her eyes. "And you had no right to destroy it simply because you were afraid that for once in your life you might have to live up to someone's expectations of you!"

"Perhaps it wasn't living up to those expectations I minded but dying for them!"

"Oh, that's right. I forgot you were a self-proclaimed coward without an ounce of honor in your heart. Is there anything worth fighting for in your eyes? Anything worth dying for? Anything noble enough or dear enough to justify risking your precious neck?"

You.

The word rose from somewhere deep within his soul but never made it past his lips.

"No," she said when he didn't answer. "I didn't think so. Well, in that case, I'm afraid I'm going to have to dismiss you."

"Pardon?" he asked softly, feeling the edges of his temper growing dangerously frayed.

"You heard me the first time. You're dismissed. Your services are no longer required. I'll find my own way back to London, thank you very much, even if I have to walk every step of the way."

Simon felt something within him grow deadly cold and hot all at the same time. "You owe me," he said.

Shaking her head as if she couldn't quite believe his audacity, she marched over to where Robert the Bruce's chicken crate sat. It was fortunate the cat was not in residence at the moment because she heaved it upside down with a frustrated grunt and tugged at the bottom of the crate until it popped off to reveal a secret compartment.

She tore fat bundles of pound notes out of the compartment and hurled them at him until they rained down like confetti between them. "Take it! Take it all! Your half of the dowry. My half of the dowry. I don't care anymore. You can spend it on your liquor and your gambling and your whores. I hope you squander every halfpenny of it and die of French pox in some opium den somewhere!"

Tossing the crate back to the ground, she turned and marched toward the archway.

Striding over the veritable fortune as if it were so much garbage beneath his bootheels, Simon caught up with her halfway to the archway, grabbed her by the upper arm and dragged her around to face him.

Gazing deep into her startled eyes, he said, "I wasn't talking about the money."

Chapter 17

Catriona gazed up into Simon's heavy-lidded eyes. They'd never looked quite so green. Or quite so ruthless. His grip on her arm was equally implacable, offering no compromise or hope of escape.

She licked her suddenly dry lips. "I paid you what I promised you. Every penny of it and more. What else could you possibly want from me?"

"You owe me a wedding night, remember? It was part of our little devil's bargain and you can't make a deal with the devil without expecting him to show up to collect one day." The husky note in his voice deepened. "Or night."

Her breath caught in her throat. "Surely you don't mean—"

"And why not? Didn't you just take great pains to remind me that I'm a man without honor? Without scruples? Unfortunately, you can't say the same for yourself. Which is why you have no choice but to honor the promise you made to me."

Catriona felt the steely jaws of her own self-righteousness snap neatly shut around her heart. Knowing his answer could very well break what was left of it, she asked softly, "And if I refuse, will you take what I owe you by force?"

He studied her face as if giving serious consideration to the notion before finally shaking his head. "No, I won't." He leaned down, his lips brushing a tingling swath across her ear as he whispered, "But I will know you're an even bigger coward than I am."

He released her arm and stepped away from her, giving her every opportunity to bolt.

She stood her ground, glaring at him defiantly. "May I have some time to prepare myself?"

"Of course," he replied, both gentleman and rogue to the bitter end. "Take all the time you need."

When Catriona finally worked up her courage to approach the moonlit grotto she and Simon had

shared the night before, it was to find it transformed. Simon had combined their blankets and
laid them over a thick bed of moss to make a
cozy bower. He'd even managed to find several
stubby tallow candles left behind by Kieran and
his men and planted them on top of the tumbled
stones. Their flickering golden glow mingled
with the silvery spill of the moonlight.

He turned as she approached, unable to completely hide the flicker of surprise in his eyes.
Despite his preparations, she knew that he had
not really believed she would come.

She drifted toward him, nervously smoothing the simple linen skirt of her nightdress. Her
skin was still slightly damp from bathing in a
nearby spring and the gown clung to her in unexpected places. Given its chaste white hue, she
expected him to make some clever quip about
Joan of Arc going to the stake. But he simply
watched her, his eyes shadowed by those thick
gilt-tipped lashes she had always both adored
and envied.

He wore only a pair of buff trousers and an
ivory lawn shirt hanging open to the waist. His
long, narrow feet were bare and his tawny hair
hung loose around his face. Despite the scars and
shadows life had etched upon it, the masculine
beauty that had so beguiled her as an innocent

girl was undiminished. She feared that if he offered her even one tiny morsel of tenderness, her hungry heart would forgive everything, resist nothing.

Keenly aware of his gaze following her every move, she brushed past him and lowered herself to the bed he had prepared for her. She tried not to remember all of the romantic fantasies she'd once had about going to her husband's bed for the first time. Especially since in most of those fantasies, Simon had *been* that husband.

She reclined on her back, fixing her gaze on a star that hung just below the graceful curve of the moon. "If you don't mind, I'd rather you have done with this as quickly as possible. I know you're supposed to be some sort of master of the art of love, but if it's all the same to you, I'd just as soon dispense with the . . . pleasantries."

"Pleasantries? You make it sound as if I were going to invite you to come 'round for tea, then leave you with my calling card."

"You know what I'm talking about. I'd rather you just take your satisfaction and go."

She could almost hear the frown in his voice. "With absolutely no thought to yours?"

"Isn't that what men prefer?"

"Not this man." Simon lowered himself, prowling over the top of her like some sort of great, golden jungle cat until his face replaced the moon in her vision. "So what you're asking me to do is just lift the skirt of your nightdress, take my pleasure, then cover you back up when I'm . . . finished," he said, repeating those naïve words she had spoken to him at her uncle's house.

"Yes, please," she said fiercely. "That's precisely what I'm asking you to do."

He studied her thoughtfully before nodding. "Very well. God knows I wouldn't want to disappoint you again."

Drawing in a shuddering breath, Catriona turned her face away and closed her eyes. Spying on her uncle's tomcats and stallions might have taught her the mechanics of what he was about to do to her, but its dangerous power remained a mystery to her.

She did her best not to flinch when she felt the warmth of his knuckles brush her calves. He caught the hem of her nightdress and slowly folded it back, leaving her naked from the waist down.

She heard his sharply indrawn breath, felt the heat emanating from his body. A helpless whimper escaped her as his hands glided down to the inside of her knees, gently lifting and parting them until her thighs fell open.

As the cool night breeze caressed her like a lover, she realized she had made a terrible miscalculation. She was even more vulnerable now than if she had been naked in his arms. There was nothing she could do to stop his eyes from drinking their fill of her in the moonlight.

"Christ, Catriona," he breathed. "I didn't think you could get any prettier than you already were."

She kept her eyes squeezed shut and bit her bottom lip, both dreading and anticipating what was to come. But she did not anticipate her shiver of pure delight as his lips found the exquisitely sensitive spot on the inside of her knee.

She gasped as the moist heat of his mouth flowered against her flesh, tracing a tingling path up her quivering thigh. His hands encircled her ankles like a pair of velvet-covered manacles, luring her legs even farther apart, making her even more vulnerable to the enticing seduction of those kisses. He kissed his way up each creamy thigh in turn until her every breath was a sigh and her thighs were falling open of their own accord.

Catriona was so dazed she didn't realize his hands had left her ankles until she felt one of them gently brush the damp nest of curls between her thighs. She gasped as he delved deeper, spreading the tender pink petals he found there

until he could dip one finger into the nectar welling between them.

"Oh!" Her eyes flew open as a sob of raw pleasure shuddered through her. She tried to sit up,
but he seemed to be holding her pinned to the
earth with nothing more than the weight of that
one finger. "What are you doing to me?"

Simon lifted his head to meet her eyes, the
beautiful planes of his face both hard and hungry. "Exactly what you asked me to do. I'm taking my pleasure."

With that, he lowered his head and put his
mouth on her. Catriona moaned deep in her
throat and arched off the blanket, but there
was nowhere she could go to escape the bliss
he would give her. After only a few strokes of
his nimble tongue, she was arching into his
mouth instead of away from it. She dug her fingernails into the blankets and whipped her
head from side to side, rendered both blind and
incoherent with need as he mated her with his
mouth, using his tongue to take full possession
of her.

Simon wasn't just taking his pleasure. He was
taking her will and making it his own. He was
taking her heart and shattering every wall she
had erected around it. He was taking her soul

and giving it a taste of heaven that would haunt her to the end of her days.

The sweet, hot flicker of his tongue over the swollen bud at the crux of her curls was like a living flame whipping her into a fever of lust. When she tried to writhe away from it, he curved his big, warm hands around her bottom and held her still, forcing the flames even higher. At the exact moment they threatened to consume her, he closed his mouth around that tender bud and gently suckled, sending a rush of unspeakable rapture cascading through every nerve ending of her body.

It seemed to roll on and on, as did her broken wail of surrender.

Feeling as if she'd been flung up to the heavens to touch the stars, then dropped to float gently back to earth, Catriona slowly opened her eyes.

Simon was gazing down at her, the glint of triumph in his eyes unmistakable.

She lifted a hand to his cheek, unable to stop herself from touching him. Eyeing him solemnly, she said, "I was right about you. You're an un-scrupulous villain without an ounce of honor in your heart."

"That may be true, sweetheart," he whispered, cupping her face in his hands. "But tonight I'm also your husband."

As his mouth came down on hers, feeding her an intoxicating taste of her own pleasure, she tangled her hands in the wheaten silk of his hair and kissed him back, wrenching a groan from deep in his throat.

Taking his groan for the invitation it was, she shoved the shirt from his shoulders, allowing herself to revel in touching him as she'd always dreamed of doing. He was a male marvel of sinew knitted over muscle—warm and smooth, supple and strong. Desperate to taste what she was touching, she tore her mouth away from his kiss and pressed it over his heart. He tasted salty and unbearably sweet all at the same time. Her greedy tongue couldn't get enough of him.

After shedding his shirt with an impatient shrug of his broad shoulders, he dragged her to a half-sitting position and tugged her nightdress over her head.

He gazed down at the pale globes of her breasts with an oddly beguiling combination of reverence and lust. "I don't think even your be- loved Robbie Burns ever composed any poetry worthy of such a sight." He lifted his eyes to her face, the corner of his mouth curving in a rakish grin. "But perhaps you'll let me put my own tongue to the task."

As he leaned down and circled one blushing

nipple with the very tip of his tongue, Catriona discovered she had neither the will nor the desire to refuse him. Her head fell back in surrender as he proved once again just how eloquent that tongue could be. Without wasting a single word, he lavished attention on each of her breasts in turn, using the taut flick of his tongue, the moist heat of his lips, the gentle scrape of his teeth, to compose a glorious sonnet to her feminine charms. She could only clutch at his hair and clench her thighs together when he drew one of her nipples into his mouth and suckled her deep and hard, skirting the boundary between pleasure and pain and sending a shadow of that earlier delight rippling through her womb.

His equally accomplished hands stripped away his trousers. Before she could steal so much as a peek at what he had revealed, he gathered her tenderly into his arms and laid her back on that bed of blankets and moss, pressing his naked body to hers and drinking one kiss after another from her lips.

There was something timeless about being here in the moonlight in this place. In this man's arms. With their breath mingling in wordless sighs and their naked limbs entwined, they might have been any lord and lady throughout all of history, drunk with the carnal pleasures of love and all of its intoxicating possibilities.

When he pulled away from her, she clutched at the smooth muscles of his back in protest.

"It's all right," he murmured, pressing a soothing kiss to her temple. He reached up to a shelf created from a fallen stone and retrieved a small lacquered box. He lifted the lid to reveal a delicate glass flask nestled on a bed of silk. As he drew out its stopper, the rich exotic smell of myrrh scented the air, mingling with the heady musk of his own desire.

"I'm afraid I can't make myself smaller for you, since you've had the opposite effect on me since the moment you walked into my jail cell. But I can"—he dragged the cool, hard stopper between the flushed softness of her breasts, leaving a glistening trail of oil—"ease things along."

As his meaning became clear, Catriona both blushed and scowled. "I suppose you carry that around in your portmanteau just in case you run across a virgin you'd like to seduce." Utterly fascinated, she watched the faintest hint of color creep across his high cheekbones. "Why, Mr. Wescott, are you blushing?"

Simon blew out a sigh and raked a hand through his hair. "I'm going to share a deep, dark secret with you that could very likely ruin my reputation if it got out." Leaning down to her ear, he whispered, "I've never had a virgin before."

Her eyes widened in disbelief. "Truly?"

He nodded solemnly. "You're my first."

She smiled, feeling ridiculously pleased by the revelation. "I suppose that makes you something of a virgin yourself." Patting his chest, she said, "Don't worry. I'll strive to be gentle with you."

"Please don't," he growled, catching her lower lip between his teeth and giving it a tantalizing little tug.

She thought he might smear a bit of the oil on his fingers, but he surprised her by tilting the bottle and pouring it freely over her belly and thighs.

"Oh!" she exclaimed as the oil began to trickle between them.

Led by his thumbs, Simon's hands followed its path, gliding downward over the incredibly sensitive hollows just above her hipbones, stroking upward until her thighs fell apart. The oil seemed to warm beneath the hypnotic friction of his touch and the sensation of his hands on her made Catriona feel deliciously decadent, like some pampered harem girl or Queen Esther being prepared for the King's pleasure.

He kept up that maddening circling and stroking until the whole world narrowed down to that silky little triangle between her legs. The one place he wasn't touching.

He had told her once that if she would give him ten minutes, he would make her beg. But it had taken less than five. "Please, Simon," she moaned, dying for his touch. "Oh, please . . ." She turned her face into her hair, but there was no place to hide from this terrible wanting.

He was not without mercy. At her breathless urging, he used both of his thumbs to part those silky curls and follow the glistening path all the way down to its ultimate destination.

He used the pad of one thumb to stroke the oil around the mouth of that fragile opening. She could feel herself blooming like a flower beneath the kiss of the sun, eager to take whatever he would give her.

She bit back a sob of pleasure. "Is this one of those creative perversions you've been known to practice?"

"No, but this is," he whispered, sliding that thumb deep inside of her.

Catriona let out a low moan, as if her very soul were being torn from her in exchange for some unspeakable pleasure. Aided by both the oil and the tears of joy her own body was weeping, he slid his thumb in and out of her, ravishing her tenderly but thoroughly in a bold imitation of what was to come.

And still he wasn't done with her. Just when Catriona thought she might very well swoon from the primal power of it all, he brushed his forefinger ever so lightly against that swollen bud he had suckled earlier. That was all it took for her body to erupt in a fresh rush of ecstasy.

The tremors of delight were still coursing through her when he withdrew his thumb from her, leaving a raw emptiness that ached to be filled. As she felt the solid weight of his manhood against her thigh, she knew he intended to do just that.

Suddenly it didn't matter how many women he had bedded in the past. Tonight he was hers. Only hers. All hers.

The thought made her feel both wild and bold. "Wait," she commanded.

His startled gaze flew to her face. His voice was hoarse, barely recognizable as his own. "If you've decided not to abide by our bargain, you'd best tell me now."

She reached for the bottle of oil, poured a generous amount over her palms, then reached for him. He threw back his head and sucked in an agonized breath as her small hands struggled to enfold him. She used both hands to smooth the oil over his rigid shaft, as stunned by the length and breadth of him as she was beguiled by the flickers of rapture that danced over his face in the moonlight. His eyes were closed and his lips pulled back from his teeth in an expression that was both feral and beautiful.

She was boldly stroking the oil over every inch of him when he captured both of her wrists in a viselike grip.

"Don't you like it?" she asked, unable to hide her dismay.

"That's the problem, angel," he murmured, easing her to her back and covering her with his shadow. "I like it far too much. And if you keep doing *that*, I'm not going to be able to do . . . *this*."

She gasped with shock as he sheathed himself in her all the way to the hilt in one masterful stroke. She suffered a sharp pain as if he'd cleaved her with a genuine blade. Despite all of his efforts to prepare her, her untried body could barely contain him.

He kissed her sweat-dampened brow, breathing as if he'd been running for a very long time.

"I'm sorry, sweeting. I swear I only wanted to give you pleasure, not pain."

She let out a disgruntled little snuffle. "I think I liked your thumb better."

He cupped her face in his hands and gazed down at her, his eyes glowing with a fierce tenderness that made her heart clutch. "I promise to do everything in my power to change your mind about that."

Knowing that was one promise he would delight in keeping, Simon braced his weight on both hands and began to move within her. She was exquisitely tight. Exquisitely hot. Exquisitely his. It wasn't as if she was the first virgin he'd ever had. It was as if she was the first woman he'd ever had, the only woman he would ever want.

He took her with long, deep, slow strokes, gliding in and out of her as if he had all night to devote to the act. Although he would have liked nothing more than to close his eyes and surrender to sensation, he couldn't resist watching her face as her pain began to melt into flickers of delight.

Before long, her lips were parted in a soundless sigh, her cheeks were flushed, her eyes glazed with pleasure. When she began to lift her hips to answer each of his thrusts with one of her own, Simon had to squeeze his eyes shut and clench his teeth against a ragged moan, in danger of losing his legendary mastery over his own needs.

Catriona ran her hands over Simon's sweat-sheened chest, marveling that she could be joined to such a beautiful male creature. The throbbing between her legs had faded to a dull ache that only made her more exquisitely sensitive to the friction between their bodies.

Both Aunt Margaret and Cousin Georgina had led her to believe that kisses, caresses, and whispered endearments were to be desired, but the marriage act itself was something to be stoically endured—the price a woman must pay for a man's affection.

But apparently someone had failed to tell Simon that, because the pleasure he was giving her now was even deeper and more powerful than the bliss he had offered her with his mouth and hands. She felt taken. Possessed. As if she might never truly be her own again. As if she would do anything for him, let him do anything *to* her, no matter how shocking or forbidden. If he was a master of the art of love, then tonight she was his willing and eager pupil.

She cupped his face in her hands, forcing him

to look at her, to really see her. "You've given me everything I wanted, Simon. What do you want?"

"You," he said hoarsely. "Only you."

Then there was no more time for words, no more time for thought. There was only that driving rhythm where their bodies were joined.

Simon clenched his teeth as he drove himself into Catriona with reckless abandon. It was as if her touch had unleashed a wildness in him that he'd been fighting to tame his whole life. For once, instead of seeking his lover's pleasure, he was seeking only his own.

Which made it all the more extraordinary when he heard Catriona cry out his name, felt her taut, velvety folds convulse around him in a paroxysm of ecstasy. Rapture came rolling through him like thunder, driving all reason before it until all he could do was collapse on top of her, shuddering and spent.

They lay there for a long time in each other's arms, their chests heaving, their breath coming in ragged gasps. Catriona's voice was still tinged with awe when she finally managed to wheeze out, "Now I know what Jem and Bess were screaming about."

"And now I remember what it's like to be two-and-twenty," Simon mumbled into her hair.

Catriona's eyes widened as she felt him harden

anew deep within her. "Why, Mr. Wescott, you can't be serious!"

He lifted his head, a rakish glint in his eye. "Why, Mrs. Wescott, I've never been more serious in my life."

Chapter 18

*C*atriona awoke to the delicious sensation of Simon stroking her breasts. Pressing her rump to his groin, she snuggled deeper into the warm cup of his body before murmuring, "It's really quite reprehensible of you to fondle me just because you believe I'm asleep and can't defend my virtue."

He slid his other hand between her legs and began to stroke her there as well. "You're absolutely right. I should be deeply ashamed of myself. Just what do you intend to do about it?"

She gasped with delight as he slid his longest finger into her. "Hmmmmm . . . I don't know. Pretend I'm still asleep?"

She closed her eyes, but it was impossible to

pretend for long. She couldn't muffle her sighs and whimpers of pleasure as he tugged gently at her nipple, couldn't stop herself from arching against his palm as his hand had its wicked way with her.

"The first time we met," he murmured, brushing his lips over her nape with a possessive tenderness that made her shiver, "I believe you tried to instruct me in the fine art of lovemaking, did you not? What was it you said? That the male simply bites the back of the female's neck to hold her still while he mounts her from behind?"

Catriona shuddered anew as Simon nipped the back of her neck at the precise moment he slid into her from behind.

"You never told me what comes next," he whispered in her ear, buried to the hilt in her but not moving a single muscle.

"This," she replied breathlessly, rocking against him in a rhythm older than time. "Only this."

A short while later Catriona lay cradled in the crook of Simon's arm, deliciously drowsy but not wanting to waste another precious moment of the night on sleep. His hand played in her hair, twining first one curl, then another, around his finger. As the chill had deepened, laying a sparkling layer of frost over each fallen leaf and blade of grass, he had drawn the blankets up around them both to create a cozy nest.

"I thought my tender young heart was going to break when you smiled at me on the docks the day you returned from Trafalgar," she confessed. "I was sixteen years old and somehow I just knew that you were going to sweep me into your arms right in front of Alice and all the world and proclaim your everlasting devotion."

"I'm afraid I was a bit distracted." He gazed up at the shimmering sweep of stars, his profile inscrutable. "You weren't the only ghost from my past in the crowd that day. My mother was there as well."

Catriona frowned, thinking she must have misheard him. "Your mother? I don't understand. You told me she died."

"I told everyone she died. But the truth is that she finally found a wealthy lover who wasn't married. Oh, she swore she was leaving me with my father for my own good—that I had reached the age where I needed a man's influence in my life and that he could give me a home and a future she could never hope to provide." A short, bitter laugh escaped him. "When she left me at the solicitor's office, she held me as if she would never let me go and cried the prettiest tears you ever saw. But she forgot that I'd seen her cry those same tears in dozens of different roles over the years."

"What if they were real?" Catriona asked softly. "What if she truly believed she was doing what was best for you, even if it broke her own heart?"

"Then she was a bloody fool," he said flatly. "I would have been better off living on the streets, picking pockets and peddling my body to strangers to make my way in the world than living off of my father's charity. The only thing he despised more than her was me."

Catriona gently stroked his chest but could do nothing to soothe the ache in her own heart. "What did you do when you saw her on the docks that day?"

"The same thing I would have done for any pretty woman. I winked at her and kept walking. By the time I glanced back, she was gone. I heard later that she had married her lover and was living a respectable life in Northumberland." He slanted her a rueful look. "I've never told another soul that she's alive, not even my father."

"That makes two secrets I'm bound to keep," she replied solemnly. "That your mother is alive and that you're not given to ravishing virgins."

He rolled on top of her, lacing his fingers through hers and imprisoning her hands on either side of her head. The fierce look in his eyes took her breath away. "But I am given to ravishing you."

"After tonight," she whispered, opening her legs for him, "that's no secret."

Simon stood at the edge of the cliff, watching dawn sweep across the vale below. The wind stirred his hair and tugged at the edges of his open shirt. Puffy little clouds tinged with pink drifted through the brightening sky, so close it looked as if he could reach out and touch them. But he knew that if he tried, they would melt through his fingers like the vapor they were.

He'd left Catriona sleeping in their nest of blankets, half a smile deepening the dimple in her left cheek. He'd had ample experience creeping out of women's beds before they awoke. He would usually slip silently out of their bedchambers, boots in hand, and never allow himself to suffer so much as a twinge of guilt. And why should he? He'd always given them exactly what they wanted from him and left them with a kiss on their brow, a smile on their lips, and a fond memory to cherish when the winter winds blew cold and their beds were empty.

But none of them had been his wife.

He certainly hadn't treated Catriona with the delicate consideration a wife deserved. He had treated her like an experienced courtesan purchased solely for his pleasure. He had treated her the way his father had probably treated his mother.

Now he could add despoiler of innocents to his lengthy catalogue of sins. He couldn't even blame the whisky this time. Although it had been the most intoxicating night of his life, he had been stone-cold sober when he took Catriona to his bed.

It hardly soothed his conscience to know she had been right. It would have been much kinder to take her quickly and without care to satisfy his own selfish needs and make her despise him. Instead he had used every seductive skill at his disposal to give her a night of pleasure she would always remember.

And one he would never forget.

Catriona wandered out of the ruins of the great hall, wearing only her rumpled nightdress and a sleepy smile. She glanced up at the tender robin's-egg-blue of the sky, shocked to see how high the sun had already climbed. Feeling deliciously decadent, she yawned and stretched with all of the lazy grace of Robert the Bruce. She was stiff and sore in muscles that had never been used before, but that only made her feel more like a bride who had been well loved by her groom.

An off-key whistling drifted to her ears. She cocked her head to the side, her smile deepening when she recognized the bawdy Scots ditty Simon had sung in the inn on the night of their wedding.

She followed the cheery sound to the spacious meadow that had once been the courtyard of the castle to find Simon leading the team of nags toward the wagon.

"Good morning, sunshine," he said, tossing her a cocky grin. "I thought you were going to languish in bed all day. I was getting ready to poke you awake."

She returned his grin with a dimpled smile of her own. "As I recall, you already did. Several times during the night."

To her surprise, he didn't respond to her naughty jest with a wicked *bon mot* of his own. He simply led the nags around to the front of the wagon and began to back them into the shafts.

She frowned. "What are you doing?"

"Hitching up the team. I'd like to be well clear

of this place before Eddingham and his battalion of toy soldiers arrives. We've a long journey ahead of us if I'm to return you to your uncle's house by the end of the week."

She blinked. "You're taking me back to my uncle's house?"

"Naturally." He devoted all of his attention to sliding a leather harness over one horse's neck. "Where else would I be taking you, now that my job is done and all of our debts are settled?"

Catriona sucked in a breath that felt as if she were inhaling ground glass.

If you truly know what sort of man I am, then you also know I'm perfectly capable of making love to you without loving you.

Simon had tried to warn her, but like the romantic fool she had always been, she had failed to listen.

A stinging shame whipped through her heart. She was no different from any of the other women he'd seduced. She'd fallen beneath the spell of his artful touch and honeyed tongue just as they had, eagerly trading her innocence and her pride for a night of carnal pleasure in his arms. For one agonizing moment, she didn't know who she hated more—him or herself.

But that was before she noticed the muscle

twitching steadily in his jaw. A muscle that made a mockery of his easy grin and a lie of every word coming out of his beautiful, treacherous mouth.

"I know what you're trying to do," she said, folding her arms over her chest.

"I'm trying to hitch up these horses—and I do use the term loosely—so we can get on the road before the sun goes back down."

"You're trying to pretend that last night didn't matter. That *I* don't matter."

After tugging the cinches tight, he straightened to face her, blowing out a long-suffering sigh. "I had hoped to spare us this awkwardness. I should have known this would be one of the perils of making love to a virgin. They tend to wax sentimental over the slightest bit of male attention."

"Is that what you gave me last night—*the slightest bit of male attention*? Because I would have sworn it was more than that. Much more."

He lifted his hands as if to ward off a blow. "Please tell me you're not about to declare your undying love for me again. I'm flattered, but it's really growing a bit tiresome."

"Stop it!" she snapped. "You don't mean a word of what you're saying."

He cocked one tawny eyebrow at her. "Of course I do. I may have spent my formative years backstage at the theater, but I'm not *that* accomplished an actor. If I was, I'd be competing with some tenor in tights for the lead in *Don Giovanni* instead of standing out here arguing with you."

Catriona could no longer keep the tears from her eyes or the plea from her voice. "Why are you doing this?"

Simon crossed to her and tenderly cupped her cheek in his hand just as he had done that day in the barn. Now more than ever, his touch sent a shiver of irresistible yearning through her. "You're a beautiful girl, Cat. What man in his right mind wouldn't want to make love to you? I saw the opportunity and I took it. It may not have been the most scrupulous thing I've ever done, but there's really no need for tears or recriminations. In the end, we both got what we wanted."

"Did you?" she whispered, tasting salt as a tear trickled into the corner of her mouth. The mouth he had kissed with such unbridled passion throughout the endless night. "Is this what you want? Or is it what your father made you believe you deserve? What are you afraid of, Simon? Are you afraid I'll walk away from you just like your mother did? Is that why you let me—and all of those other women—into your bed but never your heart? So you can always be the one to walk away?"

He gave her cheek one last lingering caress, then turned away from her and did just that, leaving her with no choice but to let him go.

Chapter 19

imon felt an unexpected pang of grief
when Catriona emerged from the ruins
of Castle Kincaid looking every bit as proper and
reserved as she had on the day she had marched
into his jail cell. She wore a dove-gray walking
gown of sturdy merino. Her strawberry blond
curls were no longer loose and tumbling around
her shoulders, but confined beneath a prim little
bonnet with a brim that cast her eyes in shadow.
She might have been any London lady strolling
down Royal Street on a Saturday afternoon shopping expedition.

There was no sign of the girl who had stood
on the edge of that snow-swept cliff with arms
spread wide to embrace the world, no sign of the

woman who had kicked up her heels and danced a Highland reel to the joyous skirl of the bagpipes, no sign of the wild child who had warmed his bed and his heart throughout the long, sweet night.

She handed him her portmanteau without a word. Before he could toss it in the back of the wagon and offer her a hand, she had hiked up the hem of her skirt to reveal an enticing glimpse of lace-trimmed stocking and clambered up onto the wagon's bench without his assistance.

She stared straight ahead. "Is this going to cost me extra?"

"Pardon me?" he replied, wary of the clipped edges that had returned to her speech.

"Since returning me to my uncle's doorstep wasn't part of our bargain, I'd like to know ahead of time if I'm going to be expected to perform any extra *services* as payment."

Simon tried to clear his throat, but it turned into a full-blown cough as his lusty imagination provided painfully vivid images of several *services* he'd love for her to perform. "That won't be necessary," he told her when he could talk again. "You still have ample credit on account with me."

She folded her gloved hands in her lap. "I left Robert the Bruce in his crate. Would you mind fetching him?"

Only too eager to escape the arctic chill of her profile, Simon returned to the ruins of the great hall. Robert the Bruce huddled behind the slats of the chicken crate, looking utterly miserable at being deprived of his freedom.

Simon crouched down in front of the crate and looked him in the eye. "Sorry, big fellow. Having been in Newgate, I know exactly how you feel."

He was on the verge of picking up the crate when he caught a glimpse of something familiar out of the corner of his eye. It was Catriona's beloved plaid, tossed carelessly between two heaps of stone that had once been a corner.

Simon rescued the garment and draped it over his shoulder before carrying Robert the Bruce back to the wagon. After situating the chicken crate on the seat next to Catriona, he held out the plaid to her. "You left this behind."

Catriona continued to gaze straight ahead, ignoring his offering. She had treasured the sentimental scrap of fabric with every ounce of girlish devotion in her heart. But she wasn't that girl anymore. Simon had finally succeeded in making a woman of her—not by taking her to his bed, but by casting her out of it.

"I know I left it behind," she said briskly. "It's old and worn out. Why should I walk around draped in rags when my uncle can buy me all the shawls I need?"

Simon frowned. "But I thought it was all you had left of your family. Your brother."

Catriona swung around on the seat, giving Simon his first clear look at her face. Although her eyes still looked a little puffy, she had splashed away every last trace of tears from her cheeks. She was pale but resolute, each of her freckles standing out in stark relief. "My family is gone and so is my brother. Leave it, please. *I don't want it.*"

Simon slowly withdrew his hand, then walked around to the back of the wagon. He fingered the soft woolen folds of the plaid, unable to bring himself to toss it away like so much garbage. Catriona had lost so much in this place. Her dream of reuniting her clan. Her last scrap of faith in him. Her innocence.

After checking to make sure her attention was occupied by the cat, he gently folded the plaid and stuffed it beneath one of the bolts of tartan in the bed of the wagon.

He climbed up on the bench, noting that Catriona had resituated the crate so it would rest between them, abolishing any possibility of her thigh bumping against his or his elbow accidentally brushing the softness of her breast.

He flicked the reins on the horses' backs, urg-

ing them into motion. As the wagon jolted its
way down the rocky path that led to the road, it
was Simon who cast a glance over his shoulder
at the lonely tower standing sentinel over a pile
of rubble. Catriona continued to stare straight
ahead, not looking back even once as they left
the ruins of Castle Kincaid and all her dreams
behind them.

After suffering through three days of strained
silence and two nights of sharing a campfire
with Catriona but not a bedroll, Simon would
have given anything to hear her chattering on
and on about some particularly fetching red
squirrel or aspen tree. Her frosty demeanor was
agony to endure when he now knew just exactly
how *warm* she could be.

When they rolled into Edinburgh on the third
day, the boisterous noise of the carriages clattering over the cobblestones, the draymen swearing
at their massive wagons, and the street vendors
hawking their wares sounded like music to his
ears—a welcome reprieve from Catriona's stony
silence.

Already anticipating how heavenly it was going to feel to sleep in a real bed, he left her sitting
in the wagon while he went into the Cock of the
Walk Inn to arrange for their lodgings.

When he emerged, he was already dreading her reaction to his news. "We have a slight problem. I'm afraid they only have one room to let for the night."

"And why would that be a problem? We *are* still man and wife, you know. At least until the bishop declares otherwise." As Catriona offered him her gloved hand so he could help her climb down from the wagon, he realized it was the first time she had allowed him to touch her since they'd left the castle.

Simon's hopes for a bed were not to be realized. Catriona and Robert the Bruce claimed the handsome four-poster the minute they sashayed into the room. Unlike the modest bedstead in Gretna Green, there would have been ample room for all of them had Catriona been inclined toward generosity. Since she was not, Simon was left to spread a wool blanket over the rather musty-smelling rug in front of the hearth.

While Catriona and her cat cuddled beneath the fluffy down counterpane, Simon lay on his back on the floor with his hands behind his head, listening to the cozy crackling of the fire and trying not to think about how badly he ached to sink into both the feather mattress and his wife.

He supposed he should be grateful that she hadn't made him sleep in the stables with the nags.

The sound of her tossing about on the mattress and rustling between the sheets, then sighing with contentment, only added to his torment.

He had nearly drifted off to sleep when one of those sighs was followed by, "I've been thinking about our little bargain, Mr. Wescott, and I suppose I should be grateful to you."

"You should?" Simon replied, his eyes popping wide open.

"I most certainly should. After all, how many women can claim they were tutored in the arts of love by one of the most legendary lovers in all of England?"

"There's no need to flatter me," he replied with mock seriousness. "All of *London* will do. I've heard there's a fellow in Bath who can tie a knot in a cherry stem with his tongue with his hands tied behind his back."

"Hmmmm," she said after a thoughtful pause. "Perhaps I can talk Uncle Ross into summering there."

Scowling, Simon propped himself up on one elbow.

"I'm sure my next husband will appreciate all of the skills I learned from you, especially that clever little trick you taught me to do with my mouth."

He would have sworn he wasn't the jealous sort, but the thought of her putting that mouth on another man made Simon want to hunt down that shadowy figure from her future and kill him where he stood.

"Or perhaps I won't ever marry again," she added cheerfully. "After spending time with you, I can certainly see how it must be quite liberating to take a succession of lovers without suffering any of the ridiculous foibles of love. All pleasure and no pain, as it were."

If that was true, Simon thought, then why did both his head and his heart feel as if they were about to explode?

He sat up. He might have been away from the gaming tables for well over a fortnight, but he hadn't forgotten how to call his opponent's bluff.

"Perhaps it's not too late for you to take advantage of me," he suggested, rising to his feet.

Catriona was reclining against the pillows with Robert the Bruce curled up at her feet. As he padded toward the bed, she shrank against the headboard, her wary eyes gleaming in the firelight. She'd tried to tame her curls into two neat braids, but several of them had escaped to riot around her face.

"Whatever do you mean?" she asked as his shadow fell over her.

"I'm offering you the chance to take full advantage of my knowledge. Over the years I've discovered there are very few skills within the arts of love that can't be improved with diligent practice." He touched one fingertip to the flawless Cupid's bow at the top of her lips, then followed it around to the plump pillow of her bottom lip. "Including those involving that beautiful mouth of yours."

She closed her eyes briefly and drew in a shaky breath, an enchanting blush rising in her cheeks. "Weren't you the one who told me that enthusiasm counted for more than skill?"

"Indeed it does," he said, lowering his voice to a husky whisper. "But just think how irresistible you'll be if you can bring both to the table."

Simon brushed his lips against hers before he could confess that she was already irresistible. If not, he wouldn't be drinking of the honeyed sweetness of her mouth again, wouldn't be straining against the front of his trousers with such force that he could almost hear the seams ripping, wouldn't be about to make the second biggest mistake of his life.

As he lowered himself into her open arms, Catriona stretched out her foot and nudged Robert the Bruce right out of the bed.

Catriona awoke on her stomach with one arm dangling over the foot of the bed. She lifted her head, shaking her tousled hair out of her eyes. Sunlight was streaming through the window, warming the curves of her naked body. Robert the Bruce was eyeing her malevolently from the blanket in front of the hearth.

"I'm sorry, old boy," she whispered. "You know I'll always love you best."

He gave her the cut direct by lifting one paw for an aloof lick, no more convinced by her lie than she was.

She rolled to her back with a gusty sigh to find her husband sprawled crossways across the feather mattress beside her, lightly snoring.

She propped herself up on one elbow, a helpless smile curving her lips. The morning sunlight gilded every inch of Simon's lean, well-muscled frame—from the whiskers that were beginning to stubble his jaw to the long, narrow planes of his feet.

She supposed he had earned his rest. He certainly hadn't allowed either one of them any sleep during the long, luscious hours of the night. It was as if he were determined to wring every last drop of pleasure from her, leaving her limp and sated and utterly in his thrall.

At one point during the night he had left her lolling in the bed—still half dazed by their most recent coupling—while he slipped into his trousers and went downstairs to beg some fresh strawberries and a dish of cream from the innkeeper. She had thought it all madness until she discovered just what he intended to do with them.

A crooked smile touched her lips. She had never dreamed that love could be so sticky and so sweet all at the same time.

He had taught her any number of lessons in the arts of love during the night, the most decadent of them involving the bedposts and a pair of her silk stockings. The very memory sent a dark shudder of delight through her, especially when she remembered how she had taken her own revenge after he was through with her and she had wriggled free of her bonds.

She had been baiting him deliberately last night, only to end up tumbling recklessly into her own trap. She had thought to give him a tantalizing taste of exactly what he would be missing for the rest of his life, not realizing until it was too late that she was the one who wouldn't be able to resist feasting on him one last time.

She smoothed a lock of hair from his brow, her smile fading. Although she had desperately wanted to believe otherwise, he was the same boy she had fallen in love with all of those years ago. He was beautiful. He was tender. He was utterly ruthless when it came to pursuing what he desired. And he would always choose the pleasures of making love over the perils of falling in love.

She leaned over and touched her lips to the scar on his brow, already regretting that she couldn't be more like him.

When Simon awoke near noon to find both Catriona and her cat gone, he refused to panic as he had the morning after their wedding. He scrubbed his teeth and took his time washing up and dressing. He ran his fingers through his hair, giving it the artfully disheveled look most women seemed to prefer. He tied a knot in his cravat with deliberate care, pausing to admire his reflection in the looking glass over the washbasin.

He was confident that when he went downstairs, Catriona would be waiting for him, tapping her little booted foot impatiently as she berated him for sleeping half the day away.

But what he found instead was the red-faced innkeeper holding out a folded piece of vellum sealed with a dab of cheap wax. "Yer lady asked me to give this to ye as soon as ye came downstairs."

Simon took the missive, turning away before he could see the pity in the man's eyes. He walked out onto the pavement, utterly oblivious to the jostling crowds or the vehicles clattering over the cobblestones only a few feet away as he unfolded Catriona's neatly penned note and read:

My dear Mr. Wescott,

Your services (while every bit as impressive as rumored) are no longer required. Robert the Bruce and I have decided to take the mail coach back to London. We'll be able to travel twice the distance in half the time. My uncle will be in touch with you as soon as the arrangements for the dissolution of our marriage have been completed. Until then, I am . . .

Catriona Kincaid Wescott

Simon gently folded the letter and tucked it inside his waistcoat next to his heart, telling himself it was for the best. Catriona had spared them those awkward parting moments they might have endured in London. There would be no need to apologize for not making promises he could never hope to keep, no need to murmur endearments he would be whispering in another woman's ear before the week was out, no need to touch his lips to hers in a kiss they both knew would be their last.

He ought to be grateful to her for behaving with such maturity and sophistication.

So why did he feel exactly as he had on the day his mother had left him on the doorstep of her solicitor's office?

It was his eldest daughter's bloodcurdling screech that first alerted Roscommon Kincaid to the arrival of the mail coach. Although the unearthly sound was one he had been hearing ever since Alice had been in napkins and realized it would make anyone within earshot give her whatever she wanted just to make it stop, it still made him grit his teeth and itch to clap his hands over his ears.

Leaving an ugly blot of ink on the accounts ledger he had been reviewing, he jumped to his feet and barreled from the study, moving with remarkable alacrity for a man of his girth.

He supposed he ought to be grateful for any break in the monotony, no matter how vexing. Ever since Catriona had eloped with that scoundrel, it had been deadly dull around the estate. He'd managed to escape to the stables for a few hours to witness the birth of a new foal, but most of his time had been spent trapped in the house listening to his wife prattle on and on about her latest piece of needlework while Alice mooned over some comely young buck she'd met at Lady Enderley's ball last week.

He hadn't realized how much he enjoyed verbally sparring with his quick-witted niece until she was gone. Now he had no one to debate Scottish rights with him or argue that Bonnie Prince Charlie might have been able to hold on to the Scottish throne if he hadn't ignored the battle advice of his best commander and chosen to fight on open, marshy ground. He hadn't even had a decent game of chess since Catriona left.

As he reached the entrance hall, an underfootman rushed in front of him and threw open the front door, plainly fearing he was on the verge of charging right through it.

His wife was standing on the steps of the sunny portico, a handkerchief pressed to her lips. Alice stood at the bottom of the steps, pointing at the tree-lined drive.

At this distance, her screeching was slightly more coherent, if not any more pleasing to the ears. "It's her, Papa! It's *her*, I tell you! The horrid little beast has come back to ruin all of our lives, just as she did the first time!"

Ross blinked at the dusty mail coach parked in his drive, wondering if he'd dozed off at his desk and somehow traveled back through the years. A slender girl was alighting from the back of the coach, her bonnet slightly squashed, her gown rumpled and travel-stained, a smudge of dirt on her cheek and a disgruntled-looking cat in her arms.

He drifted down the steps toward her, still doubting his senses. "Catriona? Child, is that you?"

She lifted her chin to offer him a tremulous smile. "Hello, Uncle Ross. I've come home."

Before he had time to absorb that startling bit of information, she burst into tears and flung herself into his arms.

Chapter 20

"They say 'e 'as a cock like a battering ram, you know."

"Oooh, do they, now? It's a shame 'e didn't marry 'im a wife who knew what to do with it. I 'eard he could pop a woman's corset strings just by lookin' at 'er, if you know wot I mean."

"Ha! My Billy 'as been lookin' for my corset strings for nigh on three years now and still 'asn't found 'em. I gotta pluck 'em myself if I want 'em popped!"

"I also 'eard one woman weren't enough for 'im. That it took two at a time to satisfy 'is ferocious appetites."

"That wouldn't be a problem, would it? As long as one o' them was you and one o' them was me."

As the young parlor maids dissolved into lusty gales of laughter, Catriona cleared her throat sharply and stepped into the drawing room.

The maids' ruddy faces went even redder. One of them snatched up a feather duster and began to wave it over a pier table, while the other one bobbed up and down in a graceless curtsy. "G'day, miss. We was just going."

"I dare say you were," Catriona replied frostily as they ducked out of the room, nearly tripping over each other's feet in their haste to escape.

As they scurried toward the kitchens, their muffled giggles floated back to her burning ears.

It wasn't the first time in the past month she'd entered a room to overhear the servants whispering about her and her scandalous marriage. She was rapidly growing tired of skulking around her own home, dodging snickering maids and leering gardeners. Those who could read had gleaned the details of her impending annulment from the more lurid scandal sheets. The others were content to get their gossip secondhand, while browsing the vegetables at the village market or smoking around the kitchen fire after their duties were done.

Just as she'd predicted when she proposed her plan to Simon, *she* was the laughingstock of the city, not him. No one could believe she was dissolving her union with one of the most shameless Lotharios in London because he had failed to perform his marital duties to her satisfaction. Several courtesans and women of ill repute had already come forward in the scandal sheets, gleefully offering to testify on his behalf.

Fortunately for all of them, that would not be necessary. Thanks to her uncle's influence and the church's public loathing of Gretna Green weddings, the bishop had agreed to grant them an annulment by the end of the month. Since the banns had never been read and their union had been blessed by a blacksmith, not a clergyman, it could easily be argued before the ecclesiastical council that it was not properly sanctioned by God.

Normally the annulment process took three years, at the end of which time the court could appoint two of the most highly skilled courtesans in the land to *test* the groom's virility. It wasn't difficult for Catriona to envision the disastrous outcome of *that* particular challenge.

To ensure her uncle's cooperation, she had been forced to tell him everything that had transpired between her and Simon. Well, almost everything. She had neglected to mention that they had consummated their little sham of a marriage, not once, but twice. Or numerous times, if one counted each event separately.

There was much speculation, both in drawing rooms throughout the city and between the pages of the scandal sheets regarding the nature of her own obvious *failings*. Was she so cold that a man's touch failed to warm her? Had she caught her bridegroom in bed with another woman on their honeymoon and decided to take her revenge by besmirching both his manhood and his reputation? Some had even dared to insinuate that perhaps it was a woman she preferred in her bed, because surely no female with *natural* inclinations would be able to resist the carnal charms of a man like Simon Wescott.

Catriona wandered around the elegantly appointed drawing room, oblivious to the radiance of the sunlight spilling through the tall French windows. Soon it would be as if she had never been Mrs. Simon Wescott. Never spent two glorious nights in his arms and his bed.

Until a fortnight ago, she had harbored the secret hope that those nights might have borne fruit. She had even allowed herself to entertain a fantasy that had Simon strolling into some London ballroom to find her heavy with his child. But the arrival of her monthly courses had destroyed that hope and given her a painful reminder that dreams such as those belonged to the naïve girl she had been, not the woman she had become at Simon's hands.

Trying to ignore the piercing ache in her heart, she wandered over to the bookshelf. With the last of the Kincaids scattered to the four winds, she could no longer take comfort in the Scottish ballads collected by Sir Walter Scott. Against her better judgment, she slid a slim volume of Robert Burns's poetry off the shelf. She flipped restlessly through the pages until a familiar stanza caught her eye:

> *As fair art thou, my bonnie lass,*
> *So deep in luve am I;*
> *And I will love thee still, my Dear*
> *Till a' the seas gang dry.*

The page blurred before her eyes. Catriona slammed the book shut, remembering how Simon had recited those very words to her with such tender conviction in the ruins of the great hall at Castle Kincaid. When she had been gazing into his smoky green eyes, it had been easy to believe he spoke from the heart. But now she knew they were only pretty words—designed to win a heart, but not keep it.

She shoved the volume of poetry back on the

shelf and took another restless turn around the room. With any luck, she would perish from boredom before her broken heart killed her. She feared it was only a matter of time before she started pasting seashells on pieces of colored paper or stitching hackneyed homilies on samplers like Aunt Margaret.

She was almost beginning to regret not accepting Georgina's invitation to visit Georgina and her husband at their town house in London. But she knew the gossip would be even more virulent there, the jests at her expense more difficult to ignore. She was already dreading traveling there at the end of the month to appear before the ecclesiastical council.

Footsteps sounded in the corridor. She turned eagerly toward the door, absurdly grateful for the interruption.

A liveried footman appeared in the doorway. Inclining his bewigged head, he said, "There's a gentleman to see you, madam."

She could not stop her heart from leaping with hope. Smoothing her skirts, she fixed a shaky smile on her lips and said, "Send him in, please."

The footman stepped aside, intoning, "The Marquess of Eddingham."

Catriona's heart plunged right back down to

her toes as Eddingham swept into the room, carrying his walking stick in his white-gloved hand. His smug smile was every bit as infuriating as she remembered.

"Shall I ring for some tea?" the footman asked.

"That won't be necessary," she replied, giving their uninvited guest a frosty look. "The marquess won't be staying for tea."

"Very well, madam."

As the servant bowed his way out of the room, it was all she could do not to grab him by the ear and command him to stay. She would have welcomed a chaperone, but now that she was a matron, they did not require one.

Eddingham sketched her a graceful bow. "Miss Kincaid."

"That would be Mrs. Wescott, my lord."

"Ah, yes." His dark eyes sparkled with malicious amusement. "But not for much longer, from what I hear."

When she didn't offer him a seat, he sauntered over and sank down on the settee, propping one boot on the opposite knee. She reluctantly took the chair across from him. She folded her hands in her lap and gazed at him sullenly, not caring in the least if he found her totally lacking in social graces.

He was the first to break the awkward silence. "I thought you might like to know that I've just returned from the Highlands."

"Indeed? I trust the fresh air was a boon to your disposition."

"I found it to be quite invigorating. I thought you might also be interested to learn that there was no need to flush those pesky Kincaids or their outlaw leader off my land. Apparently they were so lacking in spirit that they scattered like frightened sheep at the mere mention of my name."

"I've heard you have that effect on women as well."

His smile showed signs of fraying around the edges. "You disappoint me. I had hoped that matrimony might have tamed that haughty tongue of yours."

"Not every man finds it necessary to cow a woman's spirit just to compensate for his own lack of it."

He sighed. "Contrary to what you may have been led to believe about me, I am not a petty man, *Miss Kincaid*," he said, his tongue deliberately caressing the name. "I've always taken great pride in not holding a grudge."

"That's very comforting, given that during our last exchange you expressed the passionate wish that I might burn in hell."

He continued as if she hadn't spoken. "When I heard of your recent *misfortune*, I immediately asked myself how I could be of assistance."

Catriona was beginning to regret declining the footman's offer. She would have loved a pot of hot tea to dump in Eddingham's lap. "How very benevolent of you."

"I plan on returning to the Highlands within the next fortnight to demolish the pile of rubble that sits on my land. It's nothing but an eyesore and my advisers have assured me that the land can be easily transformed into prime grazing for a flock of Cheviot sheep."

In the blink of an eye, Catriona saw the lone remaining tower of Castle Kincaid silhouetted against a starlit sky, heard the majestic song of the bagpipes soaring into the night, felt Simon's hands on her bare skin as he laid her back on a bed of moss and made her his wife in more than name only.

"I don't see why that should concern me," she said stiffly. "My uncle assured you that we were no relation to the Highland Kincaids."

His voice softened. "It should concern you because I was hoping to take you with me."

She blinked stupidly, hoping she'd misheard him. "Surely you're not trying to propose to me again."

His laugh was short and unpleasant. "Oh, I don't think you'll find any fool willing to wed you now. Your sordid association with Wescott has tarnished your reputation beyond repair. You're damaged goods, Miss Kincaid, and unless you decide to embrace a life of spinsterhood or ply your wares on the street, the most you can hope for is to become the mistress of some wealthy man before you go to fat or your looks begin to fade."

Catriona didn't realize she'd stopped breathing until tiny little dots appeared in front of her eyes. "Are you hoping to be that man, my lord?"

He pursed his lips in a regretful little moue. "It wouldn't do to be seen with you on my arm in London, of course, but I can build you a pleasant little cottage on my land in the Highlands and visit you there when I grow bored of town life. I think you'll find that I can be a very generous master . . . if you strive to please me, that is." He lowered his gaze to the swell of her bosom, one gloved hand caressing the shaft of his walking stick. "And I can promise you that, unlike Wescott, I'm definitely *up* to the task of pleasing you."

Catriona simply stared at him for a moment before smiling sweetly. "Oh, my husband pleased me very much. He has a cock like a battering ram, you know."

Eddingham's gaze flew back to her face. "Pardon me?"

His strangled words devolved into a violent fit of coughing, giving Catriona another reason to regret not serving tea. If he had been nibbling on a crumpet, he would have sucked it right into his lungs.

"That's right." She sighed wistfully. "Why, my Simon could pop my corset strings just by looking at me. As long as he was around, I never had to worry about plucking them myself." She blinked at him innocently. "I've often heard it said that it took two women to satisfy his ferocious appetites, but he assured me that I was all the woman he needed."

The marquess sprang to his feet, his face going from bright pink to scarlet with rage. He was gripping his walking stick as if he'd like nothing better than to flog her with it. "You may be a woman," he snarled, "but you're no lady."

She rose to face him. "And you, sir, are no gentleman."

"A fact you'd do well to remember if we ever cross paths again." Giving her one last sneer, he strode toward the door.

"Don't worry, *Ed*," she called after him. "I'll do my best to stay off the riding trails at Hyde Park."

Eddingham froze a few steps from the doorway, then slowly turned, all the color draining from his face.

"Oh, Simon told me all about your poor fiancée's unfortunate accident. What a terrible tragedy that must have been! She was so young, so beautiful . . . so very devoted to you."

The marquess didn't say another word. He simply turned and stalked from the room, the tails of his coat flapping behind him.

Catriona's knees didn't betray her until she heard the distant slam of the front door. She collapsed into the chair and clapped a hand over her mouth, torn between laughing and crying.

"Oh, Simon," she whispered. "How you would have enjoyed that!"

Simon hadn't enjoyed anything for a very long while.

Oh, he went through the motions—prowling through the gambling hells in Pall Mall and off of St. James's until the wee hours of the morning, laughing at the ribald jokes made at his expense, and accepting the toasts to his legendary prowess with a lusty grin and a round of drinks for the house.

As for himself, he hadn't had more than a few sips of wine since his drunkenness had nearly cost Catriona her life. As long as he had remained deep in his cups, the jokes had been hilarious, the women beautiful, the games thrilling. Without the glowing haze of intoxication to soften its seedy edges, he felt like a stranger in his own life—an actor portraying the role of incorrigible rakehell to please his adoring audience.

In a perverse twist of fate, he couldn't seem to stop winning at the tables. He'd paid off all of his creditors and still managed to parlay what was left of Catriona's dowry into a small fortune. The Simon Wescott of old already would have squandered most of it at the tailor's or purchased some gaudy bauble to woo a woman into his bed. But less than a week ago, he had found himself lingering outside the barred windows of a banking establishment. Before he had even realized what he was going to do, there was an account with his name on it and a rapidly growing balance.

Although no one would have guessed it from his suave demeanor, he was in a particularly savage temper on the night he strolled into one of his favorite haunts in Pickering Place.

I should be celebrating, he thought as he wended his way through the haze of stale cigar smoke that hung over the room, his eye on the faro table. In just a few days, the bishop would grant Catriona her annulment. He would be a free

man once again. Free to gamble all night, free to
swill liquor until dawn, free to take any woman
he wanted to his bed.

Any woman but his wife.

He inhaled a choking lungful of the smoke,
suddenly feeling as if someone had strapped an
iron band around his chest. He would have sworn
he hadn't taken a single decent breath since returning from the Highlands. He was too con-
scious of the black clouds of soot belching from
chimneys and hovering over the city, the hint of
sewage whenever he passed a narrow alleyway,
the cloying perfumes of the women who flocked
around him every time he walked into a room.

As Catriona had so aptly predicted, her ridiculous accusation had only enhanced his reputation. Everywhere he went, he was besieged by
women only too eager to prove her a liar.

One of those women was heading his way at
that very moment. He slid into a chair at the faro
table, giving the other men gathered around it a
curt nod. He recognized the approaching woman
as a randy courtesan with a fondness for whist
and the dangerous habit of settling her debts
with her sexual favors. As she slipped up behind
him and twined her pale, powdered arms around
his neck, he could still smell the scent of the last
man she had taken to her bed.

"Hullo, Simon. I was hoping you'd be here to-night. I've missed you terribly and I'm in the mood for some *deep play*," she purred, imbuing the innocent words with a meaning never intended by the wide-eyed dealer.

As the man popped a card from the faro box and flipped it onto the felt-lined table, Simon said, "I'm afraid the only play I'm interested in tonight is right here at this table."

"You're just trying to make me beg, aren't you?" She touched the tip of her tongue to his earlobe, her hands wandering farther south with each word. "I remember how much you always liked it when I begged."

As her small, greedy hand cupped his crotch, his body reacted reflexively to her touch. But instead of the familiar rush of lust, all he felt was mild distaste tinged with pity.

Shooting the dealer a sheepish look, he caught her wrist and gently disengaged her. "Now, don't be naughty, Angela. You know very well that I'm a married man."

She snorted. "I wish your wife was here right now. I'd like to give her a piece of my mind. Then she could come upstairs with us and I'd show the lying little baggage how a real woman pleas-ures her man."

Simon turned to look at her, something in his

frank gaze making her take a step away from the table.

"Well," she said, while patting her upswept cinnamon-colored curls, "I'll leave you to your game for now. If you change your mind, I'll be over at the whist table."

When Simon glanced over at the whist table a few minutes later, she was already licking another man's ear.

He slid a slender cigar out of his waistcoat pocket and allowed the dealer to light it. If he was going to be stuck breathing the stuff all night, it might as well be fresh.

He was just beginning to settle into the rhythms of the game when a man's shadow fell over the table.

Simon glanced up, blowing a stream of smoke from his nostrils. "Philo Wilcox," he drawled. "The last time I saw you, you were running across a meadow after I shot you in the arse for cheating at this very table."

Philo settled himself gingerly into the chair next to him, still favoring his left buttock. "I couldn't sit down for months. That was rather unsporting of you, don't you think?"

"No more unsporting than you sprinting for the trees in the middle of a duel. Would you have preferred I shot you in the head?"

Philo sniffed, his long face growing even longer. "It might have spared me the indignity of being labeled a cheater and a coward."

"But you *were* a cheater and a coward," Simon pointed out, flicking a bead of ash off his cigar.

"And now, thanks to you, everyone knows it." Philo cast a furtive look over his shoulder. "If the proprietor catches me in here, he'll have me tossed out on my ear."

"Then I suggest you take your leave before I'm forced to call him over."

Philo's pout shifted to a horsey grin. He clapped Simon on the shoulder. "Oh, don't be that way, old friend. I was hoping you might help me turn my luck around."

"How? By offering you a pillow to sit on?"

"Well, you see—it's like this. Me and some other young bucks have made a wager in the book over at White's on which one of us will be the first to bed your bride after you bust out of her leg shackles."

The cigar dangled from Simon's lips, completely forgotten.

Lowering his voice, Philo leaned closer. "No matter what she claims, we know you broke her in right and proper. After the appropriate amount of time has passed—maybe a fortnight—we thought she'd be eager for some more saddle-play. Since

I put all my money on me, I was hoping I might be able to coax you into arranging a little introduction. If she's still speaking to you, that is."

One minute Philo was smirking at Simon. The next he was flat on his back on the floor with blood trickling from the corner of his mouth and Simon standing over him, fists clenched and the knuckles of his right hand still stinging.

"Hey! That wasn't very sporting of you either!" Rubbing his jaw, Philo started to get up, but when Simon snarled and raised his fists again, he settled back on the floor, plainly deciding it was the wisest course of action.

Through the roaring in his ears Simon could hear the echo of Catriona's voice: *Is there anything worth fighting for in your eyes? Anything worth dying for? Anything noble enough or dear enough to justify risking your precious neck?*

He'd been searching his entire life for that very thing, only to turn his back and walk away when he'd finally found it. He had been afraid to believe, never realizing that Catriona had enough courage and faith for the both of them, enough love in her beautiful, generous heart for even a scoundrel like him.

As Simon's lips curved in an exultant grin, Philo whimpered and lifted his hands to block his face. But Simon simply turned on his heel and started for the door, determined to fight for what he wanted for the first time in his life.

His path was blocked by a massive bull of a man. The hulking fellow was so blistered he was already swaying on his feet. "Hey, you! What'd you do to Philo? He's my friend!"

Simon's eyes widened as they traveled up, up, up to the man's gargantuan head. Apparently God, with His delicious sense of irony, was going to give him a chance to prove his devotion to Catriona by dying while defending her honor right here on the floor of this seedy gambling haunt.

As the man swung one ham-handed fist at his head, Simon ducked, thinking what a damn shame it was that she would never know of his sacrifice.

Enraged by the near-miss, the behemoth grabbed Simon by the cravat and jerked him off his feet like a rag doll. He was drawing back his colossal fist for a blow that probably would have dislodged every tooth in Simon's head when Angela sprang up from the whist table and flung herself on his back with a feline yowl.

Yanking at the fellow's hair with both hands, she shrieked, "Don't you hit his pretty face or I'll tear your ugly mug right off with my fingernails!"

Another fellow jumped up from the hazard table. "You there! Don't you dare hit a lady!"

Simon was too busy trying to choke in a strangled breath to point out that Angela was neither a lady nor in any danger of being hit. On the contrary, it was his attacker who appeared to be in imminent danger as she wrapped one arm around his thick neck and sank her sharp little teeth into his ear.

He roared with pain and released his death grip on Simon's cravat. All hell broke loose.

Tables, dice and cards went spilling over as the club erupted in a full-out brawl. It no longer mattered whose side anyone was on. There was only the primitive joy of fists meeting flesh, chairs and bodies flying through the air and the satisfying crunch of bone against bone.

Simon ducked a flying chair. Out of the corner of his eye he spotted Philo scurrying toward the door on hands and knees. Unable to resist the temptation, he ducked through the melee, arriving at the front door just in time to give Philo a sharp kick in the rear. He went sailing out the door with a girlish squeal.

Simon was dusting off his hands when a man jerked him around by the sleeve of his coat and drew back a beefy fist.

Simon held up both hands. "Not the face, please."

The man nodded politely, then buried his fist in Simon's stomach.

Simon doubled over with a pained grunt. "Thank you," he wheezed out before ramming the top of his head into the man's chin. He followed that with a wicked right-left combination he'd perfected while sparring at Gentleman Jackson's, laying his opponent out flat.

Before he had time to savor that triumph, a chair came down across the back of his head, splintering beneath the force. He dropped to his knees, a shower of stars exploding in his vision. He was still trying to shake them away when a wiry, sun-bronzed hand appeared in front of him.

Wary of any offer of help, he squinted suspiciously up at his potential savior. Kieran Kincaid's rawboned visage slowly came into focus.

He blinked. He must have taken a much harder blow to the skull than he realized. But if he had to hallucinate, why couldn't it have been a smiling Catriona bending over him instead of her surly clansman?

Kieran wrapped a hand around his arm and hauled him to his feet with surprising strength.

Rubbing the back of his head, Simon scowled

at him. "Where in the bloody hell did you come from?"

"Scotland," Kieran replied shortly. "Before that, me mum said I was just a twinkle in me da's eye."

"How did you find me?"

Kieran shrugged. "To be honest, it wasn't much of a challenge. All we had to do was visit every brothel, alehouse and hellhole in London. It's been real rough on me and the lads."

As a freckled boy in a grubby tunic went sailing headfirst out the door, Simon realized that Kieran hadn't come alone. At least a dozen of the Kincaid clan had slipped into the club and gleefully joined the fray.

"I heard ye were lettin' Catriona give ye the boot." Kieran shook his head in disgust. "And I thought *she* was daft. Ye're a bluidy fool, Wescott, to lose a lass so fine."

Simon jerked his cravat straight. "You're one to point fingers. You were fool enough to let her go too."

"I know I did. That's why I'm here. To get her back."

The two men eyed each other thoughtfully, realizing they just might have more in common than they realized.

"I've been thinkin' of her more as a sister or a

cousin, but if ye don't want her," Kieran added casually, "I just might ask her to be *my* bride."

Before he even realized he was going to do it, Simon had grabbed Kieran by the front of his tunic and slammed him up against the nearest wall.

The Highlander's lips curved in a rare grin. "I allus did want me a sister."

Chapter 21

"If you'll wait here, I'll inform your father of your arrival," the aged butler said stiffly, disapproval all but oozing from his pores.

"Thank you," Simon replied solemnly. "I'll try not to steal anything."

The servant gave him a withering look before shuffling from the room. Unable to resist the childish urge, Simon poked his tongue out at the man's bony back.

He sighed, knowing he would have ample time to rob his father blind if he were so inclined. The duke had always delighted in keeping his inferiors waiting, considering it a privilege of his rank.

The butler would have been surprised to learn

that his greatest temptation wasn't to pocket one of his father's silver candle snuffers but to bolt for the door. After attending his brother's burial, he had hoped never to set foot in this house again. He'd never excelled at swallowing his pride to please his father, much preferring to take a beating at some footman's beefy hands.

Linking his hands at the small of his back, he took a turn around the room. It had been many years since he'd been allowed into the sanctuary of his father's library.

Everything was much as he remembered. The imposing octagonal room had floors of gleaming rose marble imported directly from Italy. A priceless Aubusson carpet that was dragged outside for a daily beating rested in the center of the floor. There wasn't a speck of dust to be found on any of the marble busts or *objets d'art* displayed proudly throughout the room. The only items that showed signs of neglect were the books that lined the mahogany shelves.

His father's massive desk, where discipline and punishment had been meted out with equal zeal, still dominated the chamber. Simon had been summoned there on many an occasion—for lectures, scoldings, stern dressing-downs, and for the occasional caning when his father's temper got the best of him. In truth, those were the only times his father ever really looked at him. As long as Simon was misbehaving, the duke couldn't ignore his existence. But he also couldn't be bothered to beat Simon himself and would order one of the servants to do it for him.

A huge gilt-framed portrait of Richard—resplendent in his scarlet army uniform—hung over the mantel. Simon knew he wouldn't find even so much as a miniature of himself tucked away in some forgotten corner of a bookshelf.

Despite Richard's petty—and unfounded—jealousy of him, Simon had always looked up to him. Richard was older, stronger, the apple of their father's eye. But as he gazed up at the portrait, he frowned. It was almost as if he were seeing his brother for the first time. Why had he never noticed the rounded slope of Richard's shoulders, the weakness of his chin, the squinty hint of cruelty in his pale brown eyes?

"A remarkable likeness, is it not?" his father said from somewhere behind him.

"Indeed. I almost feel as if he could reach out and box my ears."

Simon turned to face his father. Although they hadn't seen each other in over three years, he was still shocked by how much his father had aged. His handsome mane of white hair was beginning to thin at the brow and crown. His gout must have worsened as well because he was using a cane to hobble around the desk.

"I trust this won't take long," his father said, sinking into his thronelike chair. Once it had added to his regal stature; now it seemed to dwarf him. "I'm assuming you need money to pay off some overzealous creditor or pregnant doxy. I was hoping your little stint in Newgate might do you some good. Build character and all that rot. Then I heard you'd run off with that mad Scots girl. I'm not surprised *that* ended in disaster. Everyone knows the Scots are a notoriously depraved and untrustworthy lot."

He opened a drawer and drew out a leather-bound box. Flipping open the lid, he asked, "So how much do you need? A hundred pounds? Five hundred?"

Simon reached over and closed the lid, gently but firmly. "I don't want your money. You know very well that I've never asked you for so much as a farthing. I've always made my own way in this world."

"I did purchase you a commission in the navy," his father reminded him.

"To get me out from under your feet and to keep me from tarnishing your good name any more than I already had."

"It didn't work on either count, did it?"

Simon reached into his coat, drew out a folded sheet of stationery and handed it to his father.

His father snapped it open, scanned it quickly, then glanced back at Simon, hiking one snowy white eyebrow. "Do you really expect me to do this?"

Simon leaned over, planting both palms on the desk. "It's the last thing I'll ever ask of you. If you do it, you'll never have to lay eyes on me again."

"In that case," his father said briskly, looking him dead in the eye, "consider it done."

Simon straightened and started to turn away, ridiculously relieved to escape his father's presence. But then he realized this would be his last chance to ask the question that had haunted him since he was a boy in this house.

He turned back to the desk. "Why did you hate my mother so much?"

"Already going back on your word, are you? As I recall, you just promised me that this"—his father tapped the piece of stationery—"was the last thing you'd ever ask of me."

Simon shook his head at his own foolishness and strode toward the door, as eager to be free of this place as his father was to be rid of him.

He was only a few steps from that freedom when his father spoke, his voice so low Simon almost didn't hear him. "I didn't hate your mother. I adored her."

Simon slowly turned and drifted back toward the desk, each step taken as if in a dream. His father was reaching into the watch pocket of his waistcoat and withdrawing a shiny brass fob. A locket dangled from the end of it.

He offered the locket to Simon with a palsied hand. Simon took it and snapped it open to find a miniature of his mother tucked into the oval frame. She looked exactly as he remembered her—her lustrous blond hair curling around her face, her cheeks dimpled in a teasing smile, her eyes twinkling with mischief.

His father's eyes had gone curiously misty. "My wife turned me out of her bed after Richard was conceived. She felt she'd done her duty by providing me with an heir." He shrugged. "She could barely endure that part of our relationship anyway.

"Then I met your mother at the theater one night. I never meant for anything to happen between us, but she was so beautiful, so funny, so warm . . . so loving. I wanted to leave my wife. I begged your mother to run away with me. But she refused, saying it would create a terrible scandal that would ruin me and my family's good name forever. She swore she loved me, yet she sent me away that night and told me to never come back."

"What if she believed she was doing what was best for you, even if it broke her own heart?" Simon asked, echoing the words Catriona had once said to him.

As his father lifted his eyes, the mist in them faded, leaving only contempt. "Every time I looked at you, I saw her and I remembered the night she sent me away." He pounded his fist weakly on the desk, looking more like a petulant child than like one of the most powerful men in London. "She was a selfish, cruel, heartless woman! It wasn't right for her to keep you from me for all those years. By the time she sent you here, you were nothing more than a stranger!"

"I was never a stranger, Father," Simon said softly. "I was always your son."

Slipping the miniature into his own pocket, he turned and walked out of his father's library for the last time.

Catriona stood on the landing at the top of the ballroom steps, fighting the desperate urge to duck behind a potted palm. The Argyle Rooms boasted one of the most beautiful ballrooms in London. The elegant theater was over a hundred feet long. A grand screen of Corinthian columns lined the walls, supporting the cove of a ceiling painted to resemble the sky. The ethereal blue daubed with fluffy white clouds reminded her of the Highland sky on a spring day.

She closed her eyes briefly, trying not to remember that at that very moment Eddingham and his men might be reducing to rubble all that was left of her ancestral home.

A half dozen cut-glass chandeliers, each containing a dozen pink wax lights, cast a soft glow over the milling crush below. Some of the ballroom's occupants were dancing an intricate minuet to the genteel strains of Mozart wafting out from the orchestra. Others were clustered in cozy groups, fluttering their fans and sipping punch from crystal goblets. A few black-garbed dowagers were hunched over in the chairs lining the walls, whispering to each other and squinting disapprovingly through their quizzing glasses at the young people who were laughing too loudly or dancing too closely.

And in just a few minutes, they would all be whispering about her.

Catriona drew in a sharp breath and flattened a hand against her corset-clad waist, wondering how she could have allowed Georgina and Uncle Ross to talk her into this madness. When they had first presented the idea to her, she would have sworn it had merit. Since her annulment was to be final on the morrow, what better way to show all of London that her heart and pride were unscathed than to appear at an assembly ball with her head held high and a smile on her lips?

Georgina had even ordered her a special gown for the occasion from her favorite York Street modiste—a high-waisted confection of softly woven silk in virginal white.

Catriona was not immune to the irony.

In keeping with the elegant simplicity of the dress, she had woven a borrowed string of Aunt Margaret's pearls through her upswept curls.

As she scanned the crowd, she knew she ought to take comfort in the fact that there was absolutely no chance of running into Simon. It wasn't as if they would ever travel in the same social circles. He might be the son of a powerful duke, but he was still a bastard, which meant that there were some doors that would be forever closed to him.

Instead of giving her comfort, the thought made her heart feel as if the very last drop of blood were being squeezed from it.

She was turning blindly away from the ballroom, determined to flee before Georgina saw her, when Uncle Ross appeared on the landing beside her.

He linked an arm through hers and cocked an inquisitive eyebrow. "Not thinking of bolting, are you, my dear?"

"How did you know?" she asked, eyeing him sheepishly.

He puffed out his cheeks in a rueful sigh. "I saw the same look in your aunt Margaret's eyes on our wedding night."

"Are you sure you want to be seen with a woman with such a scandalous past? It might cast a stain on the noble Kincaid name."

"Don't be ridiculous," he replied, giving her arm a heartening squeeze. "I'm very proud to have such a bright and lovely young woman on my arm."

Catriona blinked up at him, surprised to feel the sting of tears in her eyes.

"Besides," he added, a corner of his mouth quirking in a grin, "you're too young to spend the rest of your life listening to Alice whine and beating me at chess."

As they descended the stairs arm in arm, her uncle's words gave her the courage she needed to lift her chin and fix a gracious smile on her lips.

Just as she had feared, the minute she was recognized most conversations lurched to a halt. Even the musicians faltered, striking several discordant notes in a row before resuming the tinkling notes of the dance. The conversations resumed at a much lower level, most of them accompanied by sharp nudges and nods in their direction.

Uncle Ross remained unfazed. Catriona followed his lead, her smile frozen on her face as they joined the dance. Her uncle was surprisingly light on his feet for a man of his size.

She caught a glimpse of Georgina and her husband Stephen beaming at them from one of the scarlet-lined boxes overlooking the theater floor, then pivoted to find Alice glaring at her with a malice equal to her sister's goodwill. Alice was partnered by a handsome young militiaman with short-cropped hair and an impressive set of side-whiskers. It seemed her cousin still couldn't resist a man in uniform.

A scattering of light applause greeted the end of the minuet. "Would you care for some punch?" her uncle offered.

Catriona regretted her nod almost immediately, as his departure left her standing awkwardly in the middle of the floor.

Like a vulture sensing a fresh corpse, Alice came swooping down out of the crowd. "I can't believe you'd dare show your face in public after you've dragged our good name through the mud by making such spiteful accusations," she hissed.

"Simon certainly had no problems performing with me."

"He never had the chance," Catriona replied coolly. "I was there. Remember?"

With a scathing "Harrumph," Alice melted back into the crowd, tossing her yellow curls.

Catriona shook her head, thinking what a shame it was that her cousin and Eddingham hadn't wed after all. They would have made a perfect match.

She glanced around to discover that her uncle had been waylaid by an old acquaintance with a reputation for repeating the same long-winded stories at every social occasion. Uncle Ross shot her an apologetic glance, but the man had already seized his arm, offering him little chance of escape and Catriona little hope of rescue.

When someone bumped her from behind, she whipped around, convinced Alice had returned after finally thinking up a witty retort. But the offenders turned out to be a blushing young couple.

"So sorry, miss," the gentleman said, tugging at his fashionable forelock.

The girl giggled and bobbed a charming curtsy. "Please do forgive us."

As they proceeded on their way, hand in hand, it was easy to see why they had nearly trampled her—they were too busy gazing adoringly at each other to watch where they were going. Judging by their youth and the simple gold band flashing on the girl's finger, they were also recently wed.

Something about the way they looked at each other reminded Catriona of Jem and Bess ducking into the forge on her wedding day, soaked to the skin but glowing with joy.

She closed her eyes against a blinding rush of sorrow. She didn't belong here any more than Simon did. There were doors that would be forever closed to her as well. Doors that led to long, snowy winter nights snuggled beneath the blankets in her lover's arms. Doors that led to a houseful of laughing, golden-haired children who looked like cherubs but had devilish green eyes. Doors that led to a lifetime of love.

Desperate to escape the prying eyes that were still watching her every move, she turned and began to wend her way toward an arch at the far end of the ballroom.

The first note from the bagpipes cut straight through her heart. She couldn't have moved if a chandelier had been about to crash down onto her head.

The ancient instrument's song soared in passionate abandon within the confines of the ballroom walls, mocking everything that had come before it as only a pale imitation of music.

Catriona slowly turned to find a grizzled old man standing at the top of the stairs, working the pipes with every last ounce of his strength. Everyone in the ballroom looked flabbergasted. Her own astonishment grew when a dozen men, all garbed in green and black tartan kilts and plaids, came marching down the stairs in regimental precision, their shoulders thrown back and their heads held high. They formed a double row at the bottom of the stairs, creating a human passageway for whoever chose to descend next.

As the piper finished his tune, leaving his final triumphant note hanging in the air, everyone stood in stunned silence for a moment, then erupted in thunderous applause. Believing the entire exhibition to be part of the evening's entertainment, the men began to whistle and stomp and shout, "Capital idea!" and "Simply smashing!"

Another man appeared at the top of the stairs. Their applause faded.

The silence was so profound that all Catriona could hear was the thundering of her heart in her ears as she gazed up into her husband's narrowed green eyes.

Chapter 22

This was the Simon she remembered from the barn—clean-shaven, clear-eyed, his hair neatly trimmed and barely brushing his collar. He was dressed as finely as any other gentleman in the ballroom, but he wore her beloved old tartan—the Kincaid plaid—draped over one broad shoulder and pinned with a silver brooch.

As the crowd recognized him, a shocked murmur went up, quickly rising to a swell that rippled from one end of the ballroom to the other.

One might be offended by his parentage if one was so inclined, but there was no denying that Simon Wescott was a gorgeous specimen of masculinity. Several of the women whipped out fans and began to frantically fan themselves, while others gripped the arm of whoever was standing closest to them, near to swooning.

As Simon started down the steps, heading straight for her, Catriona was afraid she was about to be included in the latter category. Only she had no arm to grip. No one to catch her should she fall.

This was the Simon she remembered from the docks—dashing, dangerous, an element of natural command in his every step. He looked every inch the conquering hero, determined to claim whatever prize he had won. A path magically opened between them as the Highlanders fell into step behind him.

She glanced around frantically, expecting Uncle Ross to come charging to her rescue, to denounce Simon for the scoundrel he was and whisk her away to a safe, boring life that contained no risk of having her heart broken all over again by this silver-tongued Adonis. But her uncle was watching the proceedings with as much avid interest as the rest of the crowd.

Simon stopped right in front of her, his green eyes smoldering with a passion she remembered only too well.

This was the Simon she remembered from her bed—confident in his own prowess, wildly naughty . . . and utterly irresistible.

"What are you doing here?" she asked, wishing she didn't sound as breathless as she felt.

"I've come to inform you that you're not entitled to an annulment. As your husband, I did fulfill my marital duties to your satisfaction—*and to mine*—not just once, but numerous times."

A round of shocked gasps went up from the crowd. Uncle Ross hid his face behind his hand, but it was impossible to tell if he was on the verge of laughter or tears.

Catriona folded her arms over her chest and lifted her chin. "How do you know I was satisfied?"

Simon's lazy smile set off a fresh fluttering of eyelashes and fans. "You might want to withdraw that question, Mrs. Wescott. A gentleman wouldn't divulge those details . . . but I just might."

"It wouldn't matter anyway. You're too late. The bishop has already called an ecclesiastical council. By nine o'clock in the morning, our marriage will be over."

"If it's my virility in question, I'd be more than glad to provide proof. All you have to do is step over to that curtained alcove with me for a quarter of an hour—that is, if we skip the *pleasantries*."

Several of the women tittered behind their fans. Catriona felt her own cheeks heat as she remembered just how exquisitely *pleasant* some of those *pleasantries* had been.

"Of course, the bishop might require some witnesses," Simon added. He politely scanned the crowd, raising his voice. "May we have some volunteers?"

Several hands shot into the air, all belonging to men.

"Hoot, mon, if this is how ye English go about wooin' a lass into yer bed, I'm surprised yer race hasn't completely died out by now."

Catriona blinked in shock as Kieran stepped out from behind Simon, scowling in disgust.

"If I may interrupt this touchin' little reunion before it brings a sentimental tear to me eye, I'd like to tell ye the real reason we're here. We're on our way back to the Highlands. We're goin' to drive this Eddin'ham fellow off the Kincaid lands once and for all."

Catriona scowled right back at him, beginning to feel woefully outnumbered. "And why should I care? You made it quite clear that you don't want or need my help." She waved a hand at

Simon. "Why, you already have the chieftain you wanted right here in front of you!"

Kieran and Simon exchanged a glance. Simon nodded.

Clearing his throat, Kieran awkwardly dropped to one knee, the proud set of his shoulders unyielding. Gazing up at her, he said, "Catriona Kincaid, we swear our fealty to ye as the one true chieftain o' Clan Kincaid. Ye have our loyalty, our swords, our hearts and our very lives if ye require them to serve ye and protect ye for as long as we—and ye—may live."

As he bowed his head, the other Highlanders went to their knees, one by one. The grizzled old piper was the last to bow, his knees creaking with the effort.

Catriona stood paralyzed with shock, tears beginning to trickle down her cheeks, as Simon unfastened the plaid from his own shoulder and gently laid it over hers before dropping to one knee in front of her.

Instead of bowing his head, he took her hand in his and gazed up into her eyes, just as he had in her bedchamber on the morning they left for Gretna Green. "Catriona Kincaid," he said solemnly, "from the first moment I laid eyes on you, I should have known you were the only woman in the world for me. I was too stupid and stubborn to realize it, but I fell in love with your courage, your spirit, your beauty, your wit, and now I can think of nothing and no one else. If I were a better man, I would have confessed my love to you—and to myself—before taking you to my bed. But my hunger for you was so great that no power in heaven or hell could have stopped me from making you my own."

There was a brief commotion as a woman near the punch bowl finally succumbed to a swoon.

Simon gently caressed Catriona's knuckles with his thumb. "I can only pray that you'll forgive me for taking such ruthless advantage of our bargain and will allow me to make amends by doing me the honor of agreeing to share my life, my future and my name by remaining my wife. You told me once that you felt there was no place in this world for you. Well, I'm here to tell you that there is. And that place is in my arms."

He brought her hand to his lips, kissing it with a tender fierceness that made her heart clutch, then lifted his beseeching gaze to her face. His next words were so deep and soft that only she could hear them. "I know you loved me once, Catriona. Please tell me it's not too late for you to love me again."

Too late.

The words seemed to toll through her mind like a dirge.

They were offering her everything she'd ever wanted, and for the first time in her life she was afraid to take it. She had believed for so long, hoped for so long, guarded her dreams as if they were priceless treasures. How could it be that now—when she needed it the most—her faith was spent?

How could she ever trust a man like Simon to be constant in his affections? How could she ever be sure that his words came from the heart and weren't just a stanza of some pretty speech he'd memorized in the theater? How could she keep her heart—and her dreams—from being crushed beneath his polished bootheels once again?

"I'm sorry," she whispered, tugging her hand from his grip. "I can't. I simply can't."

She turned her back on them all just as they had once turned their backs on her, determined to walk away with her pride intact, if not her heart.

She'd only taken a few steps when Simon's voice rang out. "I asked you once how long you would wait for the man you loved and you told me, 'Forever.' Was that a lie?"

Since she had no answer for him, she just kept walking.

"I'm not fighting for them. I'm fighting for you. And with or without you, we're going to Balquhidder to take back Castle Kincaid."

She stopped and turned around to find them all on their feet. Surveying Simon through a shimmering veil of tears, she said, "Then may God go with you, because I can't."

Chapter 23

Catriona huddled in the window seat of her bedchamber, enveloped in the worn folds of the Kincaid plaid. Robert the Bruce was curled up at the foot of her bed, looking equally doleful. Although another perfect spring day was dawning outside the window, it might as well have been deepest winter. She didn't even bother to open the window and invite in the balmy, honeysuckle-scented breeze. She was content to watch through the thick layer of glass as the world went on without her.

Nearly a week had passed since the ball. Simon and her clansmen should be arriving at Balquhidder any day now. She closed her eyes, haunted by a vision of Kieran's stubborn neck broken by a hangman's noose, Simon sprawled on the ground, his golden hair matted with blood.

There was a curt rap on her door. Before she could tell whoever it was to go away and leave her alone, her uncle flung open the door and came charging into the room.

He stood with hands on hips, surveying her bare feet, the rumpled nightdress she'd been wearing for four days, the dried tear stains on her cheeks, her untouched supper tray still sitting on the chest at the foot of her bed.

Sighing heavily, he shook his head. "I never thought I'd say this, Catriona Kincaid, but I'm disappointed in you."

She blew a tousled strand of hair out of her eyes. "I was under the impression that you've always been disappointed in me."

"You may have tested both my patience and my temper at times, but I was never disappointed in you, child. And I never took you for a coward. I thought you were your father's daughter."

Catriona sprang to her feet, cut to the quick by the unfairness of his words. "My father was a fool and a dreamer! You said so yourself."

"At least he had a dream!" her uncle thundered, sending Robert the Bruce darting under the bed. "If you want to know the truth, I was jealous of Davey—jealous of his ridiculous Scottish cause

and his passion for it. I was the eldest son. I wasn't allowed to defy our father's wishes and go running off to have grand adventures and chase some noble dream. I had to stay here and learn how to manage the estate. I was required to marry for duty, not love."

"Then maybe *you* were the lucky one because you never had to risk your heart or your life to have what you wanted!"

"Davey lived more in his short life than I ever will. He lived. He loved. He was blessed with two beautiful children and a wife who adored him. He may have died too young, but at least he died for what he believed in instead of dying in his bed of old age with a belly full of beef and a heart full of regrets!"

Stunned by her uncle's words, Catriona sank back down in the window seat, hugging the plaid around her.

He reached into his coat and drew out a packet of papers tied with a ragged bit of string. "I realize you may very well hate me for the rest of your days for what I've done and I won't blame you if you do, but I can't keep these from you any longer." He tossed the packet in her lap.

"What are they?" she asked, frowning down at the unbroken wax seals.

"Letters from your brother. They started arriving the month after you did and didn't stop until three years ago."

Catriona turned the packet over in her hands, then lifted her tear-filled eyes to her uncle's face. "You kept them from me? For all these years?"

"I thought it was for the best. You were so young to have known so much tragedy. I thought if you could forget the past, then you could forget the pain as well. I was wrong. I know I'll never deserve your forgiveness, but I am sorry."

With those words, he turned and trudged heavily from her bedchamber, closing the door softly behind him.

Robert the Bruce crept out from under the bed. As he vaulted to the window seat and curled up in her lap, Catriona tugged the bottom letter from the stack and tore it open with trembling hands.

My dearest Kitten,

I should have known Mama made me practice my letters for a reason. She must have known that someday I would need every one of them to remind you to wash behind your ears and to scold you for not wearing your shoes in the winter.

Catriona smiled through her tears. Her brother's teasing voice was so clear he might have been standing right next to her, rumpling her hair. She tore open one letter after another, hungrily devouring his words. The letters were filled with funny stories about Kieran and the other men and breathtaking descriptions of the Highlands in every season. Connor never once complained of being hungry or cold or being forced to steal from those more fortunate just so he could fill his belly.

She broke the wax seal on the last letter reluctantly, knowing it might very well be the last time she would ever hear her brother's voice.

My sweet Kitten,

I don't know when you'll hear from me again. We've suffered some harsh losses in the past few weeks and paper and ink are growing ever more dear. Since I have never received any reply from you, I can only hope that you have settled into the life of a fine young English lady and are enjoying all of the pleasures and privileges our uncle's rank and wealth can afford you.

A tear splashed on the worn vellum, smudging the faded ink.

No matter where you may go in this world, never forget that you have Kincaid blood flow-

ing through your veins and that anything worth crying over is also worth fighting for. I shall ever be . . .

Your devoted brother,
Connor Kincaid

Catriona sat there for a very long time, studying that untidy masculine scrawl, then jumped to her feet, dumping Robert the Bruce unceremoniously to the floor.

"Uncle Ross! Uncle Ross!" Catriona took the long, curving stairs two at a time, barely resisting the urge to slide down the freshly waxed banister.

She sprinted across the entrance hall and went dashing around a corner, nearly knocking a footman juggling a tray of polished silver clean off his feet.

Two parlor maids watched her fly past the drawing room doorway, their mouths hanging open. Catriona skidded to a halt.

Smiling sweetly, she said, "By the way, you were both wrong, you know. My husband only requires one woman in his bed, and that woman is me."

"But miss," one of them said, looking genuinely perplexed, "I didn't think 'e was your 'usband no more."

"Well, he will be again. *Very* soon."

Hiking up the hem of her nightdress to free her strong, slender calves, she took off at a dead run down the corridor.

Alice and Aunt Margaret were just emerging from the breakfast room bearing steaming cups of chocolate. Alice wasn't as fortunate as the footman. Catriona barreled right into her, spilling the chocolate all down the front of her ruffled bodice.

As Alice shrieked in outrage, Aunt Margaret exclaimed, "Oh, dear, would you look at that!" and muffled a titter behind her handkerchief.

"Look what you've gone and done now!" Alice spat, snatching Aunt Margaret's handkerchief from her hand and using it to mop at her ruined bodice.

"Ever so sorry," Catriona blurted out, looking utterly unrepentant. "You know what a clumsy cow I've always been."

The earl's head flew up as his niece burst into his study, her hair and eyes equally wild. She looked much like the barefoot wild child who had once roamed his estate with her kitten and her tattered copy of the *Minstrelsy of the Scottish Border*.

"Uncle Roscommon," she said, planting both hands on the desk and looking him dead in the eye. "If you want to atone for keeping my brother's letters from me, this is your chance. I need your help."

As the mail coach rocked its way up the narrow trail, Catriona didn't realize she was holding her breath until the lone remaining tower of Castle Kincaid came into view. It stood silhouetted against the bright blue of the spring sky, its weathered stones looking both ancient and time-less. As she saw the green and black banner fly-ing proudly from the ramparts, her jaw dropped in astonishment. She could even hear it flapping in the wind, just as her papa had described.

The vehicle lurched to a halt. She threw open the door and scrambled down from the coach, then turned to help Uncle Ross heft his own bulk to the ground.

He tested his legs, groaning with each step. "Who ever heard of an earl being forced to travel in such a crude conveyance?"

"Now, Uncle Ross, you agreed it was our only possible hope of reaching the castle before Ed-dingham destroyed both it and Simon."

He glanced back at the carriage, lowering his voice. "I just hope you appreciate how much it cost to have the driver make this little special delivery. I'd have been better off just tossing my purse to the nearest highwayman."

"Don't despair," she said, glancing around nervously at the rocky outcroppings shadowing the deserted road. "You may still get the chance to do that."

He drew out a handkerchief and mopped his brow. "My father sold his soul to escape this wilderness and now here I am, right back where he started. How on earth is a person expected to breathe up here? There's entirely too much fresh air. And sky," he added, shooting the sweeping bowl of blue a mistrustful look.

"I suppose you miss those nasty clouds of soot that always hang over the city?"

"What I miss are the comforts of my own bed and hearth. I haven't had a decent cup of tea since we departed London."

"I thought you always wanted to have a grand adventure."

He sighed. "So did I. But perhaps trying to coax your aunt Margaret into giving me a good-night kiss and finding a husband for Alice is all the adventure I'll ever need."

Catriona gave his arm a fond squeeze before glancing back at the open door of the carriage. "Will you wait here until I summon you?" she asked softly.

He squinted down at her, unable to hide his concern. "Are you certain?"

She nodded, offering him a tremulous smile. "More certain than I've ever been in my life."

"Very well. But you should know that if a highwayman comes along, I'm going to scream just like Alice."

Catriona laughed. "That should scare him off, as well as every bird and squirrel from here to Edinburgh."

Lifting the hem of her redingote to spare it from the worst of the dust, she started up the steep trail that led to the castle. She'd once ridden up the very same hill on her papa's shoulders, flush with the confidence that only a parent's love can give. She could almost feel her papa walking beside her on this day, urging her to live—and love—with the same zest that had brought such joy to his own all-too-brief life.

Her pace quickened with each step. She'd finally learned that home couldn't be found in a place, no matter how beautiful or beloved, but only in the arms of those who awaited you there. She could only pray that those arms were still waiting to welcome her.

Dragging off her bonnet so her hair could blow free, she crested the top of the hill. She had expected to walk into the disorganized chaos of full-blown battle preparations, but all she saw was a lone man stretched out on a bench of tumbled stone, a book in his hand and a blade of grass tucked between his fine white teeth. The sun burnished his hair to a ripe gold.

He glanced in her direction, his eyes widening, then narrowing. As she approached, he slowly came to his feet, his stance wary.

"So what gifts have you brought this time?" he asked. "Boots, books or bagpipes?"

Letting her bonnet tumble to the grass, she spread her empty hands. "I'm afraid all I have to offer is myself. If you'll have me, that is."

He tilted his head to study her, his eyes smoky and unreadable. "Why, Miss Kincaid, I thought you'd sworn off embarrassing speeches!"

"Only those involving the noble Highland spirit and freedom from tyranny." She nodded toward his abandoned book. "Brushing up on your Robbie Burns, are you?"

He sighed. "If I'm going to throw in my lot with a bunch of sentimental savages, I don't suppose I have any choice, do I?"

Frowning, she scanned the deserted ruins. "Just where are those sentimental savages?"

He shrugged without a trace of concern. "Around."

She dared to draw a step nearer to him. "Have you agreed to be their chieftain?"

"Only until their true chieftain comes home to stay."

"According to Kieran, Connor isn't coming back. And if he doesn't want to be found, he won't be."

"I wasn't talking about Connor."

Drawing in a breath that was shaky with longing, Catriona took another step toward him. For a dizzying moment, she mistook the thunder of approaching hoofbeats for the thundering of her heart.

Until she caught a flash of scarlet out of the corner of her eye and turned to see two dozen English soldiers racing their mounts across the vale below.

The redcoats were coming.

Chapter 24

A black cloud of panic enveloped Catriona, choking off her breath. The redcoats were coming. They were coming just as they had before, to take away everyone and everything she loved. For a paralyzing fraction of a moment, all she wanted to do was hide. To crawl into some small dark hole, squeeze her eyes shut and press her hands over her ears so she couldn't hear the dying screams of those she loved.

Then Simon's hands closed over her shoulders, pulling her out of the past and into the present. Making her believe in the future.

By the time the soldiers drove their mounts over the crest of the cliff and into the ruins of the courtyard, she was standing tall and proud at his side, no longer haunted by the ghost of her childhood terrors.

Not even the sight of the familiar black-garbed man in their midst could quell her spirits.

"Why, hullo, Ed," Simon said as the marquess slid off the horse and to his feet. His spurs jingled as he strode toward them. "I heard you were in the neighborhood. We were hoping you'd stop by for tea."

Giving Simon the cut direct, Eddingham sneered down his nose at Catriona. "I must confess that I'm surprised to find *you* here, Miss Kincaid. Or have you come to your senses and decided to accept my rather generous offer?"

Simon's eyes narrowed. "What offer?"

Catriona smiled cheerfully. "Oh, the marquess graciously invited me to become his mistress. Since I'm damaged goods, he couldn't be seen with me in town, of course. But he promised to visit my bed here in the Highlands whenever he got bored."

"How very benevolent of him," Simon said smoothly, sounding as dangerous as Catriona had ever heard him.

"You're trespassing and I want you both off my land right now."

Before Simon could react to Eddingham's demand, Catriona marched forward, boldly stabbing a finger into the starched ruffles of the marquess's cravat. "You're the one who's trespassing, sir. These are Kincaid lands and no worthless scrap of paper will ever change that. The blood of the Kincaids has watered this land for four centuries and I can promise you that every drop of that blood will cry out for vengeance if you so much as remove one stone from this castle."

"Bravo," Simon murmured. "Nice speech."

Catriona spared him a scowl before returning her attention to Eddingham. She pointed toward the road. "I'll have you know that my uncle is waiting for me at the bottom of that hill. If you insist on trying to evict us, he has every intention of suing you for breaking your betrothal contract *and* my cousin's heart."

Eddingham rolled his eyes. "You must be joking. Everyone knows that shrew has no heart."

"Then perhaps my uncle will force you to honor your agreement and marry Alice."

Simon shuddered. "A fate worse than debtor's prison, I assure you. If I were you, Eddie, I'd give the lass whatever she wants."

Eddingham bit off a vicious oath. "I'll be damned if I'm going to stand here and listen to any more of your ridiculous threats. Arrest them both!" he commanded the soldiers. "And if they resist," he added, plainly hoping they would, "shoot them."

A dozen of the soldiers slid from their mounts. Catriona took an involuntary step toward Simon's arms.

"I wouldn't be so hasty to follow the marquess's orders if I were you." Simon slipped a document from his waistcoat and handed it to the officer nearest him.

Shooting Eddingham an uncertain glance, the man warily broke the wax seal and unfolded the creamy sheet of vellum. His lips moved as he read, his eyebrows climbing higher with each word.

"What are you waiting for, you numbskull?" Eddingham snapped. "Arrest this ruffian and his whore!"

"I'm afraid that won't be possible," Simon said gently. "He works for me now."

The officer sighed and turned to Eddingham. "I'm sorry, my lord, but I am under a direct order from the Crown to arrest you for the murder of a Miss Elizabeth Markham. It seems the King has received evidence from a very reliable source— the Duke of Bolingbroke himself—that you were directly involved in the young lady's death."

As a half dozen soldiers flanked him, every ounce of color drained from Eddingham's face, leaving it as stark and white as a death mask.

He was still sputtering in shock when Catriona

turned to Simon. "Your father? You went to your *father? For me?*"

"And why not? It was about time the old goat did something for his second son."

Despite Simon's careless shrug, Catriona knew exactly what his sacrifice had cost him.

One of the soldiers had retrieved a set of irons from his horse and was attempting to clamp them on Eddingham's wrists. "Get your paws off me, you piece of filth," he snarled, struggling to twist out of the young soldier's grip. "There's no need for those. Unlike Wescott here, I'm a gentleman."

The soldier gave his commanding officer a questioning look. The man sighed, then nodded. "No irons. But don't take your eyes off of him."

As the soldier lowered the irons and stepped away, Eddingham jerked his waistcoat straight, giving Simon a contemptuous look. "Once I prove my innocence, it's you who will be in irons. For the rest of your miserable life."

He did not protest when two more soldiers stepped forward to escort him to his horse. The young soldier turned away to return the irons to his saddlebag.

One minute the pistol was in the soldier's belt, the next it was in Eddingham's hand. He gave Simon an icy smile, but the yawning mouth of the weapon was pointed directly at Catriona's heart.

"*No!*" Simon shouted, throwing himself against her.

A shot rang out just as Catriona went tumbling to the ground with Simon stretched out full-length on top of her.

They lay there for a long breathless moment, gazing into each other's eyes.

"Don't mind me," Simon finally said, giving her the crooked smile she loved so well. "I must have tripped."

Catriona's breath escaped in a shuddering sob. "Oh, dear God, are you hurt?" Her hands darted all over him like a pair of frantic baby birds, searching for a warm spill of blood.

"It's all right." He sat up, pulling them both to an upright position. "I'm not shot."

"I am."

At that matter-of-fact pronouncement, they both looked up to find Eddingham swaying on his feet and gazing stupidly at the arrow protruding from his shoulder. The pistol dangled from his limp fingers, spent and harmless.

Eddingham's knees folded and the soldiers rushed forward to catch him before he could hit the ground. Catriona lifted her gaze to the ramparts of the tower. They were lined with two dozen Highland warriors, arrows notched and bows at the ready. Their braided hair and mud-streaked faces proclaimed them ready for battle. The tallest of them gave her a solemn nod and she knew Kieran's keen aim was the reason Eddingham's shot had gone astray and missed them both.

The redcoats were also eyeing the ramparts nervously.

Simon climbed to his feet, tugging Catriona to hers. "I do believe you've overstayed your welcome, gentlemen. I suggest you take the marquess and go before the lady's clansmen decide to give you a proper Kincaid welcome."

Without a word, the soldiers began to climb astride their horses, dumping the groaning Eddingham over his empty saddle like a sack of meal.

"What will happen to him?" Catriona asked softly, as they began to file their mounts silently down the cliff trail, far more subdued than upon their arrival.

"If the arrow doesn't kill him, I suspect he'll be spending some time in Newgate. But I doubt his accommodations will be as luxurious as mine were. Or his visitors as charming."

Catriona shook her head. "Why, you sly devil! If the Scots had had you fighting on their side at

Culloden, Bonnie Prince Charlie's heirs would still be on the throne."

"You didn't really think I was going to greet them with pistols blazing and get us all killed, did you? When it comes to getting what I want, you know I don't fight fair."

"I most certainly do," she said softly, holding his gaze with her own. "So what will happen to the castle now?"

He shook his head in mock sympathy. "With Eddingham under investigation for murder, I'm afraid the Crown has no choice but to confiscate his lands. I've already made arrangements to purchase this particular tract. I should be able to get it for a song, especially when I tell them that it's still being plagued by a pesky band of outlaws."

"That would be us!" Kieran called down from the tower, where he'd plainly been eavesdropping. Several of her clansmen lowered their bows and gave Catriona cheery waves.

"And just how do you hope to pay for the land?" she asked. "My dowry wasn't *that* generous."

"A most curious thing has happened since the day you walked into my jail cell. It seems my luck at the tables has turned. To put it bluntly, I can't lose. Which is why my next gamble is going to be on the flock of Cheviot sheep Eddingham has so thoughtfully arranged to have delivered to our doorstep."

She shook her head, still shaken by how close she had come to losing him forever. "Why did you jump in front of the pistol that way? You could have been killed."

He arched one mocking eyebrow. "Isn't that what heroes do?"

She gazed up at him with her heart in her eyes. "What if I don't want a hero? What if I want a husband?"

Before Simon could respond, her uncle came stumbling into the ruins, wheezing like a consumptive. When he saw Simon and Catriona, he lurched to a halt and clapped a hand to his heart. "When I heard the shot, I feared the worst. What are you trying to do? Give an old man an apoplexy? You scared the devil out of us."

"Us?" Simon echoed, giving Catriona a disbelieving look. "Surely you didn't drag your poor Aunt Margaret all the way up here?"

"Not exactly," Catriona said. Chewing nervously on her bottom lip, she took him gently by the arm and led him toward an empty window on the south side of the ruin.

From that vantage point, the mail coach at the bottom of the hill was clearly visible. A woman had alighted and was standing next to it. She was a tall woman, still willowy and graceful despite the silver that had begun to frost her once-golden hair.

Simon was still scowling in bewilderment when she saw the tears start in his eyes. "Catriona," he said hoarsely, "what have you done?"

She shrugged. "The mail coach had to stop in Northumberland anyway. I didn't have much time, but it wasn't really that difficult to track down a legendary beauty who had once performed at Drury Lane. When I told her we were going to meet you, she insisted on coming with us. I warned her that it might be dangerous, but she said she didn't care as long as she got to see her boy again."

She released his arm, dashing a tear from her cheek. "If you can't forgive me, I understand. But I thought that maybe you could try to forgive her. She left you because she believed it was for the best. I left you because I was a coward who was afraid you'd break my heart again."

When Simon turned to look at her, she took a step backward, unnerved by the stark ferocity of his gaze. But her every fear melted away when he enfolded her in a fierce embrace. She threw her arms around his neck, holding him as if she'd never let him go.

"Ask me again," she whispered in his ear. "Ask me how long I'd wait for the man I love."

"How long would you wait for the man you love?" He drew back to look at her, smoothing her hair beneath his trembling hand. "How long would you wait for me?"

She smiled up at him through her tears. "Forever and a day."

He shook his head. "You'll never have to wait for me again because I'm never going to leave you."

Cupping her face tenderly in his hands, he brought his mouth down on hers, sealing both their vows with a kiss.

A jubilant cheer went up from the Highlanders on the ramparts as they welcomed the chieftain of Clan Kincaid home to stay.

Epilogue

Catriona reclined on the rumpled sheets, feeling deliciously decadent as her husband popped a tart strawberry dipped in sweet cream between her parted lips. Her nude body was still flushed with pleasure from their most recent bout of loving.

She welcomed another strawberry into her mouth, chewing with relish. "You know—I've always heard that reformed rakes make the best husbands."

Simon propped himself up on one elbow and cocked a lecherous eyebrow at her. "Who says I'm reformed?"

She sighed with delight as he leaned over to lick a dab of cream from the corner of her mouth.

Instead of gambling at cards and dice, the man who had once been the most notorious rakehell in London now speculated on stocks and sheep. He'd managed to amass a tidy fortune with the same keen wit he'd once displayed at the gaming tables. He only drank when toasting his wife's devotion and beauty. His carnal appetites were still insatiable and there was always a wench in his bed, but these days that wench just happened to be his adoring wife.

"You'd best be reformed," she warned him, "because if you so much as wink at another woman, I'll take my finest pair of silk stockings, tie you to these bedposts and . . ." She leaned over to whisper something in his ear.

His eyes widened even as his lips curved in an appreciative grin. "I do believe, my darling, that when it comes to perversions, you might be even more creative than I am."

"Why don't you let me show you?" Catriona purred, dipping two fingers in the cream and reaching for him.

Someone banged on the door. They looked at each other and groaned.

"I'm so glad you insisted we put a lock on our bedchamber door," she whispered.

"Not nearly as glad as I am."

"Just ignore it," she instructed. "Maybe they'll go away."

She was reaching for him again when the banging resumed, more forceful than before.

Simon swore, knowing what he had to do. While Catriona tugged her nightdress over her head, he slid out of the bed and into his trousers.

They'd built their manor house around the original ruins of Castle Kincaid, turning the tower into their bedchamber. The windows afforded them a sumptuous view of the snow-capped mountain peaks and the vale below.

Simon padded to the door, half a dozen yellow and orange kittens scampering at his heels. Robert the Bruce might spend most of his time napping on the hearth now, but he'd still had enough coal in his stove to father this latest litter.

Before Simon could get the door all the way open, two wee ones came sprinting into the room, flinging themselves onto the bed with the same joyful abandon as the kittens. A litany of questions came tumbling from their lips.

"Mama, why do you have your nightdress on backward?"

"Mama, can I have a strawberry?"

"Mama, why can't *we* eat strawberries in bed?

"Mama, why are you all sticky?"

"Mama, why is Papa glaring at me that way? Is he mad?"

Simon relaxed his scowl. "Of course I'm not mad, poppet. Mama and I were just taking a wee nap."

"May we take a nap with you, Papa?" his daughter asked, her hair more strawberry than blond and her solemn gray eyes as impossible to resist as her mother's.

"Of course you may," he said, trudging back to the bed with a long-suffering sigh.

"I don't want to take a nap," their golden-haired son announced, bouncing up and down on the heather-stuffed tick. "Please, Mama," he implored, twining one of Catriona's curls around his chubby finger, "don't make me take a nap."

She rolled her eyes at Simon. "He's a shameless flirt just like his father. Only yesterday I caught him trying to steal a kiss from one of Donel's little girls."

Simon whisked his giggling son up in his arms, tickled him until he begged for mercy, then stuffed him under the blankets. "You're going to have to learn that you can't get everything you want from a woman just by batting your eyelashes at her and stroking her hair."

"I don't know why not," Catriona retorted with a smile. "You do."

They'd just gotten the children to stop wriggling and go to sleep when another knock sounded.

"You've got to be joking," Simon said, throwing back the blanket and padding to the door.

This time it was a footman with a letter on a silver salver. "This just arrived in the post for Mrs. Wescott."

"Perhaps it's a letter from your mother," Catriona suggested hopefully. "Maybe she's coming to stay and look after the children again."

"Lord, I hope so," Simon muttered, handing her the letter.

She turned it over to study the return address. Simon drew closer, his fascination growing. He'd seen that look on her face before—on the day they were wed for the second time and on the day each of their children was born.

"What is it, darling?"

She glanced up at him, her face alight with joy. "It's from my brother. It's from Connor. He's alive!"

Simon leaned over the bed as she tore open

the letter with shaking hands. As she scanned its contents, all of the color slowly drained out of her cheeks.

She lifted her stricken eyes to his face. "Oh, Simon, we have to do something! He's writing to say goodbye. They're going to hang him!"